THE GODS MUST BE SAVAGE

Kiára Árgenta

Copyright © Kiára Árgenta 2021

All rights reserved. This book or any portion thereof may not be reproduced or used in any manner whatsoever without the express written permission of the author.

First Printing, 2021

Publisher: Independent Publishing Network.
Publication date: First Printing, 2021

ISBN: 978-1-80049-865-5

Author: Kiára Árgenta
Email: natalijamagyar@gmail.com
Address: 16 Meadow Street, CF11 9PY, Wales
Please direct all enquiries to the author.

Kiára Árgenta

Kiára Árgenta grew up in Paris before moving to Wales where she studied Russian at university. She worked as a journalist before leaving to live in Spain, then Hungary and Italy. She currently lives in Milano and is a full-time writer.

Her other novels are
Infinity,
Fragments,
Opera,
Resurrection,
Lucia and Spirit.

AFTERSHOCK

One of the most beautiful ladies I have ever seen is lying on the stone outside an apartment block in Roma. Her long raven hair fans out on the pavement and her perfect face gazes towards the heavens.

She looks calm in repose, and she is draped over the marble as if an artist or photographer arranged her; elegant golden legs neatly to one side, one hand wrapped round her gold bag and the other gently resting on her chest. Her nails are polished and a shade of deep burgundy. On her left hand I see the glittering of a large diamond ring.

At first, I think she is sleeping, but stepping closer I see that her eyes are gazing up at the night sky. Maybe she decided to lie down to enjoy the view of the sprinkling of stars and the sliver of crescent moon.

Stars such as these, when they hang so low and bright on a warm evening in Roma, demand an audience.

Beneath the woman's glamorous red coat, a darker red liquid is forming in a large circle, and I start to feel I cannot breathe. Something is horribly wrong with this image.

I hear people running with urgency, running towards us. I kneel next to the woman; she is warm and her perfume hangs like a sweet dense cloud in the air.

I call her name, touch her face gently, hoping she will look at me and smile, but those lovely dark eyes continue to stare at the sky. Her long black eyelashes do not flicker once.

Someone is screaming, somebody help! Help my mamma!

She does not hear me, does not move.

I am jolted awake with a bolt of electricity.

The nightmares are the same every night.

The recurring nightmare of my mother's death snakes into my dreams almost every night in various forms, even though I did not witness it. I was in Roma and had an indescribable sense of uneasiness that night. Something was horribly wrong, and I felt fear without being able to trace the source.

The next morning, my Auntie Luisa woke me to tell me the news. I did not eat for a whole week, maybe nothing until I arrived back in Paris.

After the funeral, I returned with my father to the apartment in Paris.

I could not be in the Eternal City with all my eternal pain, so I ran away.

Except all I did was bring the pain with me. It arrived on the next flight; unclaimed baggage delivered straight to my door.

Sometimes I have those sad, searching dreams when I am looking for her and I hear her voice crying for help, but I cannot reach her. I call for her and she is just too far away.

My beautiful opera star mother was shot dead by my stepfather outside an apartment block in Roma, as he was about to face trial for the abuse she had suffered at his hands for years.

Yet because he was a powerful advocate in Italia, he was walking the streets before trial.

She should have been free; she was finally divorced from him and yet the justice system failed to keep her safe. Instead, he was free.

I know she had dreams about her death and the fact he was being charged for attempted murder and domestic violence was no consolation. She could never truly be free.

Her final night on Earth was beautifully warm, one of those spring nights in Roma where the air is full of the aroma of flowers and hope. She too had hope in her heart, having returned from her concert in Montpellier, feeling a new beginning was waiting for her.

As she stepped out of her taxi, she forgot her golden rule; always ask the driver to wait until she was safely in the apartment block.

She was transfixed by the magnificent spray of stars and delicate crescent moon.

Just for a few seconds, she allowed herself to stand alone in her beloved city as she admired the sparkling new diamond on her hand. Those few seconds cost her so dearly.

Andrea, my stepfather, is serving a life sentence for murder but that is no comfort to me, to anyone and everyone who loved the great Marina Valentino.

Me and my father are alone in Paris, unable to make sense of the desolation, this savage hole left in our hearts. I am 16 years old and in a depressed state of shock.

I am unable to face crowds of young people with all the noise and happiness, so I do not go to school. I am brittle and angry and hurting. The sun shines every day and so the world seems even crueller for it.

My father is rehearsing for his next Opera, but his heart is not in it.

My half-sister, Catalina, is eleven years old and alone in Milano at ballet school, wanting to starve and dance until only her bones remain, as if she can erase herself out of existence.

François had just given my mother an engagement ring when they were performing in the concert in Montpellier. She had finally allowed him into her heart after 17 years, finally felt able to trust and love totally, if only for one night.

François is so devastated and says he does not think he can continue as an opera singer. He has no soul left to give to the stage.

My mother was already an Italian star when they first met in Geneva over a Christmas run, but then she moved on, hungrily seeking the next lover.

She seemed unable to allow herself to feel content, claiming that her Opera demanded constant drive, a crazy wanderlust where she soared higher into the dizzying heights of fame.

When I was four years old and she was performing in Paris she had dated François, but free-spirited and impulsive as she was, she rejected both her him and her fiancé and married my evil stepfather.

I never understood her life choices. She hardly knew this handsome advocate before they married.

I feared him from the moment I met him, just knew he was bad news.

Over the years, we spent a lot of time in Paris, but my mother could never stay still; the peripatetic life as a famous opera star was the main reason, but also because she wanted to be free, or tried to be safe.

She flew wherever the work took her, sometimes dragging me along, sometimes running away from my stepfather.

Marrying this violent and possessive man had made the wildly impulsive side of her more extreme, as if she had reach further for freedom, for success. She also lived in fear, afraid of his aggression and stalking. As a star, she could never hide.

I persuade François that my mother would be devastated if he quit his career as a top European tenor because of her.

'If the roles were reversed, she would sing full of heartbreak from her loss. She would perform even better than before.

If you leave the Opera stage, it will break your heart twice. I will not let you quit, François because performing is in your blood.

Do it for her, for your Marina.

If you do not go to La Traviata rehearsals tomorrow, I will drag you out of bed and into the elevator.'

'You would, wouldn't you, Fiorenza?' he asks.

'Damn right. I am falling apart too, but you are going back to the stage. Just do not sign up for any comic operas. Laughter is going to make you feel worse.'

He looked at his schedules and immediately cancelled several comic operas he had for the next three years.

François never said I had to attend school if he returned to the stage, so I spent my days with a married lover when François was in the Opera House. I was naïve and thought Alain loved me in my grief-stricken haze. Alain was free in the days as he worked as a television producer mainly at nights or weekends.

I was beautiful and it was purely physical for him. Although he did not care much for his wife, he had no plans to divorce her.

I had framed photos of my mother, beautiful and forever immortal in her opera roles and adorned the living room so it was like a shrine. Then I moved on to the bedrooms and kitchen.

I placed all the DVDs of her operas on the shelf; the recordings from various opera houses and the films she made on location.

The only good to come out of her fatal marriage to my stepfather was my half-sister, Catalina.

She had hidden Catalina from my stepfather, after Andrea had beaten her so badly and ran away to Paris.

Poor Catalina reminded my mother of Andrea, so she abandoned her with François and the au pairs and continued her worldwide Opera touring. By her own admission, she was useless with children until they were about three years old and were pretty dolls.

My stepfather ordered a DNA test when he discovered the existence of my sister, so the Italian courts ordered my mother to have Catalina stay in Roma for school holidays from the age of four.

Parental rights were granted even to violent men. Andrea loved Catalina and that was enough to satisfy the court.

Except it dragged my mother back into the violence; she could not just leave my sister in the apartment. Catalina had screamed as if my mother were leaving forever.

She had to return to this evil husband for nights at a time until Catalina was ten years old.

Each time she tried to divorce Andrea, he threatened to kill her.

My mother also remained loyal to Roma Opera and refused to turn down work, even though her safety was at risk in the city.

'It is where I started my career and I am their top soprano,' she would say.

'I cannot cancel work.'

It was eleven years before she could finally divorce Andrea, when Catalina was ten and could refuse to see her father by law.

Most nights, when I am thrown out of bed by my savage dreams, I go to François and sit in his room.

It is that ghostly hour between 03.00 and 04.00, the loneliest hour in the world. We sit up and drink coffee and talk.

'I wish there had been a way to save her,' he always says.

'Maybe if that evil man had still been allowed to see your sister, it could have saved Marina.'

I am not convinced.

'Remember he was facing trial for everything he did to her. He never would let her win; he was already looking at a long prison sentence.

He still would have murdered my mother. He lost Catalina because she decided not to see him,' I tell François.

We go round in circles. The truth is nothing would have saved my mother.

My stepfather waited so long to kill her because as long as she remained alive, he could make her suffer. And like the true sadist he was, he took great pleasure in hurting her.

PARIS

When spring melts into summer in Paris, this is the magical time when I love the city the most.

I am now 20 years old and confident. My mother's loss still burns, like a flaming shot of absinthe.

I feel as if my insides are on fire at times.

I always was the image of my mother but now, in the mirror, I only see Marina Valentino.

It is as if I am haunted by a ghost who has taken possession of my body; sometimes when I forget and catch sight of myself in the Opera House mirrors, my heart races.

It is at night, dressed in her beautiful evening outfits, that I most resemble my mother.

Many people would give anything to look like the famous Italian diva so many adored, but it disturbs me.

I have to remind myself it is me, Fiorenza. I am Fiorenza.

I have just completed my first year at university, where I am studying law and hoping to become a criminal advocate. My father meets us backstage at the Opera; me and my three-year-old daughter.

Black haired and dark eyed, she is every bit as pretty and precocious as I was at her age.

I named her Marina in the hope that she could be a reincarnation of my mother, maybe become an opera star herself one day.

Alain, the married lover who was 15 years older than me, threw me away as soon as I told him about the child.

'Sorry, Fiorenza, but you should get rid of it,' he told me, as if Marina were a piece of garbage.

'I thought you loved me,' I had said, in tears.

'I liked you, but I do not need this,' he told me. 'I have two boys

and they are enough trouble.'
I was wept over him for a few weeks, comforted by François.
And then I got over him so fast because I had to think of Marina.
My father did not get angry or tell me I had ruined my life, having a child at 17 years old.
'We will manage, Fiorenza,' he told me that Christmas.
'Your mother would have screamed at you. Then she would have gone to see Alain and turned her rage on him,' François said.
'But I am not angry, Fiorenza. Well, I am angry with Alain, but I am not going to confront that man. Fine, he is gone. You can have someone so much nicer than this married lover.'
François said I could still go to university, still be a success. I quit school that Christmas and studied at home.

When I had Marina the following May, everyone in my family in Italia condemned me as a sinner.
Auntie Luisa told me I was a careless slut.
Luisa blamed my mother; she was promiscuous from a young age, forever in men's beds.
At least your mother had Opera and was rich and famous. You have nothing at 17 years old, Fiorenza, Luisa told me in her phone call.
I blame my sister for setting a bad example. She never even knew which of three men was your father.......
And François is not to be trusted with a temptress like you
....
I put the phone down, furious that she spoke badly of my mother and accused my father of incest.
My mother had been such an inspiration to millions through her Opera, and because she spoke out publicly about the years of domestic violence she had suffered.
The Italian Parliament amended the laws after her much-

publicised murder, which dominated the news and chat shows for a long time.

What was referred to as 'Marina's law' would bring sweeping changes to the legal system, enabling women who had violent partners to be safe before trials and to get the justice they deserved.

I never watched the news as her death was given a lot of coverage in France as well as Italia.

She had been a resident performer at Paris Opera.

Everyone in France knew of Marina Valentino.

I could not tell François about Luisa, only that she had insulted my mother.

He was angry. 'Marina was her sister. How dare she speak badly of her!'

He reached for his phone.

'No, please do not call Luisa,' I told him. 'She is nothing to us.'

He hesitated.

'Please, François. Luisa is just a bitch. Let it go. We do not need her.'

Luisa and my mother had never got on. Luisa had been so jealous of her older sister's beauty and success: Marina the beauty, the champion gymnast and then Marina the glamorous opera star.

My auntie never forgave my mother because I spent the first few years of my life living with Luisa and Uncle Giuseppe as Luisa was unable to have children.

My mother with her Catholic beliefs would not burn in Hell for having another abortion.

I was four years old when my mother announced she was taking me back and I would travel to wherever she performed in the world.

It had broken her heart to give me away. She said she had no time in her life and hated children, but the hard diva front was just that; she loved me so deeply it hurt.

She had no time for Giorgio, my cousin, when Luisa finally had a child of her own.

I still spent many holidays at my auntie's house, so for her to turn against me now seemed a total betrayal.

I was grateful I had my father and an au pair to help me when I had my daughter. I had no living relatives on my father's side. His parents had died when he was in his twenties, and he was an only child.

My c-section scar became infected, and I was also depressed, missing my mother very badly and crying every day. Loredana was our Sicilian au pair and she stayed over every night and was so good with my daughter.

She reassured me I would be fine, that it would get easier.

I did not realise that she did not like François, although she never showed it, and she was deeply jealous of me and our extravagant lifestyle. Over time, her jealousy became stronger; she resented our wealth and beauty and was even jealous of my mother.

As my mother's lovely presence was immortalised in our apartment, I knew when Loredana saw the photos of this opera star every single day in every single room, her heart burned with envy.

When I finished school, Marina was two years old, and I had top results to study law at university in Paris. I thought surely all my relatives in Italia would realise I had not ruined my life.

'You cannot win as a Catholic, Fiorenza. If you had an abortion, your family would say you will burn in Hell, yet if you have the child, they brand you a sinner,' François told me.

I was still a sinner as they truly believed my daughter was the result of incest. My once sweet little sister accused me of being an 'incestuous tart'.

Catalina shocked me the most because she grew up in Paris and even though she was Andrea's daughter, François had always treated her as his own.

François is still regarded as one of the most handsome men in the Opera World.

Co-stars always love to be scheduled with him, even though he says he never wants to date anyone after my mother.

He is dark like me, with black hair, dark eyes, tanned skin, and a toned physique. He says he needs to look good to maintain his place as Paris Opera's finest tenor in his early fifties.

Like my mother, he feared younger singers rising fast and taking his place; men faced just as much pressure to look toned and beautiful as women.

My auntie always said that being the daughter of two opera stars had ruined me and turned me into a little diva.

Luisa told me endlessly when I was a child, in the hope that I would be a good Catholic girl, about my mother sleeping with men at 17 years old.

'Your mother was wild, your grandfather forever screaming, your grandmother crying.

Marina flounced around, loving attention from men.

I am sorry to say this, but she was a slut.'

'She was a girl, Luisa. These older men, my grandfather's friends, were taking advantage of her too,' I said.

'No,' Luisa said firmly.

'Your mother's beauty will be her downfall. Giving her body to so many.

Nothing good comes of a promiscuous woman. Remember this, Fiorenza and learn from it. Dress modestly and not like a femme fatale like your mother.'

When my mother was beaten by my stepfather, I thought life seemed to be stacked in favour of men.

My evil stepfather had many lovers and had two or three

children with various women in Roma.

I never knew what they saw in him. He was charming, handsome and rich, but he was horribly cruel underneath a thin veneer of chivalry.

My relatives were also angry with me and François because my mother's grave was in Paris.

She had requested her resting place was to be here, near François. I had no idea; I assumed she would want to rest in Roma.

Maybe Roma was tainted with the violence which had cast a shadow over her life for so many years.

Catalina inherited the Milano apartment as she attended ballet school in the city since the age of ten. I was happy to inherit the Napoli apartment and the two other apartments in Roma were sold. Catalina forever gloated that my apartment in Napoli was worth less than her Milano apartment.

I loved the Napoli apartment, which is why I decided to keep it as a rental and not have the estate agency sell it. Even if I never went to Napoli, it was a comfort to think of it, overlooking Vesuvius in the lovely Santa Lucia district and right by the Opera.

It was rented to a surgeon I had only spoken on the phone, but I knew Rosalia would be taking special care of it. She worked long hours and said she loved having a beautiful bright apartment in Napoli. Her job was stressful, and she arrived in the city from Torino, not knowing the area at all.

I love the place, Fiorenza. If I lived in another district, I could not be happy in Napoli, she told me.

François stayed in the Milano apartment when he performed at La Scala, but Catalina was frosty towards him. She seemed to resent sharing the space.

How many ballet students her age lived by La Scala? How many Milanese people lived in such a prime location?

If I was spoiled, Catalina was worse.

I do not know if this child is my niece or my sister, she had said about Marina.

François was so angry with Catalina for her comments.

I just thought, I lose everyone in my life, so I lost my sister too.

'Who is this?' Marina asked me the first time I took her to the grave in Paris.

'It is my name. Mamma?' She looked at me and gripped my hand. I knew it scared her, as if I had brought her to own tombstone.

'Don't be afraid, my love. Just lay those red roses on the stone. Remember the beautiful lady in all the photos at home? She was my mother, and I gave you her name.

She had the blackest eyes you could ever see on a person, just like you.'

Marina liked to see the photos of my mother on stage or the DVDs of operas although she was too young to concentrate.

'But where is she?' she demanded, as she placed the flowers.

'Come out!' She patted the stone.

'She cannot come out, Marina. She is in Heaven. I am sad, but she is watching over us.'

I pointed at the sky.

Marina had not understood. 'Is she an angel?'

'Yes, she is an angel.'

'You are sad, mamma,' my little girl said, touching my face.

'I miss my mother,' I tell her, scooping Marina up in my arms.

'Maybe we can see her?' she said.

I looked up at the grey sky and wondered if my mother could see us.

THE GODS MUST BE SAVAGE

    The storm clouds moved in a year ago when I was 19 years old. I travelled to Italia for the first time since my mother's death to see if my relatives would see me and my daughter. I could tell them all about my success and how I would begin studying at university that autumn. All I did was study, care for Marina and visit Paris Opera to watch my father perform.
    I never had friends in Paris.
    Now seemed a good time to surprise my relatives in Roma although François was doubtful if I should arrive unannounced with two-year-old Marina. I was convinced this would work; my little girl was so pretty and charming and I was so sure they would love her if they saw her.
    She would melt their cold hearts.
    I had called my mother's friend, Anasztázia, but she was performing in Arena di Verona.
    'Oh, Fiorenza. I would have loved to have you stay! Can you come in August?'
    I could only travel this week, so it would have to be another time for Anasztázia.
    I checked into a hotel for four nights. François wanted to go with me, but he was rehearsing in Paris. He did try to persuade me that this might be a bad idea.
    I was convinced it would be a success.
    'François, once they see her, everything will change. Besides, I already booked the hotel.
    I wanted to stay with Anasztázia, but she is away. I will be safe.'
    'I am worried, Fiorenza. I do not want you hurt if they reject you. But maybe you are right; surely no one can resist Marina's charm.
    I am concerned about your safety given your stepfather's

vengeance threats.'

'We can take taxis everywhere, I promise. We will be fine,' I reassured him.

This is the moment my life changed forever.

The darkness closed over me, and the savage Gods sent my destiny hurtling into the blackness. The first shadow had already been cast with my mother's murder. Choosing to travel to Roma delivered me straight into the mouth of Hell.

I wish there were a sixth sense when we take a decision which warned us of imminent danger, but despite any misgivings, I was intent on taking this trip.

Arriving in Roma in the evening, I realised how homesick I had been: seeing the Colosseo illuminated in its glowing gold glory as took a taxi to the hotel, the thousands of years of history everywhere, the summer nights and the warmth.

As much as I liked Paris, it never ever had the same effect on me as Roma did. The city also had a magnetic pull on my mother as she was a Roman girl, so she could not stay away, even when her life was in danger. She loved this city more than anywhere.

As I left the hotel next morning, I was wearing a new white dress and I made Marina look so adorable, also in white with diamond hair slides. I was certain no one could resist her charms.

I never wore white, and I had the false hope that it would make me look pure.

My grandparents opened the door and they told me abruptly to leave.

My grandmother said my father would burn in Hell and I would join him, but my daughter would be saved.

'A pretty child but such a tragedy for her.'

'Why do you say this, Nonna?' I asked my once loving grandmother, before she closed the door.

She stared at me coldly, looked at Marina with no feeling in her heart.

'Your mother died, then you have a child just one year later?

This is a child from incest, Fiorenza. You always were a demon temptress,' my grandmother said.

'May God forgive the innocent girl and send her to Heaven.

Your mother would break her heart. She was a bad influence on you; always too many lovers but it would devastate her if she knew about you and how wicked you have become.

And look at you; dressed in white.

Fiorenza, you need to wear red, like the slut that you are.

The French have a reputation for this deadly sin.

You are going straight to Hell.'

'My father is a good man!' I screamed.

'I am going to university! My little girl is beautiful! Damn you!' I banged the wooden door with my fists.

'Mamma!' Marina said, starting to cry. 'Why are these people so nasty?'

'It is okay, my love. We go to see some other people now and they will be nice.

These people are old and bitter.'

I wiped my tears away. They always were religious, but I could not believe their rejection of Marina.

My auntie opened the door with a face like marble. She told me I could not enter her sacred house with my 'sin'.

A French man alone with his beautiful teenage daughter will inevitably put her in his bed. Especially as you are your mother's image.

'His sin is yours too, Fiorenza. You always were a temptress, just like your mother………

I cannot believe I brought you up for the first three years of your life.

Your diva mother took you away and this ruined you.

You were brought up an Italian Catholic and look at you now.

I am sorry your mother was hurt and then murdered by that evil Andrea, but she was hardly an example of how to live a decent life.'

'Wait….please see us,' I said, holding Marina.

Luisa stared at my pretty daughter with no compassion, no softness in her eyes.

'Fiorenza, take your inbred child and go back to Paris.'

My Uncle Giuseppe stood behind Luisa and his expression was sad. I know he wanted to see me, but Luisa was in charge. My mother was her sister, so this was her decision.

My cousin, Giorgio, who was Luisa's son and once like a brother to me, was sent upstairs.

As Luisa shut the door, I felt such rage and I picked up a rock from the garden.

Marina asked, 'mamma, what are you doing?'

I hurled the rock straight through the glass in the top of the door.

Luisa opened her shattered door, and I screamed a whole load of curses at her.

'I hope you burn in Hell, Luisa! My mother hated you!'

'Get off my property, you foul-mouthed little slut or I call the police!' she shouted.

'You really are your mother's daughter!'

'Good! Better than a frigid housewife! All you did with your life was make lousy pottery!

You are useless!'

I walked away with Marina who kept asking questions: why was I crying, why are they so mean and shouting? Why did I throw a rock?

'It is okay, my love, we will be okay.'

'But mamma, they are not nice.'

'No. Let us go back to the hotel and forget these people, my sweet girl. You are tired.'

If they had been cool and invited me in and we had a frosty but civilised talk, I could live with it, but to call me a slut and to insult my father and my mother. I was so angry and hurt.

Marina said, 'don't cry, mamma' as we took a taxi back to the hotel.

I had been sure they would soften seeing my daughter in person.

I knew my mother had been promiscuous, but she was so beautiful, everyone wanted to be with her and in the theatre world, she had many handsome co-stars.

I had hated her for not knowing who my father was for so many years, but I would do anything to have her back with me.

I had an old school friend look after my daughter as I needed to sort out some paperwork in the bank and Marina was tired, so I left her in the hotel room with Giovanna. At least Giovanna was happy to see me.

'Just look at you two in lovely white dresses!' she had exclaimed. 'Your daughter is a princess, Fiorenza.'

I was already depressed about this trip to Roma. François was right; I should not have come.

Thank God Marina was not with me when I was attacked.

I try to not to relive the horror, so I never speak of it. It all happened so fast; the two men had followed me for a few streets, and I felt uneasy.

But it was daytime, and I was in central Roma. I was in a depressed fog after seeing my relatives and not aware of my surroundings. Roma had been my home city for the early part of my life and seemed safe to me.

I was reliving the horrible visit to my relatives when I decided to take a short cut down a quiet back street.

I forgot my promise to my father to take taxis everywhere. I was dragged into a car by the men so fast, without anyone seeing. I was so shocked I did not even scream until the car sped away.

One pressed a gun to my head as the other drove us away. I was convinced they would kill me, that this was mistaken identity. I was not the person they were looking for.

'No! I have a little girl! Please, please let me go!' I screamed. 'You have the wrong person!'

'Shut up,' one told me.

'I have money! Please just stop and I will get you money!'

'Be a good girl then and you can see your daughter again. Be bad, and you will never see her.'

We were fast heading out of the city.

I got more and more hysterical I would never see Marina again until they told me, 'Fiorenza, we are not going to kill you.

We will drive you back to the city, but we need something from you first……'

This is when I knew my stepfather had arranged it all. That they were going to do to me what he had always threatened to do. What he threatened my mother with on her honeymoon.

'Please just let me go and I will not tell the cops, I swear! Take my jewellery and money and just let me out!'

'No, no, dear Fiorenza. That is not on our order list,' the older man said.

'Such a beautiful girl does not need to pay us with money. We will pay you, lovely flower.

And you look so much like your mother. Andrea was right. He told us your mother was a total whore.

Are you a whore too? Beautiful yet slutty?

Is this why you are dressed in white? To pretend you are not a whore?'

'God, no! Please do not hurt me! I have a little girl,' I said to them.

They dragged me into an abandoned warehouse on the edge of the city and I begged them to stop.

I was terrified, already knew they were mafia and I thought, they are going to rape me and then kill me, leaving me in this wasteland alone.

'Stop screaming! Shut the fuck up!' the one with the gun said, slapping me across the face.

I closed my eyes and let them do what they want. Let them do it without a struggle. If I fight, they could kill me. If I was not a good girl, they would find my daughter, they told me repeatedly.

'She is a whore,' one said.

'Women scream and fight back, but not whores. She is just like her mother.'

They laughed. Tears ran down my face. I did not cry out, just played dead, let them take everything from me.

It was less of a challenge to them if I lay as still as a corpse.

I had gone to the cathedral to pray to God afterwards, after they drove me back to some depressing wasteland in the city's outer boundaries and left me near a bus stop. I called a taxi in a daze and all I remember is the taxi driver wanting to take me to the cops or a hospital, as I had clearly been attacked. My white dress was dirty and torn.

'No, take me to the cathedral, the one at the end of the avenue. I need to pray.'

I went to God to beg for his mercy and spare me any more suffering, spare my daughter suffering but I was suddenly full of rage as I kneeled at the altar.

I thought of my mother taken so violently from me and the world, my relatives turning against me and now this attack on me.

Soon I would have nothing left if this was God's work.

'The Gods must be savage,' I said, as I ripped off my crucifix and dropped it on the marble floor of the cathedral.

'So savage to make us suffer so. I came here to pray and I find no peace.

Where are you? How could you let all this happen? My mother and her suffering and now me?

How can you let them do this? I am never coming back in here.'

No one was around to hear my blasphemy, only an older lady at one of the smaller altars at the back of the cathedral, lost in her own grief.

I got up and walked out of the cool shell of the cathedral. I had no faith left in a higher power.

The men had taken photos of me, sitting like a broken doll, my dress round my waist, tears streaked on my face, hair wild as they posed next to me laughing.

Fiorenza is a fitting name for a girl who seems fresh as a flower. Your stepfather will love to hear all about it.

The photos were to show my stepfather in prison they had carried out his orders. My mother knew what he threatened to do to me since I was five years old, but I think even she thought and hoped that his words were evil threats to control her.

That even Andrea was not capable of raping a child.

I almost wished he had done it himself. He was handsome and it would have been less disgusting than these brutish men.

I felt awful for these thoughts, as if rape is acceptable if your rapist is handsome.

These two men were rough and dirty. My only consolation was they did not kiss me, and they used condoms so they would not leave DNA for a rape test. Not that I would report them to the police anyway.

I knew the consequences for me and my daughter if I reported it.

When I was trainee advocate, I wanted to tell colleagues rape can be less horrible if the man is good-looking, but this went against everything we are taught as lawyers; no man has the right and rape is rape no matter how handsome or charming the rapist.

I also never wanted to expose my own attack. I kept so much of the damaged Fiorenza hidden.

I had such a mask for the world.

Many of my clients would also tell me it would have been less traumatic if their attackers were less disgusting.

I understood them, but I knew I could not say anything except, no man has the right to hurt us.

To this day the smell of cigarettes and sweat on a man fills me full of fear, even stage crew, smoking outside Paris Opera. I never have this feeling with women who smoke.

As I wander the streets in a daze that day in Roma after renouncing God, my insides hurting from the attack and people staring at me in my torn dress, I realise I am still holding a roll of euros.

They had stuffed it down my dress when I was put in the car to return to the city.

I earned that money, they said. My daughter would be safe as I was a good little tart, as I had made my stepfather very happy. He will cherish the photos, Fiorenza. He will be so disappointed he did not have you himself.

One thousand euros. I should burn it, but I do not. I can use it for my daughter. I have enough inheritance and I hate myself taking mafia money, but what good is burning it?

And as I just renounced God, I am not giving it to the church.

No, I will buy gifts for my father and my daughter. I earned it with my suffering, after all.

I buy Marina beautiful dolls and a big dollhouse with no thought as to how I get it on the flight.

As they count the notes in the shop, I feel dirty and ashamed, and I think this money is probably forged for sure, but they accept the hundred euro notes I hand over without question.

'Are you okay?' the sales assistant asks. 'Did something happen to you?'

I realise as I look in a mirror next to the cash register, that as well as my torn dress, my face is spidered with make-up from my tears and my raven hair is wild.

'My mother died, I was crying in the cathedral,' I tell her.

'I tore my dress in the cathedral door.'

The assistant says she is very sorry. 'I hope your little sister likes her gifts,' she says.

She watches me leave looking concerned.

Fiorenza you are a little slut.

Andrea said ever since you were a little girl you were a provocative little tart.

But he will be so, so jealous. You should visit him in prison, he would love to see you…...

I throw up in the street after I leave the toy shop. I hear an old lady asking am I ill, do I need a doctor?

No, I tell her. I am just a little dehydrated. She calls me a taxi as she thinks I am really sick, as I sit on the pavement with this dollhouse.

'For your little sister, cara?' she asks me.

'Yes,' I tell her.

My friend, Giovanna is in the hotel with my daughter. I am late and I say sorry, I got sick and threw up in the street.

'Oh, Fiorenza! Your pretty dress! What happened? Did someone hurt you?'

'I tore it in the cathedral when I went to pray. I was crying over my mother, pulling at my hair with anger. I just felt so emotional, that's all.'

I hand her a bracelet I bought her, but she is worried, knows by the state of me I have been attacked. But I will not speak.

'Fiorenza, you have a fever? Marina is sleeping but you should sleep too.

Do you need a doctor? Do you want me to call the cops?'

'No, really,' I tell her. 'I need to sleep it off.'

'Drink some water, cara,' she tells me handing me a bottle from the minibar.

I hug her goodbye. I want to tell her what happened, but she is young and happy.

She feels bad enough when I tell her my relatives did not want to see me, but not the details.

I just say they are angry because my mother's resting place is in Paris.

'Stay in touch, Fiorenza,' she says as she leaves.

'Maybe your relatives need a bit more time.'

I doubt all the time in the world could repair our relationship.

I place the dollhouse next to my sleeping daughter and then sit on the floor in the shower, and cry and cry as the water rains over me.

I throw my white dress in the trash and swear never to wear such the colour again.

I would never report the rape for fear of worse vengeance from Andrea and it would tarnish my law career if I went to trial.

I knew that I could never have justice, just like my mother.

I want my mother so badly right now. It would have destroyed her if she knew what they did to me.

When Marina wakes up, I am fresh and changed into my usual black outfit.

She is thrilled with her toys and does not notice how quiet I am. We eat in the hotel.

I am horribly agoraphobic, terrified the men will come back for my daughter.

I manage to take her round in a taxi to see the sights as we cannot just sit on the balcony of the hotel, but I do not dare get out. She is delighted by the Colosseo. Besides, it is too hot for sightseeing. I just ask the taxi driver to wait outside the beautiful places.

Luckily, Marina is so transfixed by her dollhouse and new toys, she is not begging to go out. I order room service for us.

When I arrived home in Paris, I was traumatised. I told my father it was the rejection of my lovely little girl by relatives who once loved me.

François hugged me. 'I am so sorry, my love. Maybe it was too soon?'

'I threw a rock through my auntie's glass door.'

'Fiorenza!' he laughs. 'You really did that?'

'Yes, they insulted my mother and I hate them all. I never want to see them again.'

'Fiorenza, in time……..'

I know François means well but I tell him no time will heal this. Never again.

I do not know it, but me and my Italian family will never meet again. Even when my grandparents are killed in a road accident some years later, I will not be welcome at the funeral.

By then I will be heartless, unable to care.

I saw Alain in the street, outside the Opera only a few days after returning from Roma.

I had virtually forgotten my daughter's father.

Three years on, I am a totally different person, had not even thought of him.

I did not even know he liked Opera. This is my district of Paris, although he does not live so far away. I am angry as he is invading my space.

'Fiorenza! I tried to contact you many times.' He moved to kiss me.

I stepped back, clutching Marina's hand tightly.

Goddamn liar, saying he called me.

'And this is…….' he looks at Marina with interest and kneels next to her.

'My Marina,' I tell him.

He is acting nice probably because I am even more beautiful. I know him too well.

He touches Marina's hair. 'So pretty, just like your mother. You know I always wanted a daughter.'

'Really?' I ask him, sarcastically.

'You did not even call to see if I had a daughter or son. You are despicable.'

Marina is quiet and holds my hand tight, knowing I am angry, not understanding why.

Alain stands up again and he looks so sad. But I am not buying this.

'Listen, Fiorenza, I am sorry. I feel so awful. I have thought of you, and I did call. On my life I called you.

I left messages and you never called back. I knew you were angry or had changed your phone number, so I wrote to you.'

'Liar,' I tell him.

I did change my phone number as I could not bear thinking he was going to call, but I still doubt he tried to call.

'I sent five letters,' he says sadly.

'I sent them to your apartment. I thought maybe you just wanted the child and not me.

I even thought about visiting your apartment.'

'I did not get letters,' I tell him angrily.

'My father hates you. He would have thrown you off the balcony.'

'Mamma?' Marina says, puzzled by this confrontation.

How can I believe a cheating husband?

'She is lovely. I would ……..'

I cut him off mid-sentence.

'Alain, you made your choice and I made mine.'

'Fiorenza, please listen; I am telling you the truth. I am divorced now and live alone so….'

'You are not playing that card, Alain. I was 15 years younger than you.

I was suffering so much after my mother's death. Thank God I had my father to help me, and I am wealthy so I can care for my little girl.

She does not need you.'

Marina stares at me silently and looks at Alain.

'I would like to see you. It was difficult with my wife and.….,' he tells me.

'Well, I hoped I could see you at the Opera. Maybe we could..…..'

He has got to be kidding.

'I do not care for excuses, Alain!' I tell him.

I have no feelings for this good-looking man who is pleading with me.

He only wants me because I am confident and beautiful and now, he is in a weaker position, if he is telling the truth about the divorce.

'Alain, this is my district of Paris!' I wave my hand across the space. 'Not yours!'

'I really want to see my daughter,' he tells me.

Maybe because Marina is so pretty, he wants to see her. She does charm many people.

'We have to go,' I say, picking up Marina.

'Who is he?' she keeps asking.

'Fiorenza, please..…..' he calls. 'One evening you could join me at the Opera?'

'Alain, my father is a resident soloist. I attend Operas with him. And I need to think about you seeing Marina. I do not want her hurt.'

I walk away and do not look back.

'Mamma, who is he?' Marina asks again.

'Just a friend,' I lie.

'But….'

'We are going to buy ice cream, remember?'

One day she will ask who her father is just like I asked my mother. I thought Romeo was my father when I was three years old. In fact, I thought many men could be my father.

I want Marina to have stability, to know her father. My life was like a circus.

I adored my mother, but at times I hated her for constantly needing a lover.

Which is why I have Alain's name on Marina's birth certificate.

I had 'unknown' on my certificate, and I was so angry with my mother even when I knew François was my father.

'Unknown' sounds brutal. Maybe she could have listed all the contenders.

Then all I want is to see her again.

Mamma, all I want is to see you again. I want you to meet my little girl.

IL DIAVOLO

It is ten months after my attack and I am ready to confront the cause of it, or more like the person who ordered it, the one who stole my mother's life.

On the outside, I am a success. When people meet me, they think I have it all.

They are so wrong. There are oceans of pain which ebb and flow within me.

I am doing well at university and my home life is happy, but I have savage nightmares and flashbacks every single night about the rape, about my mother's death.

I have panic attacks, cannot go anywhere unless I take a taxi. I am fortunate in that I can afford taxis, but I need to see this bastard who tore open my life. No point wasting money on a shrink.

I need answers.

One last time, I tell myself. One last visit to Italia.

I worry about taking my daughter to Roma, but I do not want her left with the au pair for a week as she is too young. My father is rehearsing in London, and this is the only free week for me, so I arranged to stay for nine days with Anasztázia.

Anasztázia is delighted that I will visit with Marina. I am 20 years old and feel I aged five years since last year. I will not tell Anasztázia about the attack. I do not even want to tell her much about the visit to my stepfather in prison, although she knows I plan to go.

When I speak with my father on my cell phone, he assumes I am in Paris. I do not want him to worry when he is busy with rehearsals and performances for Faust.

He will find out I went back to Roma, as Marina will talk but I will pretend I only went to visit Anasztázia, nothing more.

Anasztázia is a big star with Roma Opera, but she has not been performing in France for a few years, wanting to stay close to Italia. She has been grieving badly after my mother's death, cutting engagements if she felt they were too far from Roma, just like François.

Anasztázia has not aged at all with her china doll complexion; so pale, blonde and beautiful but her spirit is sad. Her large blue eyes are tearful at times.

She tells me Paris is in her future schedules.

Anasztázia told me in wonder how I look just like my mother, my daughter like a young version of me. She said it looked as if this 'Marina' gene had been passed down through generations.

'My God, Fiorenza! You daughter even has those same almost black eyes as your mother! She is gorgeous!'

I smile.

'She would be so proud of you studying at university, planning to be an advocate.

I am sorry we lost touch......'

She blinks back her tears.

'I would love you to visit Paris,' I tell her.

'I promise,' she says.

'You are worried about Roma, Fiorenza?'

I nod. Especially with Marina with me.

'Andrea is in prison. He will never be able to hurt you or your daughter. You are so brave to face him, Fiorenza.

It is late and you must be tired. Come on, baby; we can eat a little now. Only talk of the prison if you want to. You have tomorrow free to think when I am in work.'

'Tell me all about your rehearsals, Anasztázia,' I say.

As she talks about Pagliacci, I think of my mother who was so afraid of clowns, she never performed the role of Nedda in this short self-reflexive opera.

'You know my mother was afraid of clowns, so she never

performed in Pagliacci……..'

Anasztázia smiles. 'I know. My character is stabbed to death by a clown, her husband.

She is cheating on him with one of the other clowns.'

'That was my mother's worst fear; to be stabbed to death by a clown,' I say.

'Oh, Fiorenza,' Anasztázia says, looking so sad.

'A husband murdering his wife in the Opera; oh, God I did not think. I am so sorry.'

'No, it is okay, really.'

She squeezes my hand, and we are quiet after that.

Anasztázia was in love with my mother, and it must have hurt when she found out that François was my mother's real love.

Poor Anasztázia did not know about my mother's double life in Paris or even about my half-sister, Catalina. My mother had stayed with Anasztázia as she had many engagements with Roma, and she was going through a terrible divorce. My stepfather had already tried to kill her several times.

I know my mother found it hard to trust even François around that dark time.

She felt safe with Anasztázia, safe in her apartment high above the city.

The next day, after taking the train north, there is Il Diavolo, as I call him now.

I wonder should I just turn round and leave.

He looks content; clearly prison is treating my stepfather well as he appears handsome and arrogant. This evil man looks as comfortable as if he were sitting at home, not serving a life sentence for murder.

The prison guards did warn me. He has no remorse. You should not see him.

I said I had to face him. It was destroying me not to confront this man.

My mother had been afraid, even in Paris. She seemed forever on the run, not just because of her nomadic lifestyle as an opera star. She should not have had to suffer so.

I am doing this for her too.

'Well, what a nice surprise,' Il Diavolo says, with a cruel smile.

'I got your photos. Such a lovely white dress, Fiorenza.'

I feel ill thinking of that day in Roma.

He pushes a coffee towards me, urges me to have some of his finest biscotti.

'After all, it has been a while,' he tells me. 'We should catch up.'

The urge to spit in his face is rising. I take a fucking coffee.

'You know the photos are nothing to do with me. Your men raped me.'

He looks at me with no feeling at all.

'It should have been me, Fiorenza.

I told your whore of a mother on our honeymoon. But she did not listen.'

'Don't you dare call my mother a whore when you ended her life!' I shout.

I try not to lose it, but I am unravelling. I hate him so much, have lost my fear.

He unclenches my fist and I snatch my hand away.

'Why did you have to kill her? Why did you want to hurt me ever since I was a child? I came here to ask you myself!'

His face darkens.

'Your mother; she was a tart. And she stopped me seeing my own daughter.

She kept Catalina from me for three years, then thanks to your father testifying in Roma, I still could not see my little girl for another year.

They said I was violent.'

'You beat her when she was pregnant! She could have had a miscarriage!

You nearly had no Catalina.'

He has nothing in his eyes showing remorse.

'Well, I guess she really thought Catalina was from her French lover since she had so many men in her bed.

She poisoned Catalina's mind and anyway, Fiorenza, I gave Marina enough warnings that if she divorced me, she would die...'

'She cheated because you hurt her. She could have loved you if you treated her well!

You hurt her so badly she ran away. Catalina chose not to see you at the age of ten.

You only wanted Catalina to stay during school holidays, so my poor mother had to stay in the apartment. You were kind to Catalina but God, my mother suffered.

And Catalina despises you!'

He stares at me like I am garbage and says nothing for a few minutes.

He leans forward, closer to me.

'You are a whore, Fiorenza; having a child so young...such a pretty girl, yes she will be as beautiful as....'

'You leave my daughter out of this!' I am so angry he dares to even mention her.

He stares at me.

'You are looking so like your mother. I bet that French father of yours finds it hard to control his urges around you.

And your mother had to die; I told her what I would do to her, and to you, when she tried to run away on our honeymoon.'

He says this in a satisfied way.

'She left because you beat her!

And you dare insult my father; he treated my mother like a goddess!

All you do is hurt women!'

'Bitch, little bitch. Why are you really here, Fiorenza?' he says, eating his biscotti.

I want to tip the plate over his head.

'To show you that I am not broken and to ask you why you killed my mother.

I will be a lawyer in a few years, so I can put men like you away.'

He reaches for my arm and laughs in a nasty way.

'My dear Fiorenza, our system is stronger than one female advocate! You will never change Italia or France.

You take care of your little girl in Paris.

The world is a dangerous place for little Marina.

But you are a clever little bitch as well as beautiful. I can give you some contacts if you are nice…'

He touches my hand.

I get up.

'Stick your fucking biscotti and your contacts! I do not want any mafia involvement, Andrea!

How the hell do you even know my daughter's name?'

'You just told me, Fiorenza.

See you are not as smart you think, but then you would name her after Marina.

She would hate you right now for lying in her bed, taking her place……'

He looks at my body in a satisfied way, licks the biscotti crumbs from his lips.

I want to slap him, beat him and have him beg for mercy.

'You know nothing! I want justice for the woman whose life you made hell!

You hurt her so badly from her wedding night on! You never needed to!'

He looks thoughtful, as if he half considers taking back time and treating my mother well.

'My sweet flower, you have taken her place in your father's bed. Is little Marina from François too?

I only killed her but you stole her life. She would break her heart.'

I cannot answer him as he disgusts me so much.

'I am fucking leaving!' I get up.

'Fiorenza! Please wait!'

I hesitate.

'Can you bring me Catalina?' His face is almost soft.

'Why?'

'Because she does not answer my letters.'

'You murdered our mother! You broke her heart; your beloved Catalina.'

'I can help you,' he says. 'Please, Fiorenza…..'

Visiting time is over.

'I do not want your help,' I say.

'Fiorenza, do this for me and I can make sure your little girl is safe.'

That is a direct threat. I turn to him.

'I can call her tonight, but I cannot drag her here.'

Then I lean over him feeling such hatred.

'Andrea, never ever threaten my daughter again. I mean that.'

I walk away burning with hatred and my stomach churns.

I throw up outside the prison gates; he makes me sick.

As I had returned to Anasztázia's street in Roma, I felt drained.

I realised I had not eaten since breakfast, only had a few drinks on the long train journey.

I shivered as I was about to enter the apartment block, realising that tonight was near the anniversary of that fatal night four years ago.

My mother had been standing right here in the spring air,

admiring the starry sky.

As she felt full of renewed hope, three bullets hit her in the chest. Just a split second and the world changed. A life of such success so brutally cut short.

Andrea would never have let her live.

And a famous diva could never be free. She could not disappear unless she gave up her Opera and she would sooner die than do this.

They tell me she did not suffer; they found her draped on the pavement as elegantly as if she were in one of her operas, her vitality and beauty intact, just like my dreams of her.

She seemed at peace.

I cannot get the image out of my head which is why it haunts me so much.

I wipe away my tears, open the main door and greet the concierge, then take the elevator to the top floor.

I manage a little of the dinner Anasztázia left in the fridge. She has already eaten with Marina and as she senses I am beyond speaking, she retires to bed to be fresh for morning rehearsals.

I go to the living room to call my sister.

Catalina is spiky, defensive and tells me I am crazy.

'I needed closure, Catalina. Maybe you should come with me.'

She screams she is trying to forget she has his murderous blood in her veins.

'You think I will ever be okay, Fiorenza? My father killed my mother!'

I tell her I understand, but if she sees him one last time, she can say everything that is hurting now.

'I know you have terrible nightmares too, Catalina, just like me. I could not rest until I saw him.'

She refuses at first but then agrees.

'I still hate you, Fiorenza but I do not want to go alone.'

I did not tell Anasztázia about the prison. She knew I did not want to talk but if I did, she was ready to listen.

I pretend I am visiting Catalina next week, as Thursday is the only day she has free.

'Fiorenza, I am very happy you stay with me a little longer,' Anasztázia told me.

BLACK BEAUTY

'Do you want to come and see people in Roma Opera? The singers were asking about you, Fiorenza,' Anasztázia says one morning, before she leaves for the theatre.

I know I would break down, as there are all those memories of my mother in the Opera.

'No, Anasztázia; it will hurt too much.

 All those memories over the years when my mother took me backstage…….I just cannot go.'

Tears fall, all those tears I should have let out.

I cannot stop crying. There is so much pain locked within me, and I cannot tell my friend half of it.

'Oh, Fiorenza, I am so sorry,' Anasztázia says.

She gets up and hugs me.

'Roma is so beautiful and yet so many memories haunt me….

It was my home city, my mother's home city which is why she could not stay away.

She would not have died maybe………..'

Anasztázia whispers gently, 'I know, my sweet Fiorenza. I tried to keep her safe here.'

'It is easier for me in Paris Opera,' I tell her.

'It still has memories, but it does not hurt so much.'

'You rest here in the apartment then. I know the pain still hurts like yesterday.'

I have a sense it always will.

As I am alone and Marina plays with her toys, I think back to the strange experience the day after I arrived in Roma. Anasztázia had returned early from her rehearsals.

My cousin Giorgio had been to visit, unknown to Auntie Luisa.

I was happy that Anasztázia finished early to distract me from the next day and the dreaded prison visit.

Anasztázia said the Lilac room was a sacred space, so me and my daughter were sleeping in the Pink room, which was safer as it had no balcony.

It seemed strange for a woman who was not religious to preserve a bedroom as 'sacred', but maybe she has become more religious. Being Hungarian and exiled, she had rejected the Catholic religion, although she still visited cathedrals for the ritual of lighting candles.

Marina was restless and wanting to explore.

'No, Marina! We are not at home. Play here with your dolls right here.'

'Please, mamma,' she said, pawing at my arm.

'Marina! This is Anasztázia's apartment.'

She looked sulky and whined.

Usually, she was an obedient child and never asked more than once.

'Let her explore,' Anasztázia smiles.

'All the balcony doors are locked. She will be safe.'

'Do not touch anything, Marina!' I call after her.

I stare at the vase of black roses on the table. They are beautiful but I think Anasztázia is very morbid to have such a colour. I like blue roses but black is funereal and there are so many vases of them in the apartment. I wonder where the hell she buys them.

She always did have a sad soul.

After ten minutes I get up. 'I better see Marina is not in trouble, Anasztázia.'

I go out of the living room. 'Marina! Where are you?'

I hear Marina's voice coming from the Lilac bedroom. She talks with her dolls, so this is nothing new.

Anasztázia follows me.

'She is in the Lilac room. I keep an altar there for your mother. Lilac is the colour of the spirit realm,' she says. She seems troubled.

'Sorry, Anasztázia. I will get her out.'

In the Lilac rom, there is a large altar where many candles are burning. Photos of my mother are placed around the altar and Marina is lost in conversation.

She stops when I walk in. I told her a million times about fire.

'Marina! Did you light these goddamn candles?' I snap.

I grab her hand, mad at her for doing this in Anasztázia's place.

'What did I tell you about fire?' I kneel in front of her.

'How many times do I tell……'

'Mamma, the candles are lit,' she tells me seriously.

She does not cry but looks at me with her beautiful eyes and they appear even blacker.

'I speak to the pretty lady called Marina. She looks like you, mamma.'

Anasztázia must have lit these candles, which is careless to leave them unattended.

'That is very nice of you to speak to my beautiful mother,' I tell her.

I study the photos of my mother in her regal opera outfits, but this room is even more of a shrine than my Paris apartment. It makes me feel a little strange, this room.

'She tells me I am beautiful,' Marina closes her eyes.

'She has a sparkly black dress and ruby crown and black eyes and hair…..'

My mother is not dressed in that outfit in these photos. 'Which photo?' I ask.

'No, in this room, mamma. Right here.'

'Marina! Why do you lie?'

The air is heavy with my mother's perfume.

I wear the same perfume, but all perfumes are different on

someone else, and this is the distinct aroma of the fragrance on my mother's dusky skin. Scent is so evocative, and I feel such nostalgia it hurts. There is a big bottle of Hypnotic Poison on the table.

Marina has put some on herself and somehow it has given her the same aroma as my mother.

'Marina! Oh Dio! How much did you spray in your hair?'

Marina looks tearful now.

I turn to face Anasztázia.

'Anasztázia, why do you leave the candles burning?'

Perfume is very flammable. The whole apartment could burn down!'

'I do not light the candles,' says Anasztázia quietly. 'And neither did your daughter. She is telling the truth about the perfume.'

I turn to face Marina. 'What are you two saying? That my mother……….'

I feel a cold chill.

'Mamma,' my little girl tells me. 'She is sad not to see you. She hugs me.'

I pick her up, the Hypnotic Poison is overpowering.

'I am sorry I was angry, my love.'

My mother always wore Dior perfume as it sounded like Dio. She said that it made her feel closer to God.

I carry Marina out of the haunted room.

I know by Anasztázia's face that she has seen my mother many times, and now Marina has.

My daughter never saw this black dress and ruby tiara yet described it in detail. It is in my closet, hidden at the back.

'Do you have a photo of her in this outfit, Anasztázia?' I ask.

'It is the jet beaded dress and ruby tiara she wore to my première in La Scala …….'

'Take Marina to the living room and I will show you.'

Something about the outfit made me feel uneasy which is why I never wore it.

Anasztázia returns with a large photo frame.

'God, Anasztázia what is this? The altar, the candles, the black roses everywhere.

I know she died outside the apartment block but……'

I cannot finish.

'That is her room,' Anasztázia tells me quietly.

She places the photo in my hands; my mother in a dressing room, when Anasztázia was in Lucia di Lammermoor première in La Scala. She looks so glamorous and happy in her jet evening dress swirling with metres of train, a ruby tiara on her loose raven hair.

She holds a bouquet of black roses.

'That is yours now, Fiorenza. I have many photos from that night.'

Marina is excited. 'You see, mamma?'

Why does she never appear for me? I stare at my mother, her black beauty, her wonderful smile.

'Thank you,' I say to Anasztázia.

'Mamma! Can we see her again?' Marina asks, before turning her attention to the cake on the table.

I have tears in my eyes.

Anasztázia sits on the sofa next to me as Marina eats her cake, not noticing how sad I am.

'Fiorenza; she has been here since her memorial concert where I saw her in my dressing room…… she places the black roses, lights the candles.

I hoped you could see her.'

I keep studying the photo. My mother never looked so beautiful.

'Anasztázia; how can I believe you? Roses and candles?'

This place is haunted.

'Your daughter saw her, Fiorenza. I promise I am not lying.'

I feel so sad and empty.

'Fiorenza, please do not be afraid,' Anasztázia says, taking my hand.

'She does not appear if you search; Marina did not go looking for her.'

'Why didn't you tell me?' I feel angry now that she did not tell me all this years ago.

'I have missed my mother so badly and now you say she virtually resides here, like some kind of spirit?'

I put my head in my hands.

Anasztázia wraps her arm around me.

'Fiorenza, listen; I have been in psychiatric wards, on strong pills. Everyone would say I am crazy.

I wanted to talk in person. Yes, you are right. I do feel almost as if she is living in my apartment.'

Marina is playing with a black rose.

'Marina! Put that back!' I snap.

I want to see my mother so much it hurts.

Anasztázia scoops up Marina and sits her on her knees.

'Listen, Marina; can you get the box of chocolates from the kitchen?' Anasztázia asks her.

Marina runs off and Anasztázia faces me with her clear blue eyes.

'Please believe me, Fiorenza.'

'I don't think you are crazy, Anasztázia, but I miss her so badly. All I want is to see my mother.'

'I am sorry,' Anasztázia says.

'But you still have some days left. Let her come to you. Dry those tears.' She hands me the tissue box.

I know I will spend every moment until we leave hoping I will see her.

The day before I leave Roma, I go to the prison one final time with my sister. We meet at Milano Centrale and Catalina stiffens when I kiss her. We take the train in silence. Catalina will not speak to me.

'Catalina!' Andrea stands up in delight. He leans to embrace her.

'Do not touch me,' she says.

'Thank you, Fiorenza. You are a good girl,' he says and gives me knowing smile.

The good girl reference is not only because I brought Catalina, but because I did not report the rape, because I pleased him very much and he has the photos to prove it.

'How are you, my love? Soon to be a famous ballerina. My you are getting beautiful......'

He takes Catalina's hand.

She does not pull her hand away, but her expression is cold.

'Why did you murder my mother?' Catalina says.

'Why did you have to kill her? You could have spared her life.'

'She was a tart, Catalina,' Andrea says.

'She was such a slut she did not know you were mine until I went to court to prove it.'

'She was not a slut! She was terrified! I know you beat her so badly from her wedding night and I decided not to see you when I was ten!

I hated having to stay with you because the court made me.

I hated it because my mother had to stay......'

'But, Catalina, you loved me too.'

Catalina is quiet. She fiddles with her bag.

Then she says, 'I did love you at times. You were good to me until I turned ten, then you got so angry when I was going to ballet school, threatened to beat me.

And I saw you rape my mother as she screamed for help!

I heard her crying! Many nights. One night you smashed a

plate over her arm.'

Tears are on her face. I take her hand.

'Catalina ....' he says sadly.

'I was seven years old when we ran away to Napoli. She was covered in injuries.

Many times, when she had to stay in the apartment for me, I heard her pleading with you.'

Catalina looks at him directly.

'Would you have raped me like you raped Fiorenza?'

I am shocked.

'I never raped Fiorenza!' Andrea says. 'I love you, Catalina. I was angry that summer because I felt you were leaving me because.......'

Catalina is losing it.

'I decided not to see you! Not my mother! I hated you for hurting her.

You ruined our lives by murdering her! I hate you so much!'

Catalina throws her cold coffee at Andrea and the guards rush over and pull her away.

'Please leave, girls. This is upsetting you,' they tell us.

'Catalina! I love you!' Andrea shouts. 'You are my daughter!'

Everyone looks at us as we are led away.

A female guard takes Catalina's arm and gently escorts us out.

Catalina is crying hysterically. 'My father killed my own mother....'

'You should not come back here,' the prison guard says. 'It will hurt you too much, Catalina.'

'We will not return,' I tell the guard. I put my arms round my sister.

In the taxi to the train station, Catalina says, 'I did love him when I was young, Fiorenza and I hate myself for that.'

'Catalina; he hated me, he hurt our beautiful mother, but he loved you. And he still does.'

She looked at me, her eyes tearful and despairing.

'Fiorenza, my father is a killer. He is in my blood.'

On the train back to Milano, Catalina lets me comfort her. She has her fingers in her mouth like a child. I am almost relieved that her ice princess mask crumbled.

She needed to let out her pain.

She never told me what she witnessed in the apartment.

But how my mother suffered to be there for Catalina.

I guess she could not trust Andrea even with his own flesh and blood; she was afraid he would sexually abuse her, or at least beat her.

It was my mother's apartment and evil Andrea lived there for eleven years, refused to leave.

As I put Catalina in a taxi in Milano Centrale, she seems composed again. I have an hour before my train to Roma.

Catalina does not offer her apartment for me to stay in, even though I have a five-hour journey back to Roma.

'Goodbye, Catalina,' I say.

She hesitates and gets out of the taxi. She kisses my face.

'I am sorry for everything I said. Please forgive me, Fiorenza.'

'Are you going to be okay tonight?' I ask her.

She just hugs me and then she speeds away in her taxi to her lonely existence.

My father stays when he performs in La Scala, but my sister is way too young to be alone.

I had asked her earlier why not have one of her classmates stay.

She looked at me incredulously.

'Fiorenza, I am going to be a prima ballerina. I have no friends.'

I had no friends apart from Anasztázia, but I had François, I had my daughter and whenever I attended shows in Paris Opera, I enjoyed mixing with the performers.

I did not feel lonely.

Anasztázia like me, is agoraphobic. She takes taxis all the time.

I saw how afraid she was when the deli below the apartment block was closed on a Sunday, and she had to walk further to buy our morning pastries.

She appeared so shaken when she came back with the cornetti, her porcelain face even whiter, I thought something awful happened.

'Hey, are you okay?' I asked her, as she rested her head against the wall.

'Panic attack, Fiorenza.'

'But in Opera you perform in front of thousands, Anasztázia.'

She nodded.

'I am safe in an opera house as it is my world. I am in control.'

I took the bag of cornetti from her hand and her palm was damp.

'Come and sit down.'

I knew exactly how she felt. I took taxis everywhere in Paris. I did walk to Opera, but I was usually with my father anyway. Occasionally, I went to Opera alone, but never walked the five minutes back to the apartment at night. If I went to university, I took taxis.

My mother said agoraphobia was quite common in the theatre industry; being in theatres constantly rehearsing or performing, taking taxis to and from the hotel and never walking city streets made the outside world seem like a threatening place.

But my mother had extra reasons to be afraid.

STRIDE LA VAMPA

As I have lost my faith in God, I absorb myself in black magic and tarot cards.

It becomes a little obsessive, but as I feel I am already branded by darkness, what does it matter if I plunge further into the dark side.

Despite my fear of going to Roma one year after my attack, me and Marina were both safe, and it gave me the chance to see my cousin Giorgio and Anasztázia.

Maybe Catalina will also be the sweet younger sister again. There is hope.

Catalina had asked me tearfully on the train back to Milano, was evil inherited.

I had reassured her that our mother's DNA would be dominant, that evil is not genetic anyway.

'I truly feel we are at least three-quarters Marina Valentino.'

She was comforted by my words.

Confronting my stepfather did not bring me any closure, it merely reopened the wounds.

I lied to my sister. I just hope it helped her, if only a little.

However safe Anasztázia says her place is, it did not save my mother.

I asked Anasztázia when I was leaving for the airport, had Marina seen my mother again.

She looked at me sadly.

'Yes. I am sorry, Fiorenza.'

'She hates me,' I said. 'I wanted to see her.'

'Fiorenza; children and animals are very sensitive to the spirit world.

Marina is your mother's granddaughter. She has been looking

in the Lilac room every day.

Then, when you were visiting your sister in Milano, Marina saw 'the beautiful lady' placing roses in the kitchen. When she ran to hug her, your mother smiled and disappeared.

Poor Marina was so distressed. She does not understand.'

I feel worse.

'Fiorenza, listen,' Anasztázia said.

'It is proof there is a world beyond this life, that your dear mother lives on somehow. Hope is one thing you should never lose.'

I have allowed Alain access to Marina. After thinking about my own life, I decided that I wanted the best for my daughter.

After I return from seeing Anasztázia, I am looking for some documents in the bureau, and there are Alain's letters stashed at the back.

He was telling the truth; he was not lying about trying to contact me. Alain had wanted to see me, to see his child. The last letter was sent a week after I had Marina, resigned and sad. He asked me to call, but he guessed I hated him.

Just knowing Alain did care might have eased my depression.

François had no right, no right at all.

When he returns from London, Marina tells him excitedly about my mother and the Lilac room in Anasztázia's place.

He smiles when she says, 'the lady who looks like mamma.'

'Anasztázia was always very spiritual,' François says, assuming Marina saw a lot of photos, just as she does in our apartment.

'Yes,' I say. I am quiet. 'She was in love with my mother.'

I want to ask him why he hid my goddamn letters. It will have to wait until Marina is in bed.

'I worried she was in love with Anasztázia, but you know your mother, Fiorenza.

She was a free spirit.

She loved Anasztázia but not as much as Anasztázia loved her,' he says.

Marina talks constantly about 'the lady who loves black roses'.

François says to me that Anasztázia is a little morbid with black roses.

'The photo Anasztázia gave me as a gift was from opening night for Lucia di Lammermoor in La Scala. My mother gave Anasztázia a bouquet of black roses.

I am putting this one above my bed.'

He stares at the image of his beautiful Marina Valentino and says despite her smile, it is almost like a premonition of her death: this gothic black outfit, those hideous black roses, her last time at La Scala.

'I would hate to get black roses in the Opera,' François tells me.

'My mother liked it,' I say, defensively.

'She gave Anasztázia those roses in La Scala and once, for Tosca opening night, Romeo gave her black roses.'

François looks sad and reflective because I mentioned Romeo.

He does not like to be reminded of her past, although Romeo lost her. She broke his heart, first by marrying my stepfather, then running off with François.

I do not understand my father's retrospective jealousy. Romeo and my mother had appeared together in the early days in Romeo et Juliette, and like star-crossed lovers, it was sweet at first.

She had called him Romeo, instead of his real name, Giacomo.

She was already famous and as her career accelerated even faster, she screamed at poor Romeo for not committing to his Art.

Her life was Opera and travelling. Romeo would not have lasted even if they had got married.

He began to resent her densely packed schedule, which was full for years, spanning many countries.

I remember her shrieking in a Paris hotel room that she was a famous diva, and that Romeo could take it or leave it.

Although she would unkindly snap at François that she was way more famous, he was more on her level than Romeo. Opera has been his life.

'Why did you hide my letters? I found them in the bureau.' I turn on him, once Marina is safely in her room.
I throw the pile of letters on the table.
'Fiorenza, I did not want you hurt. I was thinking of you.'
'When I met him last year, he told me he wrote to me!
Maybe I would have been less depressed after having Marina if you gave me those letters!
I was so messed up when I was young: my mother gave me to Auntie Luisa, I thought every man was my father, I had 'unknown' on my birth certificate which felt lousy.
I know my mother made it up to me but it still hurt.
I want Marina to grow up knowing her father.'
He tries to take my hands and I pull away.
'Fiorenza, it broke her heart giving you to Luisa. She cried for five whole days, then got so depressed she wanted to end her own life.
She adored you, she really did.'
'Damn you, François! Those were my letters!'
My emotions are all over the place.
'Fiorenza, you want the truth?
Your mother loved you more than anyone. More than me, more than Catalina.
This is why you feel so awful. She had such a special connection with you.
You lost the one person in your life who felt so much for you.'
I do not answer.
It seems strange that if this is true and she loved me the most, I cannot see her spirit.
'I worried Alain could hurt you again when you were fragile.

I am sorry about the letters, and maybe I was wrong to do this, and I am sorry if having 'unknown' on your birth certificate hurt you, but when she gave you to Luisa, it nearly destroyed her.

She just did not want a man involved in your life but she adored you.

Fiorenza! Are you getting this?'

'This is about my daughter's father! Damn you! And my mother was everything to me.

I love her like nothing else!'

'I know.'

I am full of hurt and anger.

I go to place the photo frame on my bedroom wall.

Anasztázia promised to bring some more when she visits us.

I sit on the bed and look at the photo for a long time. The sun sets and I am still there as shadows begin to fall across the room.

'You look lovely,' François tells me as I am ready to go out on my date. My first date since Alain.

I am still mad with François. I have more time to be mad as I have summer break.

I carry on pinning my hair up, beautiful raven waves of it, like my mother's.

'It is good you are going out. The only social life you have is attending my operas.

As long as it is not some married man?'

I glare at his gentle smile in the mirror.

'You had no right to hide my mail.' I jam the hairgrips in, still sulky and resentful.

François says, 'I thought I was protecting you.'

He does not know I saw my stepfather in prison twice and I took Catalina, just that I visited Anasztázia in Roma. Marina only saw the apartment, says I visited 'Auntie Catalina'.

He asks me again about my date.

'I have a date with a woman……..' I tell him, directly and wait for his shock.

'Fiorenza, as long as your date treats you like a goddess.'

He squeezes my shoulders and smiles at me in the mirror. Then I wonder, is he jealous?

Stop thinking this, Fiorenza. He is your father.

'You are early,' she smiles. 'Come in.'

I first met Natalija, the famous mezzo who broke Anasztázia's heart, backstage in Paris when I was with my father. My mother despised this ruthless Hungarian who had hurt dear Anasztázia.

Natalija is pretty much disliked by the whole Opera World for being difficult and arrogant.

She walked out on Anasztázia to go to The Met five years ago. She told her the day she was leaving that she was never returning to Roma, that after her run of Carmen in Latvia, she was flying direct to New York.

She said, it would have messed you up to know earlier, so I am telling you today.

That is one of the most heartless breakups ever. She had planned it for some time and stepped over Anasztázia, who was crying on the floor, with all her suitcases.

Natalija is very beautiful in a smoky, sensual way. She had a crush on my mother once, so she wants to date a young Marina Valentino. I am what she is looking for.

'Fiorenza! You are so like Marina! I respected you for saying no to my first offer. So many would chase after me, but you really are your mother's daughter and very fiery in nature like her.

How strange I never even knew you existed until your mother……'

'Died,' I say. 'It is okay to say it, Natalija.'

'Fiorenza; such a pretty name.'

She steps forward with a flirty laugh, kisses me, and holds me at arm's length.

'Wow! An exact likeness, except her eyes were nearly black and yours are dark brown, but other than that……...'

'I called my daughter after her,' I tell her. 'She has her eyes.'

But Natalija is not interested in my little girl. I doubt she likes children one bit.

Her long jet spirals of hair are loose, and she wears a sensational red dress. There is no denying she is very beautiful, but she is just like her signature role, Carmen. She is a woman who loves and leaves.

I would never trust her with my heart.

This is a dangerous game to play, especially because she hurt Anasztázia.

But I am lonely, and I truly do not think I could love anyone now.

I am only going to see Natalija rarely, given her schedule takes her all over the world.

I tell her about Alain, that I wanted the child, and he did not. And that is that.

'I let my daughter see him now and he begged me to go to the Opera, but I am not interested,' I tell Natalija.

'You are so strong and independent, like your mother, Fiorenza. Not just beautiful but you do what you want. I admire people like this.

But why do you never visit Italia?' she asked over dinner.

'I could see you more as I always have La Scala at least twice a year, usually three times.

Surely you take your daughter to see relatives?'

'No, they think I am a slut and there is too much pain in Roma.

Besides, my mother's grave is here, in Paris My sister lives in Milano, but I never visit her.

She is training to be a ballerina.'

Natalija is not interested in my sister. She takes my hand in the flickering candlelight of the restaurant, and she is serious.

'You know, baby; I lost my mother too. I cannot remember her, but I cried many times over her gravestone in southern Hungary.

I was just over a year old when she died. I think it turned me into a careless bitch.'

She looks sad and I finally see vulnerability under her tough front.

'I went on for years believing she took her own life because she hated me.

She jumped off a bridge in Budapest, like so many Hungarians before her. The tragedy was that she survived, but her heart was damaged. She had two heart attacks in the ambulance, but she recovered.

Then one year later, she passed away in her sleep.......'

Her eyelashes flutter and she looks down.

'I am so sorry, Natalija. You know she must have suffered postnatal depression? She adored you but she was sick.

My mother suffered very badly with depression after having me and my sister. She hated my little sister when she was a baby, but she my mother was ill. No one knew because she was just a famous demanding diva.'

Natalija says nothing for a few minutes as I hold her hand.

'I am so sorry about your mother, Fiorenza.

I never even knew she had children until I met you.

Yes, post-natal depression is terrible, and it was the reason my mother jumped into the Duna River....' Natalija wipes away a tear, then she smiles at me.

She switches back to her flirty self, sadness forgotten.

'Well, anyway, Fiorenza. Let us enjoy our evening!' she says brightly, letting my hand flop on the table. She had a careless manner, switching from vulnerable to flirtatious in an instant.

I would not trust this woman with my heart if I had any heart left to give.

'Do you have a photo of your mother?' I ask.

I am wanting to see this softer side of Natalija, not the hateful prima donna everyone talks about. The world's most famous mezzo; so young and talented and so bitchy.

She is happy to be asked and produces a picture frame from her handbag.

A hauntingly beautiful but sad-looking woman stands in a wonderful red dress in a piazza. She has long dark brown hair, but her delicate features are unmistakably Natalija's.

'Where is this piazza? Roma?'

'No. In southern Hungary, in her wedding dress,' Natalija explains.

'She and my father lived there, and I attended university in the town too. It has Italianate buildings. After her death we moved to Budapest. He was too sad to stay in the town.'

'She looks lovely,' I tell her.

'Yes,' she says.

'It is a strange thing, grief. Some want to be around the memories and others want to run away.'

It was a sensitive comment from a so-called hateful prima donna.

'Do you have a photo of your daughter?' She surprises me by asking.

'A little Marina!' she exclaims, studying the picture.

'My relatives think she is from an incestuous relationship with my father. I hate them. They refused to see me in Roma.'

'Is she from your father?' Natalija asks, twirling her hair in an interested way.

She looked at me with a beautiful but hard expression.

'Why would anyone have a child from incest?' I say, shocked.

'But incest is okay if you are both adults,' Natalija said, pushing her wine glass around.

She gave me a wicked smile.

'Can it ever be okay, Natalija?'

She had said something like if no one is underage or getting hurt.

Then she remembered a question about Opera and the conversation was forgotten.

Her casual dismissal of incest was typical of her; she had no boundaries.

For the second time in just over a week, I have another date. Natalija wants me to attend her final night in the Opera.

'Are you sure it is okay to watch Marina?' I ask my father.

'It is just this lady is only in Paris for a short time. She is wanting me to see her opera tonight....'

'An opera singer!' my father says.

'How nice! Why would I mind watching Marina? I am at home anyway and she sleeps well.

God knows you need some affection in your life.

At least your sister seems better after your visit. It was so nice of you to make the journey from Roma to see her. She sends her love.'

François does not know about the prison visit. He would be so angry with me for taking Catalina.

'Well, is she famous?' François asks.

'Very,' I say.

It is a Verdi festival for the end of season in Paris Opera. Verdi and Puccini are always my favourites. I already attended La Traviata with Marina to see François play Alfredo.

I take my daughter if it is suitable or have Loredana take care of her for the evening. After all, I have been attending shows with my mother since I was three years old.

She was a little restless in La Traviata, but I trained her to be quiet and sit on my knees, like my mother did with me. Never speak, Fiorenza. Ask me later. No chocolate until the interval.

I was bored or tired in many performances, but I never spoke, not even if we had a box alone.

Marina is a good girl. She fell asleep through most of the Opera but says she enjoyed the night.

I think she really likes the occasion; the dressing up like a princess, all the attention and meeting everyone backstage. She will be hopelessly vain.

'Il Trovatore is on tonight,' François says, then his smile fades.

We went a few days ago, me and François. I did not take Marina because it is violent, and the lyrics are so dark; all that talk of burning and vengeance. The age rating was 14 on the tickets and the director is dubbed the 'king of darkness'.

I like his inventive productions, but I do find some of the violence too much.

'You do know Elise is married?' François asks me. Elise is the lead soprano playing Leonora.

'She is a mezzo,' I tell him.

He knows who is playing Azucena tonight, the woman we saw only a few nights ago. Her reputation in the opera world is legendary; the beautiful, fiercely talented Hungarian mezzo, who is talked about for all the wrong reasons.

François knows of all the theatreland gossip and none of it is good.

'Natalija? That awful Hungarian girl? Fiorenza, you know what she did to Anasztázia?

She is poison! That girl is a diva of the worst kind.... if it was not for her beauty and incredible talent, she would be blacklisted by every opera house in the world!

In Paris, she has been despised by the entire company for Il Trovatore!'

He is angry with me.

'You never got mad when I told you I was going to have Marina! Now I date a woman you only know from backstage gossip, and you are mad? For God's sake!'

'Fiorenza, you are vulnerable. Your mother hated her!' he takes my arm.

'She was good to Natalija when she was a young opera singer, then she realised how ruthless that girl was.'

'Dating Natalija is better than being hurt,' I say, as I pick up my bag.

'Fiorenza, did Marina's father hurt you?' he takes my arm, his eyes full of pain.

'Did Alain force you, my love?'

'No, he was nice until we split. Look, I have to go!'

I slam the door and run into the elevator. I never want to tell him about my attack, have those horrible images in his head where I am broken and ruined by Andrea's men.

Il Trovatore suits my mood with its twisted tale of vengeance and angry suffering and Natalija is amazing, even better than the other night. When she performs Azucena's famous aria Stride la vampa, I marvel at the power in her voice and see how she became one of the finest mezzos in the world.

She is not just gorgeous and a fine actress, she has one of the best mezzo voices I have ever heard, if not the best. It is so unusual and rich, which is why her signature role in Carmen always sells out the minute it hits box offices.

The next morning, when I arrive home, François clearly has not slept very well. There are dark circles under his eyes.

I kiss Marina who says, 'mamma, you are so pretty!'

I take a coffee.

'You are not eating?' my father asks me.

'I already had breakfast,' I say.

'Were you on a sleepover?' Marina asks me.

'Yes, I visit a friend, Marina. I stayed for a sleepover.'

I think of Natalija and at least I do not feel dirty. I could not imagine being with a man right now.

'Fiorenza, please talk to me,' François pleads. 'You mentioned being hurt; who hurt you?'

'No one, I was only saying that a date is better than anyone hurting you.'

He rests his hand on my arm and says he better go to rehearsals. 'Are you okay?'

'Of course.' I shrug and pour Marina some more milk.

IL ROGO

My father is upset I am going to see Natalija one final time before she leaves Paris.

'Fiorenza, I do not want you to! She is much older than you and famous. People take advantage of beautiful young women.

You are still vulnerable…...'

'I was 16 years old when I dated Alain and he is about the same age as Natalija. Only you let me think he was heartless. Thanks to you I had worse depression.

I am old enough to decide who I date, and I have no heart left to break!'

'Fiorenza, I am worried about you and your moods,' he says.

'Can you speak with a shrink?'

'Stop asking! If you want me to call the au pair for Marina when I go out, fine! But this is three dates in all these years. Cut me a break, François!

Are you jealous? You want me all for yourself in your bed? Is this why you hid my letters?'

I jab my finger into his chest, confrontational and angry. I pull open my dress, showing my lingerie.

François turns away.

'Fiorenza. Please cover up.'

'Why? Look at me, François! Look at my beauty!' I laugh.

François is horrified.

'Do you really think I see my beautiful daughter in this way?

Fiorenza…... you wear her clothes, her perfume. You look like her and have her fiery nature, even her laugh…....sometimes, when I see you, I think you are her…....'

He gropes for the words he cannot truly express.

'At night I see Marina in you.'

He does see me as my mother.

'I knew it,' I say coldly.

'Fiorenza, I just miss her; it is natural to see her in you.'

The thought that has been growing like poison inside me swells to bursting point. Now I feel there is an element of truth in what my hateful relatives said. Ever since I visited Roma to see Anasztázia two months ago, I have this strange feeling.

As if I brought my mother's spirit back in my body.

But then I have been performing black magic, so maybe I attracted some malevolent energy.

I felt only a glimmer of it before, when I began attending premières as his 'date' for the evening. He wanted me on his arm, like a glamorous wife.

The thoughts are shifting and starting to form a clearer picture.

When he performed Tosca with a very beautiful Italian co-star earlier this year, I was jealous.

He had also been working away from Paris, and I asked him didn't he ever want affairs with some co-star?

'No. I do not want some shallow fling however beautiful the co-star, whatever chemistry we have.

I leave it on stage.'

'Alessia is very beautiful and only 33 years old,' I said, studying the photos in the Tosca programme.

'Surely you are attracted to her?'

'Fiorenza,' he said.

'This soprano; I do not have feelings for her. She is a good co-star and yes, I see she is very beautiful, but acting is not reality.

Your mother could perform with any co-star, however much she disliked them and still make it seem real.

Why do you worry?'

'I am jealous,' I tell him honestly.

'But why? No one would ever come close to your mother. Only you are in the same league.

If it is not your mother, I do not want them.'

'I like to be your date,' I tell him.

'You are worrying over nothing,' he had told me.

'You will always be my date, carissima,' he said, as he kissed my face.

I wanted to be with him. I was shocked when I admitted this to the mirror, late at night with the candles flickering from my black magic.

This was the first time I voiced those feelings.

And then it became all too real.

I carry on applying my make-up as François watches me.

He steps in front of me as I go to leave. I pick up my bag and coat.

'Get out of the way, François.'

'I do not want you to see Natalija. Please do not go tonight.'

'Get out of my way!' I scream. 'I am an adult!'

'You want me here so you can have me yourself? Because I look like my mother?'

I laugh in a crazy way. I think I am losing it, but the thoughts are burning deeper with a terrible intensity.

I am thinking of the flames in Il Trovatore, of the fire of burning jealousy I have.

François grabs my shoulders and shakes me hard.

'Stop it, Fiorenza! You stop this!'

I fall on my knees. 'I always slept next to you after mamma died!'

I remember how I would sleep on his big bed because of our nightmares.

'Fiorenza, I am sorry. And we fell asleep in the same room for comfort from all the nightmares, so we were not alone.

It was innocent, Fiorenza. We were both so traumatised. You would sit on the bed with coffee, and we would talk.

How can you even think of it being anything more? You were 16 years old.'

He tries to take my hand.

'Don't touch me!' I scream.

I see his face look at me with hurt. I am out of control tonight, possessed by some dark volcanic energy.

I run out of the apartment. Why am I doing this to him?

I seem to be so full of hate and venom right now. I do not feel much for Natalija; I just wondered if I would be better with a woman, but people are all the same. They all hurt.

And now I am having feelings I do not understand.

The more I try to push them away, the more they fly at me like angry mosquitoes.

After a few days I have even forgotten Natalija. It is as if I am unable to see or feel anyone in this world apart from the introspective world of me, François, and my daughter.

If Natalija had sworn undying love I would not want it right now.

The next morning when I return home, François is cold towards me. Marina is already with the au pair, and he is about to leave for the Opera House and rehearsals.

My hair is wild. I look like I have been dragged out of bed.

'I am sorry,' I say, but he does not want to look at me.

He turns away and washes his coffee cup.

'There is coffee if you want. I saved you a croissant.'

'François, I am sorry about everything I said last night.

I am so full of anger, because of losing my mother and it still burns!

You never deserved those things I said.' I sit at the table and cry.

I feel his arms wrap around me.

'Please keep talking to me, my love. And I should not have told you to stop seeing Natalija.

Listen, carissima; when you went to see Anasztázia, were you and Marina safe?

Is that it; you fear Andrea even though he is in prison?'

'Yes,' I tell him. 'We were safe and yes, I still fear Andrea.'

'Do you want to see a shrink?'

'No. Seeing Anasztázia in April is the last time I will go back to Roma. I am so sorry I left you feeling bad last night. Please forgive me.'

I kiss him as he is holding me. A real kiss.

He steps away, shocked.

'Fiorenza, please do not kiss me like that. It is too amorous. That is not how we should be.

You are my life; you and little Marina.

But your family in Italia speak poison. Catalina is sorry she said hurtful words too, but she was young.

And you and me; we are not the people your family talk about; those 'sinners'.

We are very close and that is all.'

Right now, I want to be one of those sinners.

He wipes the tears from my face, gently strokes my hair. I know he has thoughts.

I see it in his eyes, and I see it when I talk to handsome opera singers when we go backstage together.

He stares at me as if he is in love with me. In a year, I have turned into a woman, but one with no boundaries, like Natalija. As if I cannot separate dream from reality.

The stress and life events have propelled me into this abyss.

'Fiorenza, I want you to see someone to talk about this violence; you were 16 years old when your mother was killed.

You are holding too much pain within you.' François is sad

'No, I cannot,' I say.

'I have lost faith in God. I tore off my crucifix in the cathedral and I no longer pray.'

'I wish you would talk and how can anyone who has been hurt so badly pray at the altar?

No wonder you renounced God.

I always wondered how your mother could still go to church after all her suffering. But her religion was part of her life, on stage and off it.'

'François, I like our life being just you and me. Maybe I am a little in love with you.'

He smiles at me.

'No, you do not know how to love, dear Fiorenza. You love me but you are not in love.

And about me dating; it was your mother or nobody.

I was lucky to have so many years with her.'

I say, 'I would be so jealous if you dated someone.'

He looks at me strangely. 'Why? You mentioned this a few times; being jealous of co-stars.'

'You know why,' I say and push my coffee cup around.

'Ask yourself the same question.' I look at him.

He hesitates and stares at me, as if assessing his feelings and then smiles.

He does not want to face those feelings.

'Listen, dry those tears now because I have to go to rehearsals.'

He kisses my hair.

I want to be my mother for him. If it was her or nothing, I can be her.

The thought which spins around my head is relentless. It shrieks at me with an intensity which grows each day. I feel powerless to prevent the darkness closing in, until I am suffocating in the idea which I created myself.

Maybe Natalija and her lack of boundaries triggered this, or maybe it is the black magic I have been absorbed in.

I have been really digging into the dark side and performing secret spells, asking for my mother's spirit to possess me, in body and thoughts.

I do not want Natalija or Alain or any of those good-looking men or women in the Opera.

I change our lives forever and plunge us straight into the darkness, driven by the savage Gods.

Like a woman possessed, I am unable to prevent it.

Maybe and beyond this life, if Heaven and Hell exist, I will burn forever.

Burn like Azucena's mother in Il Trovatore, in that terrible funeral pyre.

But that is a long way off.

I go to his room after midnight, the witching hour, when he is asleep. I am drenched in Dior perfume, dressed in black silk and my long hair cascades down my back. When I look in the mirror, with make-up on at night, even my eyes look darker. I am my mother

I am convinced her spirit is in my body.

He is sleeping deeply so I silently pad over to his bed and get under the covers. I move closer and I feel the warmth from François.

Maybe I can just sleep here, just as we did four years ago. That would be nice. I feel safe.

Maybe this is all I am craving, just closeness and love.

'Marina?' he murmurs in the darkness.

'Amore, you came back to me…..'

Then all thoughts of innocent affection vanish. In the dark, I am Marina Valentino.

His tears are damp on my skin.

It is a terrible but lovely feeling as if I stepped off the precipice. My twisted love is driven into my savage heart like knives, and I know this is us falling to our deaths.

Then he sleeps deeply.

I stay awake listening to the silence. Eventually I fall asleep without nightmares.

Until I wake up the next morning to screaming. He is already out of the bed shouting and shaking me awake. I never saw him totally lose it like this.

'Fiorenza! Wake the fuck up and get up before your daughter does! God have mercy on my soul!

What the hell have we done?'

I am drowsy and still tired. I do not want to get up yet. He is pale and looking at me in horror as if I am a demon temptress or a vampire.

'François....' I reach for his hand. 'François, please......'

'Get the fuck up, you evil little tart!' He hauls me out of the bed roughly by one arm and I fall to the floor, like a broken doll.

'Last night you wanted me,' I say. I am tearful.

'Do not make me the guilty one, François. You wanted me!'

'Fiorenza, I was dreaming! Of your mother! I was asleep. What the fuck have you done?

What the hell have we done?!' he shouts at me.

He is still in shock, his hands over his face.

'François, I love you....' I stretch my arm towards him again and he steps further away.

'Cover yourself up right now, you little whore!' he orders.

He throws me my robe and turns away as if my body totally disgusts him. I get up, feeling ashamed and hurt.

He never called me such horrible names before.

We did something truly unimaginable, but he is turning it all on me. As if he did nothing.

'Get the hell out!' he says.

'Just get out! You are not my daughter; you are some demon

temptress in her body!'

'You did want me,' I tell him.

'I wanted you too. You do not admit to it, instead you just blame me!'

'Get the hell out before I slap your insolent face!' he shouts at me.

'I cannot look at you. You disgust me, Fiorenza.'

He turns away and wraps his robe tighter and stares out of the window.

I leave, knowing I ruined everything. The door slams. I hear the shower running for a long time.

He has been crying when he comes into the kitchen, dressed and ready to leave for his concert rehearsals for tomorrow evening's performance. I touch his hand and he moves away in disgust without looking at me. Maybe he did think I was my mother, maybe he really was asleep, dreaming of her.

All I know is we will never be the same. I hate myself. I did ruin everything.

Marina asks me what is wrong?

'François is not well,' she says.

'He does not sleep so well last night, my sweet girl,' I tell her and kiss her face.

I get her ready to see Alain. He is taking her out, but I think he always wishes I would join them.

I did go the first few times, but Marina is such a little diva that once Alain paid her attention, she loves going out with him. He spoils her like crazy, always buying her treats. She gabbles non-stop when she comes home.

I just hope he never lets her down, that this is permanent now. I sense that it is.

I do know he was so disappointed that he had two sons from his ex-wife and not a daughter.

François is going away in two days and for the rest of the time in Paris he cannot bear to be near me. I want to go to his concert.

'No way do I want you there now, Fiorenza!' he yells at me. 'No way!'

I am so hurt.

'Why are you treating me like this?' I say, when he leaves for the airport and Lake Constance.

I was supposed to go with him to Bregenz and he told me no way in Hell was I going.

He is away for three weeks and me and Marina were planning to stay for five days.

'How can we ever be the same, Fiorenza?' He looks so lost, despite his anger.

'No one has to know,' I say. And I truly believe this.

'But I know, and it is killing me!' he says angrily.

'I am an adult. I am 20 years old,' I tell him.

'And I do not think that 'I was dreaming' excuse is good enough.'

I am angry because he acts as if it is all my fault.

'Who else is in your life, François?'

'What difference does that make, Fiorenza? You need help if you cannot see it. I told you before, I do not want to date anyone! But I sure as hell do not want this! It is sick!'

'Don't leave like this. You want me to leave this apartment and never see you again?

Fine, me and Marina can leave.'

I try to hug him, but he pushes me away.

'No! Please do not touch me! I want you to stay here and forgot that night.

It did not happen.'

'I wanted it,' I tell him.

'And so did you. François! Why do you still want me here then?' I clutch my chest.

'You ruin everything!' he tells me, as he steps into the elevator.

'Why did you ruin our lives, Fiorenza?'
'Because you would never dare!' I shriek at him.
He stares at me as if he does not know me.
'Damn you to Hell on that fucking floating stage in Bregenz!' I shout, as the doors close on him.
'I hope it is stormy every night! I hope you fall in that fucking lake!'
I go back into the apartment.
I feel guilty wishing him bad luck before his performances, but he is a good swimmer. One year in Bregenz he had to jump in the lake and swim round to the back of the set during Carmen.

'Marina! Pack your suitcase. We are going to La Rochelle,' I call.
'But we go to François?' she says. 'To the lake?'
'We fight because I told him Bregenz is boring. There is no beach.
La Rochelle is so pretty, and we get to have fun. Isn't this better?'
She looks doubtful, until I show her some photos of La Rochelle. Then she becomes excited about the artificial beach and says she wants to go there instead.
Bregenz would be no fun for a little girl, and I hated that huge arena of 7,000 people with its monstrous floating stage.
I went with my mother to see François and we both hated it and hated the audience too. My mother favoured Italian box style theatres, so she hated sitting near people and got into arguments with the Austrians next to us.
I go and help Marina pack her case, tell her all about Île de Ré and La Rochelle.
It is easier for me too; to take her on the TGV instead of travelling through a busy airport. We will stay in a nice little hotel. Nothing too expensive, just a medium-priced place for the two of us.

Fuck François. When he texts two days later, he is surprised we are in La Rochelle.

I text, telling him to leave us alone.

He calls me. 'Fiorenza, I need…..'

I cut him off.

'Leave me the hell alone.'

As I lie on the beach, I remember Natalija told me her stepmother went crazy and accused Natalija of seducing her own father when she was 17 years old.

'I was sitting in my night-robe in the living room, talking to my father about my hopes for the future and that is all. Then Lilla, my hateful stepmother, arrived home and went totally crazy.

She was screaming at us both, accusing us of incest. God, I was shocked.

She made sure I went to university in the south and not Budapest. My father tried to calm her down as she was hysterical, but she always got her way. She exiled me to the South.

If circumstances were different, well……I do not see incest as such a terrible thing now.'

She twirled a spiral of hair in her fingers thoughtfully. This girl really had no moral compass.

'I sometimes think of it too,' I confessed.

'It is just a normal crush before you experience real love.'

Natalija had smiled.

'Your father is extremely good-looking, and you do look like a carbon copy of your mother,' Natalija laughed.

'Maybe you should give it a go! You are his beautiful love reincarnated.'

She laughed in a wicked way. Here she was speaking so lightly of incest, a thought which would horrify most people.

But somehow, after our conversation, the idea which had been hiding like some venomous creature in my head for months, began to form. It grew until it was taking over.

When I try to call François a few days later, he does not answer. He just texts he cannot speak now.

I am angry with myself, with God, with the whole world.

Apart from my daughter I cannot see any good in life. I turn cartwheels on the artificial beach, we visit Île de Ré and eat seafood.

Marina has a fine time. She would have hated Bregenz.

STORMS

The day François returns, he retires to his room without speaking.

'Well fuck you then,' I call through his door.

Let him sulk tonight. He was even quiet with Marina. He said he was very tired, refused her offer of a bedtime story.

We avoid each other for the rest of the week.

Easy enough as he has been in rehearsals all day and late into evening, having missed a week due to Bregenz.

When he arrives home in the evening, I make sure I am in my own room.

In the morning he is gone before I get up.

Only tonight, we are attending the open-air theatre for La bohème and the Puccini festival.

We walk in silence from our taxi.

I had arranged to attend his première some time ago, except now he really does not want me there.

The Opera will then form part of the autumn schedules in the Opera House. François is playing Rodolfo. He told me to stay at home.

I nearly did, then decided I wanted to see the show, only we argue non-stop once out of the taxi.

'Why do you always wear her perfume? I bought you some Chanel. But you wear your mother's favourite Dior.'

He glares at me as we walk towards the entrance. We are very early as he has to go backstage to warm up and get into costume.

'I like the Dior best of all, François,' I say sarcastically.

'She bought it for me as well! Now you have a problem?'

'We do have a problem, one hell of a fucking problem, Fiorenza. Do you have to wear that outfit?' He is picking an argument about my mother's clothes.

I have worn her clothes since I was 16 years old.

'It is my mother's dress and tiara. For God's sake, we are the same size so why waste money buying more?'

I had wondered about the jet beaded dress and ruby tiara, but it is a hot summer night, so I wore a gold dress and sandals. The jet beaded dress is how she appears in Anasztázia's apartment, so I feel it is a little strange. No, I could not wear that dress or the ruby tiara. It is a haunted outfit.

When I see the photo of her above my bed, I feel terrible guilt.

Forgive me, mamma, forgive me for what I did.

If she can see me now, she will hate me forever. I spend a long time when I am alone wondering exactly what she can see from Heaven.

'It is your mother's outfit,' François continues.

'You look too much like her.

You seemed to go overnight from being a lovely girl to a demon temptress. Maybe you should be praying in the cathedral right now.

He walks ahead of me, angry with me because I am attending his première tonight.

He is a goddamn hypocrite too. If I pray, then so should he.

'All this stuff is mine now. She would love to see me in her outfits.'

'If she knew what you did it would destroy her,' he says.

'What WE did, François.'

He tells me I should not attend the drinks backstage post-show.

'People already say I only have eyes for my beautiful daughter. They are innocent comments only they are not innocent now. What if they knew the truth?'

The hurt burns deeper. He is ashamed of me now. I am so angry.

'I can control myself around other people.' I march ahead.

'Maybe you cannot, François! You have the problem! Always you parade me around, stare at me as if I am a goddess!' I shout this at him.

'Be quiet! Someone might hear us,' he says, scanning the street.

There is no one near us as we are so early, only some stage crew smoking at the entrance of the open-air theatre.

'I would be proud to show you off before, but now….. Fiorenza, wait!'

'No.'

I walk away to the main entrance leaving him standing there.

The venue is not open for another half an hour, but the staff know me and let me in for my double espresso.

I do this everywhere; dress like a diva and behave in an entitled way and the staff in every Opera House allow me entry before the audience. Once I even got into a première before the President.

I am Marina Valentino's daughter after all.

She did the same, behaved like a diva when she was still a student at La Scala.

In fact, she behaved like a diva ever since she was six years old, told me she knew she would be famous.

I knew I had it all, Fiorenza. I was so hungry for it.

I knew at six years old I was destined to be a star.

God made me beautiful for a reason and God gave me this voice to split the heavens open.

As soon as the performance comes down, I do not wait for the curtain call.

I know this is unlucky; both my mother and François believed the superstition that leaving before the end of the curtain call means no applause for your next performance.

But I am not an opera singer and tonight I have to get away, not queue with the masses for a taxi.

A storm is already threatening in the distance with a few jagged lightning forks.

How appropriate, given the mood at home.

I enjoyed the Opera, but François already resents me even watching the performance.

These outdoor shows begin at 21.15, so the stage lighting can be seen in all its dramatic beauty, and because the intense summer heat makes any chance of commencing before sunset an impossibility.

It is nearly midnight when I take my taxi and I brood over the argument we had.

Loredana is surprised to see me so early.

She was fine to be here much longer and stay overnight; after all she stayed overnight when Marina was a baby. I pay her and call a taxi.

She is not afraid of being out late at night alone, but Paris is not safe.

'I did not want champagne,' I tell Loredana.

'The outdoor shows come down so late. It is hot and I just want ice-cream at home alone, not champagne and socialising.'

'Did you argue with your father again?' she asks.

'Marina said you were fighting before Bregenz.'

'Oh, that,' I say dismissively.

'I refused to go to that monstrous arena of Bregenz. I went with my mother when I was seven years old, and we both hated it.

Me and Marina enjoyed La Rochelle, just the two of us.

And as for the argument tonight; he is stressed before new performances.'

I settle on the sofa. My feet ache from the gold sandals.

The rain is threatening outside as I watch jagged forks of lightning streaking the sky and the thunder is creeping nearer.

I wondered even then how much Loredana guessed about us.

Me and François always speak Italian and French to Marina,

which is why we hired an Italian-speaking au pair, and why I was reluctant to search for another au pair.

My mother and François always stressed the importance of languages as like many opera stars, they spoke four languages. Languages are the key to freedom, my mother had instilled in me.

I had to study English and French, but I never got on with German although my mother was fluent.

Yet she hated German language for Opera.

'François also says I should not wear my mother's dresses,' I say to Loredana.

'Well, no sense in those beautiful dresses hanging in the closet and you look lovely, Fiorenza.'

She kisses me goodnight.

I sit in the living room drinking and eating gelato, the dark thoughts churning over in my head.

There is a lousy film on nearly every channel. I turn the television off and listen to the wild weather, watch the lightning split the Heavens. Storms always make me feel strange.

François arrives less than an hour later. I did not hear the taxi, or I would have run to bed.

'I am just going to bed. You can have the living room to yourself,' I tell him.

'Please leave me alone,' I say, as he follows me to my room.

I light all the candles on the dresser and do not look at him. He does not speak.

To Hell with him.

'What the fuck do you want? I want to sleep and so should you after performing.

If you cannot sleep, eat some gelato and watch a film. There is camomile tea in the pot.

Just go!'

I sit on the bed and take off my earrings, dropping them on the table with a clatter.

'You made it clear I was not welcome tonight. François, I am tired.'

He stares at me; I cannot even read his expression; a mix of sadness and something else.

'You are so beautiful. I am sorry you did not join me backstage,' he says quietly.

I do not know what he wants. I do know that I am tired of arguing.

'There is no woman alive I would sooner be with.'

He turns the key in the door.

'Get the hell out! I want to be alone!' I tell him.

I get up to unlock the door and he takes my hands.

We face each other and I am still furious at him.

'God forgive me,' he says, as he turns out the light.

'God forgive me for what I do. You look so like her.......'

Through the storm he calls me 'carissima'.

Now, there are no more lines to cross. I am condemned. I will be walking in the shadow of darkness forever.

I do not care if I burn in Hell; as spears of lightning slice the sky, illuminating the room, I feel as if I am in some strange place.

My room has become another dimension, like stepping through a mirror.

Only there is no return.

I sleep deeply and I have nightmares as the storm circles Paris. I wake up a few times and François does not stir.

I think how I am really a sinner now. I am the Devil's own child.

I swear I wake up at one point and my mother is standing over the bed. She is so beautiful, but her black eyes are full of hatred.

'Mamma,' I sit up. 'Mamma, I am sorry......'

'How could you?' my mother says.

'You are going to burn in Hell, Fiorenza!

You are stealing my life, you treacherous little bitch! I die and this is what you do!' She clutches my arm, and her voice is a harsh whisper.

I cry out and feel her grip tighten.

'He broke my heart but you, goddamn evil girl; you broke me! You will die for your sin, Fiorenza!'

She scatters the black roses she is holding over the bed. I touch them, feel the velvety petals between my fingers.

'Forgive me, please forgive me……..'

She steps back and retreats into the corner of the room. I cannot reach her.

'Mamma! Mamma, please……'

And then she is gone, back into the shadows. François does not wake up. I am kneeling on the bed and the petals are gone.

I feel like I am losing my mind. I was awake, I swear I was.

I would never have done this if my mother had not been murdered, if I had not suffered so much.

We have both turned in on ourselves until no one else really existed in our world, a terrible secret world hidden high above the glittering lights of Paris.

I remember those first nights and feel such horrible guilt and shame.

I was the temptress. I remember Andrea's chilling words about my father having to control his urges around me.

I thought Andrea was evil when he said it.

François is ill with the guilt. It is hard to exist when the one you are with loves by night and hates you each morning. When you have entered this dark world, there is no escape.

Who would people blame? Me at 20 years old or him in his early fifties with his beautiful daughter?

The circumstances have to be right for a crime; pushed to the limits, we can do something we never thought possible.

François had given everything to Opera and my mother had been his life. He had no friends either, although he was highly renowned in the opera houses across Europe and respected by his colleagues.

Once we entered this jagged and twisted self-reflexive world, there was no turning back.

I know for both of us, the nightmares are savage. He spends his waking hours in torment, whereas I am haunted in my sleep.

He is quieter, sadder in those early days. It is a fierce addiction.

Maybe he finds the ghost of his lost love and I find what I need, which some strange form of love. But it is a horribly distorted love, like a grotesque reflection in a funhouse mirror.

I am terrified of my little girl finding out.

I think both of us hope that we will stop tomorrow, next week, next month, but we do not.

Some nights we sleep apart, but inevitably, we cannot last.

He met many co-stars who wanted to be with him, but I know from the early days of his career, his first marriage had broken up and he could not settle with anyone. His profession was too peripatetic, travelling all over the world for his Opera.

It ruined relationships, he always said. My mother said the same, only she always found herself a lover.

François let her be free without jealousy; he knew she was still married to my stepfather and unable to get a divorce, then later she was with Anasztázia maybe in some romantic way or maybe not.

All François asked of her was that she would return to him in Paris.

He was the polar opposite of my evil stepfather.

She could spill croissant crumbs all over the apartment, drop clothes everywhere and François adored her. She virtually abandoned my baby sister in Paris, leaving au pairs to care for her and he accepted her failings without question.

He even pretended Catalina was his child to save her from Andrea.

She refused to stop returning to Roma and all François asked in return was her love.

I know my mother hated Catalina when she was a baby, hated her because Andrea was her father.

For two years, she hardly touched my sister, but she had been the same with me.

She believed she was a terrible mother; a promiscuous, selfish diva who was careless and capricious.

But the truth is that she would have died for both of us.

I am the image of my mother; beautiful, tempestuous, and seductive. The fact I have a little girl who looks like I did at that age truly messes with François's head. Sometimes he even calls her Fiorenza and me Marina, especially after returning from working abroad.

I know given our lives before, I never once thought that this dark thorny forest of self-reflexive desire and loneliness even existed.

And it is lonely. Horribly lonely.

I was not Fiorenza in the darkness or even in the evening. It is as though some savage demon possessed me. He called me 'Marina' and 'carissima' in the dark.

In the mornings, I was Fiorenza.

I was his shameful secret, the ruined daughter he could not even look at, in case the sight of her burned out his eyes.

I headed to London purely because I was so sick of our shouting matches. I got on the Eurostar and went to see Natalija in Covent Garden in September.

Shopping trip, I had told François and Marina.

Despite my agoraphobia, I could take trains and flights as long as no Metro was involved or walking. I still had panic attacks.

Okay, I had a good time, but I sensed Natalija was only with me because I looked like my mother.

She mentioned my resemblance several times in London.

She was beautiful and glossy and full of mischief. I actually admitted what I did, the terrible sin and she laughed. She was curious.

What was it like, Fiorenza?

Her beautiful eyes had sparkled as she called me a wicked temptress. It seemed to make me more desirable somehow.

If she told me the same thing, how would I feel about her?

Natalija was as attentive towards me as usual, yet still possessed that same careless manner.

Her casual dismissal of my terrible confession made me feel as if I could not really like or love her very much.

She liked showing me off in the Opera and yet I felt when I left London, I could have been anyone.

Anyone beautiful. She must have a whole string of lovers, even admitting how many singers in The Met wanted her.

I knew she was dating other people, but I really did not care.

That autumn, François has a lot of commitments abroad, but he is in Paris for a Christmas run of La bohème. We argue nearly every day when he is home and, in the morning, there is guilt and shame from him and resentment from me.

I had time to spend with François and Marina by the time it got to university Christmas holiday we have shouted most of the time; me and François.

I take Marina to La bohème on Christmas Eve as it is an earlier performance in the day, at 16.00 and she loves the Opera and afterwards, François seems delighted to show us both off.

One guest baritone from Napoli says, 'I thought she was your beautiful young wife, and this little princess your daughter. Italian DNA creates beautiful women.'

The Neapolitan singer says, 'Fiorenza; such a lovely name.'

'He is my papa!' Marina says in a loud voice.

'Marina!' I tell her.

'François is my papa. You know papa Alain; he bought that lovely dress for Christmas yesterday!'

The mood is strange after that.

Marina gets her gifts at home as we eat dinner and François remains quiet. She is not seeing Alain today as he promised to see his two boys, but he spent a lot on her yesterday; bought her overly expensive dress she wanted which will not fit very soon. She is turning into the spoiled little girl I was at her age.

François retires to bed early, saying he is tired.

I sleep next to Marina hoping me and François will go back to normality. Maybe we will now.

Maybe this is a wake-up call for him.

INFERNO

After François returned from performing in Faust in Munich in February, everything retreats into darkness. How appropriate given his character in the Opera sells his soul to the Devil.

I feel as if we are on an express train heading straight to Hell.

For now, we take the TGV into the July inferno of the Riviera.

There are no flames here, but there might as well be. The last few months have been turbulent.

He is in a mood as I saw Natalija for two nights last month in Brussels, where she was performing in a concert.

He thought I was seeing someone else, jealousy rising because of some imaginary lover, and it made me hate him.

I did not admit to seeing Natalija.

It was no fun and I hate Brussels; Natalija was distant, distracted and constantly checking her cell phone.

She had been in touch a few times since I saw her in London, but we did not speak that often and everything about her was so inconsistent. She told me, in the few short phone calls we had over the winter and early spring, she was ill and unable to fly. So she could not leave New York.

She did not want to discuss it.

Why I am even here? I thought as it rained, and we hardly spoke.

She did apologise for not seeing me since last September.

I did believe the illness story as over Christmas, I checked her website.

She had cancelled an Opera in Zurich in January and February to April, in The Met.

She looked thinner and her golden skin was paler than usual. I asked was her bulimia returning and she shouted she was not discussing her health.

You are not a fucking doctor! She was so angry with me.

Again, I wondered was she worth travelling even a short distance for.

Well, this could be the last time as I am not in the mood for this self-absorbed prima donna.

Then in the last five minutes before my train back to Paris, she had reverted to the Natalija I knew; coquettish, seductive, and attentive.

There was a kind of magic about her as she could be cool and careless for days and then for five minutes, her face would light up with beauty and charm.

She was like two different people.

I can make it up to you, she said brightly.

I promise, Fiorenza. I hardly left New York for six months, had to cancel Switzerland and some work in New York too. Seeing doctors and not able to travel was hard.

Next time, I will be better.

I have Madrid in September, and I am sure you can join me.

So by the time I was travelling out of Brussels, I did think it would be nice to see her in Madrid.

Or at least visiting Madrid could be enjoyable if I managed my agoraphobia.

François seems convinced that we can go on holiday to Nice and 'swear off this terrible addiction'.

He truly believes it, like a hopeless junkie.

I am not convinced that a holiday will change anything.

If being apart for five weeks when he travels for Opera does not cure us, I cannot see that the Riviera holds much promise of salvation.

As Marina is four years old, train travel to Nice is easier than flying anywhere for a holiday. François had booked us a suite in the Negresco. Even by my standards it was expensive.

My grandmother moaned at my mother for booking exclusive hotels, but my mother earned a top salary which more than covered her most expensive stays.

She shrieked that she needed luxurious rooms in the best hotels when she was performing on stage.

'I am not on a fucking holiday, mamma!' she would shout.

'I am a diva!'

Travelling worldwide, my mother had to give everything to her Opera; she worried about the saying, you are only as good as your last performance.

She told me in the early days of her career she had cried in dark, lousy digs when her salary would not cover a decent hotel.

'Nothing worse, Fiorenza, than having to prove myself in the Opera World only to return to a dirty hotel or apartment in a lousy district.

After graduating La Scala, I performed in Napoli in Tosca.

My first ever big role in Teatro di San Carlo and virtually no sleep because of the noise in the dark sunless streets. Everyone threw their garbage out of the window and shouted all the time.

There was no light or sun in those narrow streets of God knows what district.

It gave me even more drive to perform better and make it big.

Lucky for me I got famous very fast.'

Some opera houses were months late paying, so unless she had enough money saved, my mother had to take lousy digs.

By the time she was 26 years old, she was already an Italian celebrity.

But we are not performing in Nice, and a medium cost place for a holiday would be fine. We are hardly confined to the hotel room. We do not need sleep for work, or luxury for my daughter.

François insisted on the Negresco.

Besides, he never took holidays, just added on extra days in countries once his Opera run finished. Even over the summer, when he had to take fewer commitments to rest his voice, he still had to rehearse for the autumn season.

Occasionally, he performed in Arena di Verona or in open air concerts in Paris.

Bregenz was not a place he liked; he had performed there several times, but I knew he always favoured Mediterranean countries. In Bregenz, you could be anyone on that monstrous stage.

People did not attend performances on Lake Constance for the famous names, but for the spectacle of the sunset over the lake and the outsized scenery.

The receptionist at the Negresco assumed we were a family, although me and François do not share the same surname. Marina looks like me, so everyone thought I was a beautiful young woman with a sugar daddy, and this was our daughter. I retained my mother's surname for me and Marina.

I also felt to retain my Italian roots distanced myself from François somehow.

Despite all my time in Paris, I was still an Italian beauty and had appeared in a magazine advertisement for an Italian perfume, posing outside the Opera House.

It helped that I was Marina Valentino's daughter.

'Fiorenza Valentino; what a lovely name,' the chic receptionist at the Negresco said to me.

'You and your husband and your delightful little girl are such a good advertisement for us.

Be sure to use our restaurant.'

For a horrible moment I was thinking she was going to take photos for a brochure.

Our room is the best suite available and when I see its luxury, the beautiful views and enormous bathroom, all I can think of is, what a waste of money.

I am irritable and tired. I turn on the air conditioning. I put Marina to sleep, and I am tired too.

He wants to sit up and read and I am scratchy and irritable with him.

'François, just turn out the light. I am fucking tired, and I want to sleep now.'

During the night, I heard him whisper into my hair, 'Marina, carissima'.

And every morning, the same routine; he would take his breakfast silently at the table by the window. Despite this trip being his idea, he acted as if I was the wicked temptress.

This was all his idea and he resented me.

I would sit on the chaise longue with Marina to eat breakfast while François stared moodily at the blue sky outside. He would not even look at me, hardly spoke to Marina.

'What is wrong with François?' she asked many times.

'He worries a lot about his Opera,' I tell her.

One morning he totally lost his temper as I ate breakfast in bed.

'You are ruining the bedsheets, Fiorenza! What is wrong with you that you are so untidy?'

'You cannot ruin a sheet with croissants!' I snap at him.

'Don't be so dramatic.'

'Well, you have coffee too,' he continued.

'Then you will knock it over. I feel like slapping your insolent little ass.'

'You dare!' I yell.

Marina starts to cry.

'See what you do?' I ask him and scoop my daughter up. I dry her tears and tell her we will have an exciting day without him. He is no fun at all in Nice.

He hates me and hates himself and likes to go alone to the beach.

Fine. I hate beaches and it is way too hot for sunbathing, so me and Marina spend our days at the hotel pool. We lie in the shade of four-poster sunbeds, out of the fierce midday sun.

We go together one morning as Marina wants to walk in the sea. François stares at me when I take off my dress.

'Cover yourself up. You are an exhibitionist like your mother.'

'It is a fucking beach, François! I am wearing a bikini. I am hardly a slut wearing just a thong like those tarty girls.'

I look at two topless blonde girls who are letting everyone see their assets. They are over-tanned and bleached blonde. Nothing more unsexy than showing it all off. François does not even look in their direction. He hardly notices the most beautiful women.

And he hates me for it.

'You lie here and sulk then. I am going to the water with Marina! You wanted this fucking holiday in the first place!'

'You curse as much as your mother did,' he says, flopping on to his back.

'Your daughter repeats it. This is not good, Fiorenza.'

I call Marina over from the sandcastle she is building.

'François is being a pain in the ass, so we go to the sea, my love. Then back to the hotel. This sun is very bad for skin.'

The sand is burning hot, as I flip flop to the edge of the ocean carrying Marina. She asks why do I have a pain in the ass from François? Did he slap me?

I give up explaining and just say that he is miserable today. 'Probably the sun has gone to his head.'

Marina asks where the sun went, how is it in his head? It is still in the sky.

She is the age where she asks 'why' all the time. It is driving me a little crazy.

I tell her to watch me do some gymnastics.

Many people look at me as I turn perfect cartwheels and backflips in the sand.

I help Marina to do handstands and cartwheels. 'This is good for the body,' I tell her.

'I can take you to gymnastics classes. My mother was a champion gymnast when she was young.'

I want Marina to be anything but an anorexic ballerina, like my sister.

When Marina jumps on François playfully in her wet swimsuit, he snaps at her too and curses. 'Fuck!' he says. 'Marina, get off!'

He never says unkind words to her.

She is hurt by his anger and starts to wail.

'How dare you speak to her like that! I wish we had not come here! And you complain about my language?

Fine, François. You lie there and be hot and miserable. Me and Marina are going back to the hotel.

It is not healthy to cook the skin.

Lie here and turn yourself into a crocodile handbag!'

'Showing yourself off with your gymnastics for all the men!' he says.

I ignore him and walk away from this wretched man and his jealous heart.

Marina cries, still upset from his harsh words.

'Why do we come to the sea, mamma? He is so mean!'

'It is okay, darling. François is nasty today and the sun is bad for the skin. We can have fun together in the hotel swimming pool and sit in the shade.'

Although I have golden skin like my mother's which tans well, I see it as unhealthy to lie in the sun. My mother was obsessive about never letting her skin be touched by sunlight. She had lovely skin; smooth and perfect even after two children.

An Italian pharmacist told her to always wear sun factor

protection 100 cream and she did, even though she rarely went outdoors.

She feared ageing, especially in her profession, which favours beauty and youth as much as a wonderful voice. She knew if she ever let her standards slip, she could be passed over in favour of younger sopranos especially as she reached the age of 50.

Which was the main reason she was afraid to let her Italian opera houses down. She knew Italia would always favour her for being their star. Paris could pass her over in favour of a younger French soprano, who would hit higher notes and cost the theatre less.

I command a high salary. If I am not perfect, the opera houses stop booking me. That goes for my appearance too; I have to be the best, she always said.

François should still be careful. Men have tougher skin, but they can still age.

He is gone all day. I hate him so much right now.

I do perfect dives off the springboard into the hotel pool for Marina and she splashes in the children's pool, then we lie in the shade and stare at the infinity blue of the sky.

'Your little sister is such an angel,' an older French woman says to me, after I climb out of the swimming pool. She has roasted herself into a crocodile handbag the colour of darkened wood and seems intent on carrying on doing so. She smokes in the sun as well.

'She is my daughter, not my sister,' I tell her.

'My God, how old are you, dear?' She is shocked.

'Older than I look,' I say. I feel years older than my real age, but I look younger without make-up and evening dresses.

I drink two cocktails in the early evening. I wear a black floaty dress and gold sandals which belonged to my mother.

Maybe François went out to eat alone in a restaurant somewhere.

Well so what. I do not really want to see him again today.

Me and Marina eat by the poolside, then I take her back to the room to sleep.

The cocktails are deceptively strong, but I feel nice; warm and sleepy.

A sullen figure is sitting in the window of our room which is not what I need when I am in a good mood. François is staring at the ocean view and the blazing red of the sunset in the darkening room.

'You should not watch the sunset,' I tell him. 'It is very bad for the eyes.'

He says nothing.

I take Marina to the bathroom, brush her teeth and put her to bed. She is tired after swimming.

I turn off the light next to her bed.

The room is only lit by the dying sun which casts a strange red light across the walls. Arterial red.

It seems like a bad omen, just like the end of an Opera when the funeral pyre is lit, and someone will die.

'Did you eat?' the shadowy figure of François suddenly asks.

'Yes, and cocktails too,' I say, flopping on the bed to read.

'If it is so bad being in the same room as me, then the door is right there.' I tell him this coldly.

He is silent.

'Please come here. I am so sorry,' he says after a long silence.

'Stop acting as if you hate the sight of me,' I tell him, getting up.

'I am sorry. I was horrible to Marina today too. That poor little girl who jumped on me playfully.

When you were that age....' Then he stops himself. I am no longer his innocent girl.

It is getting dark, so I am beginning the transformation into his dead love reincarnated.

I exist in this twilight world as a different being, vampiric and mythical until the morning.

Then it is all gone.

'Want me to order some food for you?' I ask.

He nods. 'And I need some good white wine.'

I sit down opposite him.

'Try these moules, Fiorenza. They are perfect.' He seems to have cheered up when his bowl of seafood and bottle of wine arrive.

He places a wrapped box on the table.

'I wanted to give you this. It should have been your 21st birthday present but I had to have it made into a necklace first.'

I open the box. It is my mother's engagement ring, but the large diamond is set in a silver chain.

He bought it in Montpellier only a night before she died.

The next evening, she flew back to Roma, and he went to Paris. It seems a cursed bit of jewellery, as if its owner will die within 24 hours.

'I cannot take this.'

I snap the box shut, place it back on the table.

'She wore it for one day only. She would want you to have it. Please take it.'

He pushes it towards me.

'Please, Fiorenza. It seems such a waste not to wear it.'

I look in the mirror as I fasten the necklace. The rainbow splits of light are beautiful. It is lovely and I can wear it every day. So much of my jewellery is only suitable for evenings, as my mother bought large dramatic necklaces and earrings for premières and concerts.

No sense in tiny pieces of jewellery when no one can see it, she told me.

'Thank you,' I tell François.

Catalina does not wear jewellery. I offered her some I was wearing in Milano on the day we met, and she refused. Even after the prison visit, when she cried over me, she still did not want the pretty bracelet and necklace.

There is a storm out of nowhere that night; savage and twisted after the heat has built up all day and I dream my mother is standing by the bed.
   She is in her jet beaded outfit and tiara holding black roses.
I sit up and for the first time her face is so soft, not full of hatred. She glows as if the light is on, but the room is dark. The glow comes from her. I see all the features of her lovely face, her raven hair, how beautiful she is. But also, so like me.
The glow is so bright, it even shows the darkness of her amazing eyes. It makes her even more beautiful. Black eyes are so rare, and I wish I had them too.
'Mamma! I missed you!'
She smiles instead of spitting her fury, so maybe she really is here.
I reach for the beautiful black roses she holds and blood drips on to my hands.
   Her expression has turned dark, all the sweetness snapped out. I reach for her, and my hands have blood all over them, which is running down my arms.
'You treacherous little whore. Wearing my fucking diamond! That was my engagement ring!
A day later I was dead, Fiorenza!
May God strike you down too!'
And she walks away across the room, her jet beaded dress trailing behind her.

The next morning, I wake up and the sun is streaming in. It is late; after 11.00 and I am still drowsy. I have a bitter metallic taste in my mouth from the sleeping tablet I took in the middle of the night after my nightmare.

I touch the cursed diamond round my neck and wonder if the wearer always dies within 24 hours. There are some hours left. I still need to get through today.

The Gods have tightened their savage grip.

I am alone in the room. François has gone with Marina somewhere. Maybe to the hotel pool.

'François, I am going to get sleeping pills to stop these nightmares.

Where did you get them?'

He is lying moodily by the hotel pool watching Marina in the water.

'The doctor prescribed them when your mother died,' he tells me.

'Give me the others,' I demand.

'I only brought two with me and you had them. I try not to take them unless I am very stressed.'

'Damn you. I am getting some when we return to Paris.'

On our final night in Nice, we eat in the hotel restaurant. I hate eating out.

I always feel that restaurant food is overrated and the mark up on drinks is crazy. To see a bill for a few hundred euros for something you could just as easily prepare at home seems a waste, even though I am wearing dresses which cost hundreds or even thousands of euros.

My mother did not like eating out either.

For someone who lived in luxury, she disapproved of spending in restaurants.

She complained that it lacked intimacy, to dine surrounded by people. She never cooked but bought dishes from deli counters and trattorias.

Nowhere was better than home for a romantic dinner, she maintained; light the candles and be alone. Anyway, she did not like big portions, hated the oversized restaurant plates and pressure to order desserts.

And there is always someone to annoy me at one or more tables nearby. No, I do not like to eat around people.

I am a diva, after all, she would say.

The waiter had commented to François what a beautiful young wife he had and adorable little daughter.

It was the night I remember François saying in the hotel room, 'Fiorenza, do you think people know? Can they see?'

'No. Why would they?' I shrugged.

'I know the guilt gets to you too,' he said.

'You never speak of it, Fiorenza, but this is poison eating away at both of us.'

I stare the moon above the ocean.

'Fiorenza, when I went to Bregenz, I wished God would strike Lake Constance with lightning and kill me because I felt I deserved it.

I wished I had drowned in that lake.'

I am angry with him, trying to opt out of life like that.

'Fine,' I say

'Why wish yourself dead? How about me? Both of my parents dead, left alone with Marina; you are so fucking selfish!

What about us?

No, you cannot just wish yourself dead so easily!'

I drop my dress over the chair and climb into bed.

'François, blame me if you want, but never wish death on yourself.'

What was the point of this holiday? We were supposed to try to reclaim our normal lives only the savage Gods have tightened their grip.

It has totally failed.

'This has turned into an expensive guilt trip not a holiday trip,'

I snap at him.

'So much for a relaxing break in Nice!'

I wake in the morning, and he is gone.

'François?'

I sit up and he is at the table with Marina. He cannot look at me.

I do not exist. I feel like an empty shell; used at night and forgotten in the morning.

I take my juice and coffee and croissant and sit in an armchair away from him, away from his shame. He does not even say good morning.

To Hell with him.

I am getting familiar with this same routine, the same miserable mornings. I think I prefer it when I am alone with my daughter in our Paris apartment, and he is working abroad.

'Mamma? Are you ill?' Marina comes over to me.

'Why do you sit there?' she presses her soft little hands on my shoulders.

'I am very tired, my love. I do not sleep so well.'

François does not say a word.

He was admired for his opera career; his voice and looks and his commanding presence on the stage. For a long time, he has been highly regarded on the European circuit.

This dark awful place we now inhabit is so out of character with the François everyone knew.

Years ago, we had become his life and the life of a famous opera singer can be extremely lonely: hotels, constant touring, always working with different companies.

He did far less travel now as he had no heart to go beyond mainland Europe and had asked his agents to reschedule anywhere else after my mother's death.

And he still avoided comic opera. My mother always hated

comic operas; she said tragedy and dying made her feel energised and comedy made her miserable.

I need to die to feel alive. Dying is my favourite part of Opera, she told me.

MON COEUR S'OUVRE À TA VOIX

It was August and François had a concert in Verona. He wanted me and Marina to travel with him, but I refused. I was not taking my daughter to Italia.

'Your mother; her fatal mistake was returning to Roma. If she had given up her Italian opera houses, she would still be here. Maybe you are not safe in Italia. I worry for you.'

I tell him it was always her decision; she was an Italian celebrity after all.

'But I will never ever go to Italia again.

I miss my home country, but I cannot go back,' I say.

'Mamma, is François my father?' Marina said, as we wave goodbye to him from the balcony.

'No, my sweet girl. François is my father. You know it is Alain? Why do you ask again about François?'

'Maybe I have two fathers,' Marina shrugs. 'But I like Alain.'

'No, you have one father, Marina. Alain.

Remember you saw my beautiful mother called Marina? Remember the Lilac room in Roma?

The pretty blonde lady called Ana?'

She nodded.

'She looks like you. Is that why François loves you, mamma?'

I felt uneasy about how much Marina sensed. I had no idea if her questions were just normal children's questions, but I tried to answer as best as I could.

'François is my father.

This is our home as well as his home, Marina; you and me.'

'But people say we are a family,' she carried on.

'And why does your mamma live with Ana and not with us? She visits me here.'

'Marina she died. She lives in a kind of different world, a spirit world we cannot go to.'

'But I see her,' Marina insists.

'In my room, in the Opera.'

It is too hard to explain about my mother. Every time I try, it just confuses my daughter more.

Especially as she has seen her, talked with her, even embraced her and she is as real to Marina as I am.

When François returned from Verona late at night, he said he needed have some camomile tea and shower. He was cool towards me; did not say he missed me or embrace me.

I think he had decided when he was away that our lives had to go back to 'normal'.

However long that can last.

'I have not seen anyone but Marina since you went away. I feel so lonely,' I say to him.

All I want is a civilised conversation but that seems too much for him.

'Fiorenza, I am very tired. We can talk tomorrow....'

'Well, you go and be alone then with your miserable camomile tea! I was looking forward to your return and you are so goddamn selfish!'

Fuck him. I have a nice weekend to look forward to in Madrid.

I go to bed alone, mad at him and swallow a sleeping pill and knock myself out.

I need oblivion.

I fly to Madrid for a weekend at the beginning of September, stating that I need to be alone to clear my head before the autumn term.

Marina is fine to be left with François although he is mystified because I never do this; jet off leaving her behind. I have had those so called 'shopping trips' to London and Brussels but this is a longer vacation.

'Who is in Madrid?' he says, his jealousy rising.

'No one, but I have not been since I went with my grandmother for a Christmas run of La bohème.

My mother was performing, and I want to remember her, booked the same hotel.

I want to visit Teatro Real again, feel those memories of the past once more.'

I insist that I need a city break just to recharge before university commences; go shopping for clothes, just drink coffee and eat churros.

François is not so happy, but he does not keep asking who is in Madrid.

He believes that my Thursday to Monday city break is to recharge as he knows it is rare for me to have a chance to be alone without Marina for a few days.

Really, the reason for visiting is because Natalija is in Teatro Real in Samson et Dalila.

She called me two weeks ago when I was alone in the apartment, wanting me to attend her early première, as she had mentioned in Brussels back in June.

The season is opening early because this was not such a popular or well-known opera and La Traviata would follow on. La Traviata had sold out every night, give or take a few seats.

Box office sales were not going so well for Samson et Dalila.

I was about to refuse, remembering miserable Brussels where Natalija was moody. Then I realised that I do need to get away and get some perspective on my life.

And I like the thought of visiting Madrid.

I am afraid if I see Natalija too often, I will be under her spell.

On the Friday evening, Natalija has left my ticket at box office.

I arrived on a flight too late last night to meet and stayed in my own hotel for one night.

She had extended her welcome to staying in her hotel for the rest of the weekend, which was something.

I do not find much of this rarely performed Opera by Saint-Saëns enjoyable, especially the violence in Act Three. Despite the impressive traditional setting, elaborate costumes, and the French language, I can see why many opera houses are reluctant to slot this Opera into their schedules.

It does not sell the house.

The house is not full in Teatro Real either, despite Natalija's name commanding a sell-out at box office in pretty much every opera house.

Unless the two leads are sensational, this would be a disaster. I saw Massenet's Thaïs once, which is also another risky production, but Paris Opera had gone all out with a lavish set and two perfectly cast leads.

Natalija's co-star as Samson is a world-famous Italian tenor, so this has boosted the ticket sales, but I still count many empty seats in the auditorium on opening night.

Dressed in luxurious purples and golds, her seduction of Samson is beautiful, believable, and the absolute highlight of the evening is Natalija's Act Two aria.

When those first golden notes of Mon coeur s'ouvre à ta voix, float through the air, I know this is going to be a rarity. All my nerve endings are heightened and the music is coursing through my body, just like the dizzying sensation I had experienced when watching my mother perform Adriana Lecouvreur.

As Adriana was poisoned by the flowers, I began to feel as if the poison was flowing through my veins too; my mother had that elusive magic which cast a spell over the entire audience.

She was a true diva.

Natalija has a similar magic. I feel it in the auditorium, see how everyone is transfixed by this glorious mezzo. I have heard the aria in concerts, but only sung by good mezzos.

Natalija's tempo is far slower, perfectly paced, and velvety rich. She has complete mastery over her voice and the aria is even more haunting than I could imagine.

As I have been attending operas from the age of three, I notice when singers rush arias or transitions of notes or fail to hit a note. Natalija's intoxicating voice lingers on every note, her French clear and perfect, before setting it free to sail through the auditorium.

I have a feeling this is what hypnotism does to the body and mind.

I usually favoured sopranos as my mother and Anasztázia were top sopranos, but Natalija is way above every mezzo I ever heard. And that is before her captivating seductiveness.

Well, the girl herself could seduce pretty much anyone.

At the end of the aria, she smiles and closes her eyes as her applause lasts minutes. There are calls of Bis! but she does not break character, keeping her arms outstretched towards Samson until the applause dies down.

The reviews will no doubt ensure Teatro Real can fill the house over the next two weeks.

Later, in Natalija's hotel, I wondered whether I was just not allowing myself to feel.

For her, for anyone.

She is beautiful; the glow was back in her skin, after her mystery 'illness' and she was flirtatious and cheerful. I ask if she is better and she answers, of course. It was nothing.

I know not to ask again. She looked away as she answered, so maybe it had been her bulimia resurfacing.

She gives me her full attention, but I still feel that I am not special.

'You are lovely, Fiorenza. I am happy for you to visit me in Madrid.

You really should come to Italia more often.

We could meet in my apartment as I am in La Scala at least twice a year, sometimes Verona and I have so much work with The Met.'

So she had asked me to her apartment in Milano. Well, that is progress.

As she turned over and switched off the light, her long spirals of jet hair fell over my fingers.

She fell into a deep sleep almost instantly; we had stayed late in the Opera House as it was a big opening night and not returned to the hotel until the early hours.

I stayed awake for a long time.

I feel guilty because she hurt Anasztázia. I am betraying my friend.

I had mentioned Anasztázia earlier and Natalija said, 'nice woman but it was not right for us.

I hurt her, but I had to think of my career.

You already know about the incident in Budapest where someone traded the prop knife for a real one?

I nearly died.'

'I heard it was an accident because a stage manager failed to check the blade,' I said, shocked at what she told me.

My mother mentioned something about the incident, but I had never met Natalija then.

'That is what the Hungarian media said, so as not to damage the company's reputation.

I told the real story many times in Italia, on chat shows or news interviews.

The woman who laid the blade on the table was a jealous rival who wanted me dead in Carmen.

She is serving 14 years in Hungary.

I do not know who she is. I never wanted to know.'

Anasztázia never told me.

'Natalija, someone really did that? Someone was that ruthless in the Opera?'

She looked away.

'I thought I was ruthless; your mother knew how cut-throat I was.

But I do not want to talk about this, Fiorenza.

When I moved to Roma, I could not sing a note. So, I had that chance at The Met when my injury healed, as I also stopped my bulimia after the stabbing. I left Anasztázia.

God gave me this talent and He gave me the second chance.

I thought as Anasztázia was a star, she would get over me.

She needed too much attention.'

I believed that she just walked out on Anasztázia heartlessly.

I could understand the frustration of being with someone very needy.

My mother would never have a needy relationship at the expense of her Opera.

She dropped Romeo because he was too clingy and wanted time; time she could not give him.

After Natalija's near death experience, I could begin to see why she acted so coldly towards other performers.

Something inside this famous star had been damaged: by her mother's death when she was a child, her eating disorder and then an attempted murder.

I realise there is a lot I never knew about this superstar.

Natalija had been far cooler and more distracted over the rest of the weekend.

On Saturday after such a late night, it was after midday when we ordered room service.

We drank coffee in virtual silence as Natalija obsessed over her glowing reviews from the opening night. She had ordered every single journal and newspaper and spread them over the bed, obsessed with her own greatness.

Now and then she would say, 'Wow! Listen to this, Fiorenza!'

I left her surrounded by a sea of newsprint and went for a walk, said I had shops to visit. I knew I could manage the few designer shops if I kept the hotel in sight, despite my agoraphobia.

She hardly looked up from the review she was reading.

'Fine, see you later,' she said, spreading out another sparkling review on the bed.

'I look so beautiful,' she murmured, holding the photos up to the light.

Although she was pleased to see me return, she spent most of the evening sleeping and hardly spoke because she wanted to rest her voice for the next performance on Sunday afternoon.

On Sunday, I stayed in the hotel. There was no point watching the Opera again.

Afterwards, Natalija talked non-stop about how wonderful she had been.

I realised after a few hours I had hardly said a word.

She really was a self-absorbed diva.

She stopped gabbling about her wonderful career long enough to answer her cell phone, speaking Italian to some lover for half an hour as she lay right next to me on the bed.

It was full of romantic sentiments, as she twirled a spiral of hair in her fingers.

Ti amo, amore, she said when she ended the call.

That is so fucking rude.

She could wait till tomorrow or go to the bathroom.

'Who was that?' I asked.

'Just my husband,' she said carelessly, and got up to make a coffee.

'Your husband!' I shouted.
'What the hell did I miss?' Since when did she even date men?
She was not wearing a wedding ring but like many opera singers, she would remove it for performances and had removed it to see me.
She probably removed it as soon as she left New York, so she could cheat non-stop.

The atmosphere changed from indifferent to frosty. Natalija's lovely face looked up at me full of contempt. Her eyes were cold and resentful.
'Don't act possessive, Fiorenza,' she said.
'It doesn't suit you. I thought you were as careless as me. You know I hate needy people.'
'You are married, Natalija?
 Maybe I would not have come to Madrid if I knew that!'
She banged the cups of coffee in irritation, the first annoyance she had shown towards me.
'Since when do you even date men?' I asked.
She suddenly exploded with anger, shouting at me as I were a stupid little girl.
'He is a tenor at The Met! The most handsome man there! Only 26 years old!
 What the hell difference does it make? I do not care who you fuck!
God, you are with your own father sometimes and that is messed up! It is your life, Fiorenza and this is mine!
At least I put my wedding rings in the hotel safe!
Do you want this fucking coffee or not?'
I did not answer, so she handed me one anyway.
She got on the bed and shrugged.
'Well, I married quietly last Christmas. No one really knew, no big announcements.

We got engaged in September last year.

He is good in bed; at first, we had a real chemistry after performing Carmen.

Diego is young, a little boring but very good genetic material: Mexican, dark, so good-looking.

Makes for beautiful children.'

Bitch, heartless woman telling me all about her conquests. Her goddamn husband!

'Seriously! You hate kids! I hope you are not thinking…..'

'I already have a baby, Fiorenza!' she interrupted, stirring her coffee. She turned and rummaged in the drawer next to the bed.

'You have a child? The careless mezzo! Are you crazy?'

I grabbed her wrist.

She shook me off and glared at me, then continued to look in the drawer.

'Her name is Lucia. She is five months old.' Natalija hands me a photo.

She is in a brilliant red dress looking every bit the famous diva and holding a beautiful baby.

'She is so pretty,' I say, studying the picture, but then so was Natalija.

'Of course she is,' Natalija said arrogantly, tossing her long spirals of hair over her shoulder.

'She came from me. I am beautiful.'

Lucia is dark, like her mother and has that wonderful creamy complexion Mexican beauties have.

I could imagine Natalija studying colour charts as if she were choosing paint for her wall and deciding on café au lait. Then finding a suitable man for her requests.

Not too dark, not pale either. Oh, that colour looks nice for my daughter's skin; perfect!

'Did you forget about them when you invited me here?' I ask

her.

'Yes, I did and do not take that tone with me, little girl!
When I am working, I forget everyone.

I am not a stay-at-home mother, Fiorenza and I had to starve myself to keep working until I had Lucia in April.

This is why I could not travel over Christmas, why I was ill and cancelled performances.'

She was frosty, acting as if I was out of order for being angry.

'You are lucky she does not have malnutrition,' I snap at her.

'That is shocking, Natalija! No wonder you looked so ill in Brussels!

And you could have told me then you were married!'

Stupid woman. Stupid selfish bitch.

Starving so she could squeeze into a few more opera gowns at the expense of Lucia's health.

God, I hate her.

Natalija's eyes are cold, and she snatches the photo away.

'You should stop acting as if you are jealous. I do not owe you any explanation!

Jealousy turns me right off, Fiorenza!

So what if I have a husband and baby? You have a daughter!

My family is in New York. I am here in Madrid. With you!'

Bitch, I thought. She is not fit to be a mother.

I hated her then.

She was willing to fool around everywhere. She was nothing more than a vain greedy woman who felt entitled to everything in her gilded life.

I realised I did hurt a little. I suddenly thought this woman was every bit as awful as people said. My father was right.

I turned away and reached for my bag, blinking tears of anger and hurt away.

Her warm hand rested on my back.

'Don't go,' she said more softly. 'Please. I am sorry not to see you between London and Brussels, but I had Lucia.

I could not see you between September and June because I felt fat. I hate feeling fat.

And when I said Diego was good in bed, it hardly lasted. Short chemistry.

This is not you and me.

Do you understand? So do not feel you have to leave…..'

I turned to face her again. She was a much softer Natalija.

'I am not leaving; I was getting my book,' I tell her.

She takes the book from my hands and strokes my face gently.

'Fiorenza. I am so sorry.

Speaking on the phone to someone else was nasty of me. I would not like you to do this.

Sorry for being a bitchy diva.'

Her fingers run through the length of my hair, and her dark eyes are soft again. She smiles.

'It is okay to feel something for me, you know.

I am not just a heartless prima donna.

And I have feelings too, just sometimes I forget where I put them.'

She laughs and she is so beautiful, I feel it is impossible to stay mad at her.

'You think I invite many people back for more?' she asks me.

'And not just because I had this huge crush on your mother.'

I move closer.

'I am scared to feel for anyone,' I confess.

'And you do have one hell of a reputation.'

'I promise I will not hurt you, Fiorenza.

I am a diva, I am selfish.

But maybe I did want to see some emotion from you.

I do not love my husband.

I said it on the phone as we speak Italian, not Spanish. I never learned Spanish.

I do not love him, Fiorenza.

Not when I married him and not now.'

'But you still had this child with a man you do not love,' I said.

'That is different,' she said quietly.

She sighed, gazed into the distance as she said almost sadly, 'I just want to be the diva who has it all. I wanted a child.

I love Lucia.'

'My mother was the diva who had it all too. Everyone wanted to be her.

She had her mask for the world too.'

As I head back to Paris with new clothes I did not need and gifts for Marina, I got horribly lost on the Metro on the way to the airport. For some crazy reason, I convinced myself the journey was short, that it was a Monday afternoon, and I would be fine.

I could break this agoraphobia which was affecting my life. After all, I have taken trips to cities alone, managed to do this so one step up is the Metro.

Bad idea.

I end up after an hour's stress where my heart is bursting through my chest right back where I started. I have travelled in a loop, changing lines multiple times and in the choked heat of the Metro tunnels, nearly dying with fear.

I have the biggest panic attack ever; a Spanish businessman notices I am standing against the Metro wall, clutching the tiles like a terrified cat. I am literally frozen.

He only speaks Spanish, but he understands Italian, and I say I am not ill as he first thinks, but that I am in a state of complete terror.

He helps me out as I cannot even find the exit to Sol Metro station. We are right near Opera. I have come full circle.

THE GODS MUST BE SAVAGE

I cannot breathe and I am crazy with fear. As I sit in the heat by a fountain and pop another Valium, he asks me am I feeling better?

Does this happen a lot?

Yes, I tell him. I cannot take the Metro in Paris.

I get in a cab after he takes me for hot chocolate and churros. You need sugar, he told me.

I take his business card. I guess all men are forever hopeful.

Then I get lost again, this time in the sprawling maze which is Barajas airport and vow to never to visit Madrid again.

I see losing myself on the Metro and in the airport as some kind of metaphor for my life; going round and round in circles and never getting to the right place.

It puts a feeling of gloom into me.

MANON LESCAUT

First opera of the season and September is sizzling hot in Paris. It feels as hot as Nice in July. August was warm and then the mercury started to rise, so now the whole of Paris is enveloped in grimy city heat which shows no sign of abating.

It is sticky and unpleasant in the daytime, and everyone is in a permanent bad mood. Just like Roma, there seem to be a lot of car crashes.

I still have that racing heart feeling whenever I glide by the mirrors in the Opera House, as if I see the ghost of Marina Valentino, not Fiorenza. I imagine she is going to turn and look straight at me and it makes me shiver.

'François only has eyes for you,' his co-star in Manon Lescaut said at the première.

'What did you say?' I turn to face Louise, the lead soprano.

Is it that obvious? God, does Louise guess?

Louise smiled. 'I mean you look so like your mother. It is as if I am standing next to a young Marina. François worshipped her.

It is such a crime such a talented, beautiful star was stolen from you and the world.'

She squeezes my hand.

'These wounds never ever heal when someone is taken so violently,' I tell her.

'I miss her as much as I ever did.'

Six years ago.

I have a flashback to the funeral; how beautiful she was surrounded by blue roses with her long raven hair spread over her shoulders. Everyone was hysterical with grief, yet she looked content, just as if she were sleeping.

I am just a beautiful young version of Marina Valentino, who attends her father's operas.

'My Italian relatives do not want to see us. They are angry my mother's grave is in Paris,' I say.

'Maybe they will see the light one day soon.' Louise kissed my face.

'Un bel dì, Fiorenza.'

She then drifted away.

François rested his hand on my waist. 'What did Louise say?'

'We were just talking about my mother.'

I spend the rest of the evening feeling I want to be at home for once and totally alone, not dazzling everyone in an evening dress.

Romeo is coming to Paris.

He was once my mother's fiancé and still a resident at Roma Opera. He has never really progressed from the early days of his career when he performed alongside her.

He was a good tenor, handsome and talented and showed such potential.

Yet he was hopelessly inconsistent. My mother told me he only performed well when she was his co-star and at other times, he did not come up to standard, dragging whole productions down.

Because his performances were either brilliant or lacklustre, he failed to secure many roles outside Italia and never once performed in La Scala.

He also had two daughters from his ex-wife, so he was anchored in the city. He had no desire to take many opportunities abroad despite my mother constantly moaning at him.

'Get yourself a better agent, Romeo!

You have children, I have Fiorenza, so do many opera singers. We all have to travel!

It is part of our lives, our passion or why become an opera singer?'

She married my stepfather impulsively without even telling

Romeo, after they fell out.

Poor Romeo. She was the love of his life.

Romeo has a concert in Paris, but he also wanted to visit my mother's grave. He has been unable to move on from her death.

When I visited Anasztázia in Roma, he had been performing in Torino.

'We drifted apart, me and your mother, so I felt it best to leave her to her life in Paris,' he told me, when he spoke on the phone.

'She was always going to be like a shooting star with her beauty and fame, and I was left behind. She was so driven, so talented.'

'I know you were still a good friend to us, Romeo; that apartment I own in Napoli was one you found for her when she had been attacked by my stepfather.

You were so kind, and she adored you.'

He is quiet. He wanted to marry her, not be her adored friend.

We arrange to meet up as he only has one free evening in Paris, but I am going to watch François perform in Manon Lescaut again with Marina, so I invite Romeo and get him a company ticket.

It will be nice for him to attend Paris Opera.

It is a hot night for the end of September, even more airless and oppressive than the opening night. Marina tells me we could fry eggs on the street.

'Go and get the egg box and we try on the balcony.'

Marina drops an egg on the sizzling stone. It starts to cook. Marina laughs until François sees us.

'What the hell? Fiorenza! What are you two doing?'

'Oh, lighten up,' I tell him.

He is mad at me. He was fine on my birthday but has been moody ever since, referring to my Madrid jaunt more than once. Stupid jealous man.

François is snappy as he scrapes up the egg, telling me and

Marina we are both irresponsible children to waste food.

'It is just one fucking egg,' I tell him.

'Wasting food,' he says. 'And what do I tell you about your cursing, Fiorenza? Marina repeats everything!'

'One fucking egg!' Marina says and laughs again.

'Go to your room, Marina,' I tell her, sensing François is angry because of Romeo's visit, not the half-baked egg.

When I told him that Romeo was in the city and attending tonight's performance, he went very quiet.

'Your mother's ex-fiancé? Fiorenza, this is not a good idea.......'

I tell him Romeo is in Paris for a concert and that he wanted to see my mother's grave.

'Romeo was so good to us, and he would love to see your show.
 You did not take her from Romeo; she left him. He was still a good friend to her.

He knew my mother was climbing higher and higher with her career. He was left behind.

This is the real reason they split.'

François finishes scraping up the egg and looks at me coldly.

'It is still a bad idea, revisiting the past. And lock this door, Fiorenza!

You know about Marina on this balcony. It is dangerous.'

At times like this I am his disobedient daughter. He speaks to me and Marina as if we are both little children.

 François says very little after this and leaves for the Opera early in a bad mood.

I meet Romeo in the Opera bar before the performance. He wanted to go to my mother's grave alone, although I offered to accompany him.

He probably had personal things he wanted to say to her.

He looks almost the same; handsome with light brown hair and sad dark eyes, but not very different to the Romeo I knew. I last saw him at the funeral.

'Fiorenza! It is so good to see you.' He smiles happily and embraces me.

'But my God, you are so much like her, so much like Marina,' he says, with a touch of wonder.

'I know,' I tell him.

'Everyone says this. When I see a glimpse in the mirrors at night, it is almost as if she is reflected in the glass, not me.'

He looks at me and I know he always thinks of what might have been; married to my mother and happy with me as his stepdaughter.

Only it never works like that.

'I recognise that dress your mother wore in a concert. It looks lovely on you.

Anasztázia told me all about you; studying law and wanting to be an advocate.'

'I remember you were always so good with us.' I smile.

'And this is your little girl?' he says.

'I am Marina,' she announces. 'Mamma names me after an opera star.'

'What else could I call her? God, I miss my mother so badly, Romeo.

It never stops hurting, does it?'

I need to talk to someone who feels it too, such as Romeo and Anasztázia.

'Someone so beautiful and talented taken away long before their time,' he says, squeezing my hand.

'You are right, Fiorenza. It will never stop hurting.'

Marina is demanding his attention, so he picks her up.

'Just like your mamma, Marina,' he tells her.

'Did François ever move on?' Romeo asks me.

'No, she was the only one.'

Something about the way I answer makes Romeo probe further.

'Are you happy, Fiorenza? You must be lonely….it surprises me you say you have no lover, because you could have any man or woman on the planet.'

For a few seconds I feel he knows my terrible secret. Or knows I have seen Natalija and that would hurt Anasztázia.

But he says he worries I am estranged from friends and family in Roma, that Paris is lonely for me.

'I am still haunted by what happened and I miss Roma…...

But there are so many memories in that city.

For God's sake, Romeo! Can we just enjoy our night?' I snap at him.

'Of course, Fiorenza. I am sorry.'

I look at him, at the gold flecks in his dark eyes. He is only interested in me, that is all.

Later, when we meet up with François post-show, the atmosphere is tense. Romeo congratulates him on an amazing performance, but I know François is not enjoying this.

He graciously accepts the compliments from Romeo, then makes some excuse about 'a throat coming on'.

'He is not happy,' Romeo says, as he watches him go.

'You were love rivals a long time ago. I know he feels strange finally seeing you.

And he is always moody after a performance, especially on a hot night.

In fact, he is moody pretty much every day.'

It is dry and airless in the Opera bar, so we go for a walk. We sit by a fountain and very few people are around post-show as it is a Tuesday night.

The night air is still and beautifully warm, but soon it will slide into autumn. I always wish it could stay September forever.

As I am thinking this, Romeo punctures my mood.

'Fiorenza, if something is making you unhappy, you can tell me,'

Romeo says.

I look at Marina who is asleep in my arms.

'Like what? Everything is perfect. I have Marina and my home and my career.'

'François never stopped looking at you. You are beautiful but…………'

'Just what are you saying, Romeo?' I start to get defensive.

'He thinks no man is good enough for me, that is all!'

'I am sorry, Fiorenza but I cannot help thinking………'

His eyes are sad and serious as he takes my hand.

'You were just 16 years old when your mother died. You and François exist in this bubble shutting everyone else out. It is not so healthy for you.

You are lively and should have many friends. Does Marina have friends?'

'She is too young,' I say.

'Romeo, I do not like the way this conversation is going!

You are as bad as our au pair, forever with the questions! I do not like to be interrogated.'

Marina is scratchy after being woken up by our shouting and starts to cry.

'Come on, my love, we go home now. Romeo is being a pain in the ass!'

I turn to him.

'You have no right to come to Paris and judge me, question my life here. We are still grieving, Romeo; all of us. Life cannot be the same.'

I lift Marina into my arms, comfort her tears and walk away from Romeo.

Damn him for ruining the evening.

'Fiorenza, wait!' Romeo follows me, wrapping his arm round my waist.

'Let me walk you to your apartment at least.

I see that adorable little Fiorenza, who has become a very beautiful lady.

I am sorry that I upset you.

I have two daughters who are a little older than you. I want the very best husbands for them.

One is dating some good for nothing wannabe rock star and I hate that.'

I compose myself.

'Listen, Romeo; do not worry about me.

I would take you to see the apartment, but it is not a good idea.'

I feel as if I cannot breathe; the warm night feels airless and oppressive, just as if we were indoors.

'Fiorenza, I am sorry for you,' Romeo says.

'It is sad to lose not only your mother, but your entire family.'

I look at the sprinkling of stars in the sky to change the subject.

'September nights like these, Romeo. Don't you wish the weather would stay like this forever?'

Romeo admires the apartment block and gazes at the sky.

'How amazing to live so close to the Opera,' he smiles.

I say goodbye and Romeo tells me he will stay in touch.

He kisses me on the cheek. 'I still remember our happy days years ago.

Look after yourself, Fiorenza.'

At home I am tired, and I want to relax.

'I will just put Marina to bed,' I tell François, but I know by his silence he is in one hell of a mood.

I can sense the chill just by stepping into the living room.

François has the air conditioning on, but the chilly atmosphere is coming from him. God knows what his problem is. I try to continue talking and hope he will get over it.

'Romeo loved the Opera. You were even better than on première night,' I say, as I settle on the sofa.

He is irritable as I am eating in the living room.

'Don't you spill all those crumbs over the floor, Fiorenza. You make such a mess by eating everywhere except the kitchen. You wander from room to room with no damn plate.

Just like your mother.'

'Whatever,' I say.

'You never moaned at her. She was a goddess to you. It is only a bit of toast anyway.'

'Well, you make sure you clean it up, Fiorenza.'

He is always whining about nothing.

He finishes his tea and I talk about the Opera. He does not have much to say to me.

François is thinking of Romeo, who was once my mother's fiancé, which is crazy as he never even met him. Doesn't he trust my mother?

'I guess your throat is fine?' I ask.

'Why lie? Did you think my mother kept working in Roma Opera for Romeo?

They were friends and that was it. I can swear to that. I knew that.'

He loosens his shirt and runs his hands through his thick black hair, says nothing and then turns to look at me.

'You have been out for an hour with Marina.

It is late for the poor child. If you were going to flirt, I should have brought her home.'

François is totally irrational.

'François! He was my mother's fiancé. I hardly saw him once she married Andrea!

Romeo should be the jealous one because he lost her. She broke his heart, and she went to you.

I wanted to see him tonight, as a friend.'

François says darkly, 'you are such a flirt. Every man wants you, just like they wanted your mother. Only her heart was true.'

I sigh. 'I am so tired of this irrational jealousy. Romeo was concerned. François, do you have to make it so fucking obvious?

He noticed the tension between us.

He even asked me is everything okay with me.'

François explodes with rage.

'Our lives are none of his concern!'

'Well, we are not innocent, François.' I reach for the camomile tea to swallow a sleeping pill.

His grips my wrist.

'That hurts!' I cry out.

'Stop it! What is wrong with you?'

'You keep popping those damn pills like candy, Fiorenza! Sleeping pills are addictive. Then you sleep through your alarm, and I have to see to your daughter!'

'Oh, shut up,' I snap. 'I will set the goddamn alarm.'

He is so moody these days.

'I was stressed after performing, I am sorry.' He softens a little.

'But you were flirting with him. Why do you always have to do this, Fiorenza?'

I get up.

'I am going to bed. Fuck it.

Sit here on your own and come down off that post show adrenaline before you get into bed.'

'Fiorenza! Don't you walk away!'

François grabs my arm and twists me round to face him.

'Let go! I am tired!'

There is no softness in his handsome face, just anger.

'This red dress is like a red rag to a randy man! You should not wear such revealing outfits!' He pulls at the straps of my red dress roughly.

'Stop it, François!' I shout at him. 'What is with you tonight?

This is my mother's dress!'

This is not the François I know.

'You are acting crazy!' I am afraid of his anger tonight.

I lose my balance and fall to the floor.

'You stay away from me tonight!' I yell at him. 'You tore my goddamn dress! My mother's beautiful dress!'

'Fiorenza......' He tries to pick me up.

'Leave me alone!' I shout.

'Mamma!' Marina calls.

We woke her up. I glare at François and go to comfort my daughter who is standing in the hallway, rubbing her eyes.

'It's nothing, my love. Let me take you back to bed.' I take her hand.

'You should sleep too,' I tell François.

'Fiorenza, I am sorry.....'

I ignore him and go to Marina's room for the night.

'Mamma, your pretty dress is torn,' she touches the straps where the stitches were ripped out.

Stupid François.

'I can fix it tomorrow,' I tell her. I get out her storybook until we both drift away. I cannot be bothered to take off the dress.

'Never do that again! I do not want her to hear our volcanic domestics! What if she tells the au pair? Did you ever think?' I ask him in the morning.

'This is all on you, François!'

He pours his coffee, still in a deep sulk.

'I am so sorry, carissima.'

'Shut up now; Marina is up, and I need to fix her breakfast. Take your coffee to bed and leave us alone.'

He returns to his room without a word.

'You are so beautiful, mamma,' Marina says as she wanders in, hair tangled and wild.

She hugs me in my silk flowered kimono, my jet hair swept over one shoulder in a thick cable.

'Alain is picking you up soon to take you out. Eat quickly, my love,' I tell her.

'You had a fight with François,' she says, as I hear his door slam.

'He is strange after his Opera. Remember how he was mad about us cooking the egg?'

'Yes, but....'

'I am untidy, Marina and he hates mess. But a lot of opera singers find it hard to be normal after a show.

My mother went crazy if I woke her up early.'

I think of my mother and remember how she slept very late before or after performing.

I remember her beautiful body at rest; long golden limbs sprawled over the bed, raven waves of hair shining blue black in the light. She loved to sleep.

Nothing could wake her, and you would not want to. She was like a tigress.

She even slept through an earthquake once.

'Marina, you like to sleep too?' my daughter says to one of the photos of my mother.

I overheard the cleaner complaining this apartment is one huge shrine to this Italian diva. I told her this was no business of hers how we live.

She does not like me very much, but we rarely meet, so she is not a problem.

The au pair is the problem.

'She visits me a lot,' Marina says, breaking my thoughts.

'That is nice,' I say. I wonder if she really does see her, if she does talk to her as she did in Anasztázia's apartment.

I tell Alain that Marina is constantly announcing in a loud voice that François is her father.

Alain finds this amusing.

'Children do say things, Fiorenza. Why are you worried? I can try to see her more, have her stay over on a weekend maybe.'

'No, she is a little young, but can you try to convince her that you are her father?

She knows, but she still tells everyone at the Opera that François is her father.'

'You worry too much, Fiorenza,' he says. 'It is just a phase.'

François has left his Opera magazine open on the kitchen table. There is an interview with Natalija, all about her wonderful life and her meteoric success. It is the first interview where she has spoken about her personal life, and I know François left the magazine open deliberately.

He wants me to read this.

I guess she always kept her affairs secret before, but it was no secret in the Opera World that she was a predator who dated more women than men.

Yet here she is in her wonderful Park Avenue apartment.

The fairy-tale existence of the world's most beautiful and renowned mezzo-soprano. A fiercely talented Hungarian who married her co-star. He is a handsome young Mexican tenor from The Met, nine years her junior.

At least she told me about the marriage, but it does not make me feel any better.

The interviewer described the star who had it all: the world's most talented mezzo, her riches, her fantastic homes in New York and Milano, her wonderful young family.

Diego is described as the 'most desirable man in The Met' by this female journalist, a young tenor from Mexico City who had many female fans.

Natalija and the rising young Mexican tenor had fallen in love when he was her Don José in Carmen last year in May.

It was his first major role with The Met.

That burns to read it; fallen in love.

I read that sentence over and over again, torturing myself.

Natalija did not even love this guy, just wanted to prove she could have him.

She told me in Madrid that she was bored.

She had been engaged to him for a year and only married him because she thought it was better for Lucia. She swore it was never love for her.

Yet this interview makes everything sound perfect and now I am doubting her words.

Maybe she did love him.

As I looked at the glamorous photos of Natalija in various opera gowns with her gorgeous daughter and impossibly good-looking husband, I did feel that same stab of jealousy I felt in Spain.

They looked good together.

Even if it was one big theatrical artifice, like her whole existence.

'I did not even know she dated men!' François exclaimed.

'As for that child; poor Lucia with her unfit mother. Poor man too, trapped into marriage by such a predator. He only just turned 26 years old this summer!

She is nearly ten years older than him! God, isn't she 35 years old?'

'I am sure she will love her daughter. It takes time; she is a diva, after all.

My mother was a diva,' I remind him.

'And you would not question a man with a woman nine years younger. That is so damn sexist.'

He ignores my comments.

'You dated Natalija,' François said, looking up from the magazine.

'Does her wonderful new life upset you?'
He probably knows it does.
'Who cares,' I lied.
'As you said, she is much older than he is and she is 14 years older than me.
God, she is old enough to be my mother.'

I went to my room and cried.
I hated François, hated Diego. Then I stopped short of hating Natalija.
Even though she did not love this man, something in me was hurting.
I promised myself I would not have feelings and here I am, clearly upset and jealous.

LUCIA DI LAMMERMOOR

Anasztázia is to perform in Paris in January.

I realise just how lonely life has become, that she is the only friend I have left. I lost touch with Giovanna and Romeo is unlikely to be in Paris again.

And then there is Natalija, the one I do not want to feel anything for.

She had given me a butterfly necklace before I left Madrid.

Just so you know you are special, Fiorenza Valentino.

I cannot always see you. But I do want to return to Europe to live soon.

Then I can just guest in America. I miss Europe.

I had even started to get regular calls from the great mezzo; once a week or so, depending on her schedules. Maybe she really did like me, but I was still unable to trust her.

I had taken the train to London in December for two nights, another one of my so-called city breaks, to meet Natalija and attend her Opera.

She had reassured me about that 'nauseating photoshoot and interview'.

God, my agent wanted me to do it.

That interview, Fiorenza. Hell, I was smiling until it hurt.

I would throw up if I read those comments about me too. Please do not think that is my life; that is what my agent wants the world to see.

I thought I wanted the world to see it too. But I feel empty.

It means absolutely nothing, I promise.

Now François is beginning to wonder after Madrid; is there someone I am going to see.

I denied ever seeing Natalija again after those three dates in

Paris, but there are just too many excursions alone.
Especially cold grey London in December.
Paris is full of far more exclusive shops, so why travel to London? Christmas shopping trip, I had lied.
It had been Natalija's birthday, and I surprised her by giving her a pair of earrings from a famous jewellery designer in Paris.
You remembered, she said, delighted. No one remembers my birthday!
I should just tell François about Natalija.
Or maybe not.

'Can Anasztázia come for dinner?' I ask him in early January.
He will be at home for three of the five weeks Anasztázia is in Paris, then he goes to Barcelona for La Rondine.
'Why don't you ask Anasztázia to stay when I am away?' François says.
'That lady is very lonely. It is lonely for you and Marina too. You do not have friends, so I think it will be good for you all.'
Anasztázia is delighted when I ask her to stay. Her agents already booked a hotel for five weeks, but the dates can easily be changed as they are two weeks away.
So she agrees she will stay in the hotel for rehearsals, then our apartment for the two performance weeks.

Anasztázia appears frozen in time, as if she has not aged since I last saw her.
She is so delicate, almost too fragile for the real world. But then she inhabits the Opera World.
She told me the real world ceases to exist when you are a famous star. Your life literally becomes just rehearsals, performances, and travel.
 You only see the inside of theatres, planes, and hotels. She travels less after my mother died and she says Roma Opera makes

her feel grounded. Like François, she also cut anywhere out of Europe from her schedules.

'How is Marina, your friend?' my daughter wants to know.

Anasztázia is not surprised by her question. She brought us some more photos of my mother from that final La Scala première.

'You remember her, Marina?' she asks.

Marina nods. 'Mamma has the photo on her wall. She lives in your home.

Marina likes that dress. She wears it when she comes to my room, and I see her at the Opera.'

François looks at Marina.

He is a little disturbed because she mentioned seeing her at the Opera.

He knows my daughter found the shrine with all the photos in Anasztázia's apartment,

so assumes this is the reason.

'Marina thinks your mother lives there, although poor Anasztázia seems to believe this too.

It is understandable that we feel her presence, especially with all the photos of her in our apartment.

Anasztázia seems to be trapped in time.'

'Yes,' I tell him. 'She did love my mother.'

François does not see Anasztázia as a love rival, so he is not jealous.

Marina is only four years old, so François thinks the fact she talks about seeing my mother at Paris Opera is just a child's imagination. That she wants to see her, so she does.

After all, my daughter has grown up in this apartment where every room is adorned with my mother's image. But François hates the photos Anasztázia brought us.

He did not like that photo I placed above my bed. There is something morbid about that night, particularly as it was Lucia di

Lammermoor, where the lead character loses her mind.
 It was only two weeks before she died.
'Are we all having a sleepover?' Marina asks.
'Yes, but not tonight,' Anasztázia says.
'Mamma has sleepovers. She sleeps with François.' Marina continues.
'Marina!' I say, annoyed with her.
Anasztázia looks at me.
'I have nightmares,' I say. 'I find it hard to sleep alone in a room.'
'I never have bad dreams, but I do dream of Marina. Have you seen a doctor?' Anasztázia asks.
'Yes, but I do not want therapy.
The doctor gave me sleeping tablets which give you nightmares when you stop taking them.
I feel so spaced out the next day.'

 Me and Anasztázia sit up late and talk. We have long periods of silence as we listen to the rain outside.
 She mentions Natalija. She read that interview too, was amazed this heartless girl had married and had a child.
'I cannot believe I loved her,' Anasztázia tells me.
'And she hated kids and men! That poor young Mexican tenor.
 As for her daughter; Natalija flaunted that girl like a piece of jewellery.
 I feel sad for Lucia. She will be so messed up, like Lucia in my Opera.'
'My mother nearly had the name Lucia; it was her middle name,' I say, changing the subject.
'Your mother did not like the name Lucia,' Anasztázia remembers.
'She associated it with Lucia di Lammermoor.'
 I pretend I only met Natalija one time after watching her perform in Il Trovatore in Paris.

'She was backstage, but I was with François in the aftershow, so she had just complimented me on my beauty.

Just like your mother, she told me. But she was very nice.'

Anasztázia does not doubt my story but warns me to stay away from her.

'She is a predator, Fiorenza. You are young, beautiful and just the type she would sink her teeth into.'

'As if,' I laugh.

'I should go, I have rehearsals tomorrow,' she tells me, and unfurls herself from the sofa.

'It is lovely you asked me to stay when François was away,' she says.

She smiles as she puts on her coat, then her blue eyes are sad and serious.

'Fiorenza, forgive me, but I need to ask.'

'What?' I smile.

'You and your father sleep in the same room?' She looks around the living room, even though François and Marina both went to bed.

'When I have bad dreams. It is nothing, Anasztázia.'

Anasztázia takes my hand. 'Romeo called me. He was concerned you are lonely........'

'No, I have university and my daughter taking all my time,' I say.

'I have a lot of darkness in my life. Whatever you tell me............ Fiorenza, you can trust me,' she says, her expression sincere.

I do trust her.

Then she says warmly, 'I always feel better seeing you, Fiorenza. You make me feel like I am so close to your mother.'

'Thank you,' I tell her.

'My sister is the opposite of me. We have such different personalities.'

My mother stayed with Anasztázia after she filed for divorce from Andrea, but Anasztázia was in love with her. My mother probably loved her too. I do not know what sort of relationship they had.

I remember François feeling sad, worrying my mother had been so broken by the violence.

He thought he had lost her to Anasztázia.

She spent less time in Paris and had more work in Roma and La Scala.

The autumn and winter before her death, my mother had been badly attacked by my stepfather and stayed with Anasztázia.

I think her poor body had taken so much, she even rejected François.

Then I imagine Anasztázia falling in love with me because I look like my mother.

She is lovely, but I do not have those feelings for her. I am not even sure about Natalija.

I laugh.

'What is it?' she smiles.

'Oh, nothing, Anasztázia. Just something Marina said.'

I walk her to the front door.

She kisses me goodbye. 'Remember you do not have to take your mother's place.'

'I am impulsive, and I do what I want,' I say defensively.

She looks at me sadly. 'Fiorenza; those would be her exact words.'

I take Marina to watch Anasztázia's opening night for Lucia di Lammermoor.

Although my daughter was restless, when the haunting notes of the glass harmonica floated from the orchestra in Il dolce suono and Anasztázia's spinto voice split the auditorium, she was transfixed. For the 18 minutes as Lucia spiralled across the stage, Marina did not move.

Anasztázia was famous, but the way she can still perform this role with those sky-splitting notes is incredible. I wondered how such a tiny woman had such power in her voice.

She is legendary in this role and the whole run is sold out.

Afterwards, Marina is one of the first to speak to this otherworldly Hungarian soprano in her shimmering silver dress. She looks so cool and composed, as if she had been watching an opera, not performing one of the most difficult arias in the soprano repertoire.

'I want to be like you, Ana! I want to be an opera star!'

Anasztázia smiles.

'My God, a four-year-old loving Lucia di Lammermoor!

Marina you are very special, and you will be a star.'

But now, after her first two performances have been such a success and all the adrenaline has subsided a little, Anasztázia has five days off. She relaxes in our apartment.

'You know, Fiorenza, I went a little crazy performing Lucia in Palermo. It was the summer Natalija left me.

The night your mother came to La Scala to watch me in the role was nearly a year after Palermo.

It was the last time I ever saw her in the real world, and I conquered my demons.

She had literally scooped me off the floor after Natalija walked out.'

I feel even more guilty than I already do.

Yet Natalija had not said anything critical about poor Anasztázia, just that she was needy, and they drifted apart.

After Natalija had been stabbed and nearly lost her career, I do not feel she is totally heartless for leaving my friend to go to America. Yes, she had been cruel, but I understand her more now.

All opera singers have to make sacrifices.

'The Lucia role is a little crazy. Especially your madness aria,' I tell her.

'I can imagine the huge demands it places on a singer. My mother found it hard to play Marguerite in Faust. I think the descent into madness scared her.'

We are quiet.

'She gave me a reason to live, Fiorenza…...'

Anasztázia's parents disowned her for being unable to love men after her marriage fell apart.

She suffered a lot of depression and darkness in her life, especially in Hungary.

She attempted suicide twice, was hospitalised and as far as I know, still takes strong medication.

As for the past, she says is too dark to speak of.

'Fiorenza?' Anasztázia asks me gently.

'Please talk to me. I know whatever secret you hide from the world is hurting you…...'

I have avoided this conversation as she has been in the hotel, then performing. Now the stress has subsided, I have to face her questions.

I am carrying this darkness around and it is so corrosive.

Natalija was not the right person to confide in. She found it entertaining. I need a reaction which is more balanced.

'Life really pushed me to the limits,' I say.

Anasztázia waits and gently urges me on.

'Fiorenza, whatever you tell me is totally confidential.'

She places her hand in mine.

As I tell her everything, she listens without any reaction of shock or disgust.

Afterwards, I gaze out of the window for a long time as Anasztázia plays with her bracelet and probably thinks of her own darkness.

'Anasztázia?' I ask to break the silence.

'Can you see my sin all over my black soul?' I look at her and her expression is calm and gentle.

'I sense it, Fiorenza. But I am different to other people.

After all, you know about the Lilac room; I sense things others do not.'

I nod. 'I know.'

'It is as if I have a layer of skin missing. Life hurts, but it is good for my Opera……..……..'

I get up and gaze out of the window, unable to face her after everything I just said.

'You look in the mirror and see your beautiful mother, don't you?'

She joins me by the balcony, and places a cool hand on my shoulder, as I watch the streets below.

She speaks almost hypnotically with her delicate glassy voice.

'I see her every day in the mirror. Anasztázia! I cannot even see Fiorenza now.…….'

Anasztázia moves closer, wraps her arm round me.

'Darling, please listen to me.

Your daughter says strange things.

Okay, it could be years from now, but believe me, you never want that day to arrive when she finds out the truth.

My daughter hated me for so long: for giving my life to Opera, for missing out on her childhood.

It broke my heart.'

'I feel so trapped, Anasztázia,' I tell her. 'Every day I look in the mirror and hate myself.'

'My dear Fiorenza, this is sickness.

You have become her to him.

It must be hard for François seeing the love he lost as he is living in the past.

And you are not the demon temptress; you are not to blame. He is the one who is responsible.

He is to blame.

You were only 20 years old whatever you say about being the one who started it all.'

I turn to face Anasztázia. Her expression is of concern.

'Anasztázia, you swear you tell no one!'

'I promise but, Fiorenza, how can you live with this? It must destroy your soul.'

'My mother haunts me every night, Anasztázia. She screams at me.

 She knows what I do,' I say.

I put my head in my hands.

'She hates me, Anasztázia.'

'Listen to me, sweet girl; your mother's presence in my apartment someone at peace.

I see her and sense her; she smiles and disappears. It is very rare we speak.

The roses and candles are her work and I swear on my life I do not lie.

Once I had a conversation with her in my dressing room at her memorial concert.

Your daughter saw her. She also said that your mother appears for her in Paris Opera and her bedroom here and I believe she does see and speak to her.

She talked to her in my apartment.'

'That means my mother sees what I do at night,' I say.

Anasztázia laughs despite the dark conversation.

'Fiorenza! Spirits cannot see us in bed!

I do believe that those who die long before their time are most likely to appear, as if they are searching for something they left on Earth.'

'I guess so,' I say, full of doubt. I still wonder how much the dead really see.

Anasztázia does not know how dangerous it is for me in Italia, especially in Roma. She wants me to visit her place again.

When François returns, he is happy and wants to know all about Lucia di Lammermoor.

Marina says over dinner, 'Ana is so pretty but she has a sad heart.'

François asks why she thinks this.

'She misses her Marina,' she tells him.

I look at my daughter and think, what a perceptive little girl, knowing how Anasztázia feels.

'I want to be a star just like Ana in the Opera,' Marina continues.

'You took her to Lucia di Lammermoor?' François is a little shocked.

'Why not? It is not violent, and Marina loved the madness aria. Anasztázia one of the best in the world for the role of Lucia.

How she stretches her voice into those incredible high notes, I never know.

Marina now wants to be an opera singer.'

'Anasztázia. Does she say anything?' François asks me later.

'We talk about Opera and performances, reminisce about my mother.

I like to hear her stories from Roma, about the past,' I lie.

I thought after speaking with my friend, that François would return, and everything could be normal, our lives magically back to how they were years ago.

I had been performing some dark magic on the balcony again, trying to unbind us from this relationship, but clearly it has messed up.

It has become stronger if anything. I have managed to bind him to me instead of unbinding.

I should not be invoking dark forces when I do not fully understand what I am doing.

I discover some framed photographs François carries with him as I unpack his bag.

At first, I think they are my mother but looking closely, two are of her and the other two are of me at Paris Opera.

I put them back in the bag. It is not just the fact he carries these photos, but because even to my eyes, me and my mother are identical when dressed for the evening, give or take a few years.

She looks much younger, and I look older.

I have become my mother.

Anasztázia is right; he really is stuck in some crazy time trap.

It makes me feel unsettled and I go to make him a coffee. As the coffee bubbles on the stovetop, I obsess over this situation I created. This is all my fault. I brought in the dark forces.

You have become her to him, Anasztázia said.

'Here is your coffee,' I tell him, leaving it on the bedside table. 'I have to go.'

I see the black shine in his hair in the light and wonder if he will ever turn grey.

'You should have woken me,' he says, looking at the clock.

'You were tired. I have to get to class, and Marina's au pair took her to school already.'

'You unpacked my suitcase?' he asks.

'You are so kind, carissima. I cannot believe it is already February. Time just melts, the seasons merging into one as I do opera after opera.'

'I left your bag, I did not want to look through your personal possessions,' I lie.

'I have to leave now.'

He smiles at me, runs his fingers through the length of my hair. 'What would I do without you?'

'I will see you later,' I tell him.

He seems to be oblivious to everything else outside our bubble, as if he is truly living in the past.

I worry about what Marina says to the au pair.
I should have changed the au pair long ago, but I would need to make sure Marina was happy with a new one and that would take interviews and time.
Loredana also makes wonderful Sicilian food, and I want an Italian speaking au pair.
I use Italian with Marina as it is so important for to speak her native tongue. French is easier as she uses it in school and with François, although I feel Marina is equally competent both languages.
If she is serious about wanting to be an opera singer, languages are essential.
Loredana helps her with Italian written exercises when I am busy.
As Italian grammar is complex, I want to ensure her written work does not suffer.
So, I keep resolving to deal with the au pair issue another time.
I wish I had listened to my instincts and changed the au pair when I felt uneasy.
As I take the elevator, I stare at myself in the mirror wondering who the hell I am and what it is I really want.

Marina has helped François make a cake and thank God she is chirping on about papa Alain. She saw him yesterday and he treated her in the toy shop.
Alain is good for her.
He wants to see me, but I tell him only Marina is to see him, depending on his work schedule.
If he works weekends, he is good about making it up and seeing her after school on a weekday.
I was afraid he would let her down, but he seems more attached

than ever.

She is spoiled with ice cream and sweets and clothes, but that is a minor problem compared to everything else in my life.

Every single night, I am afraid to sleep, afraid of the dreams which will not stop; dreams of my mother cursing me to Hell for my sin.

I keep thinking of me as a little girl, precocious and confident and how I dreamed of being a star.

Now everything is hopelessly tangled and savagely ruined.

Sometimes I feel such anger; Andrea stole my happiness by murdering my mother, having me attacked.

He is directly responsible for this terrible chain of events, which is why I am lying in this bed of fucking lies, hating myself, hating what I have become.

Why did she have to die?

Why did she have to go back to Roma that night?

Where is God?

But as I already know, the Gods must be savage.

CARMENCITA

Catalina visits at the end of February for five days and it is the first time I have seen her since we went to prison nearly two years ago. Hearing how Catalina witnessed the violence Andrea inflicted on my lovely mother disturbed me so much. My poor little sister.

Catalina, once so cold and vicious tongued, hugs me like she did years ago.

Her hair is no longer a glossy dark brown but as black as mine.

As she has my mother's almost black eyes, she looks more like her now.

Her fair skin appears slightly golden, and she tells me has been applying fake tan, to lose her father's Venetian colouring. She wants to distance herself from Andrea.

My sister looks like a fragile fairy-tale princess, but it is sad that she is clearly starving herself.

She also has none of the precociousness I had at her age.

I am 22 years old and bitchy and mean. Catalina is a sweet innocent girl.

'She just told me about your prison visit to Andrea when I collected from the airport.

What were you thinking of, Fiorenza?' François confronts me in the kitchen as Catalina plays with Marina.

'The poor girl is messed up enough!

She told me you went twice to the prison when you stayed with Anasztázia.

How the hell could you see that evil man who stole…….'

He is crying.

'He stole our mother!

He fucking stole her from me, from you and Catalina, and

everyone who loved her.

I had to confront him about my mother's death and then he asked me to bring Catalina the next week.

He said my daughter would be safe if I did.'

'Fiorenza! How could you even be in the same room?!' François says.

'That evil man who ruined our lives!'

I shriek at him. 'We needed to do it, François! Me and Catalina! We had to ask him why he killed our mother!'

'Stop shouting, Fiorenza. I do not want Catalina to hear,' he says.

'It helped Catalina. She needed to confront him. He is her father and she saw things she should never have to see,' I say quietly.

'Oh, Fiorenza; you mean she saw Andrea hurt your mother? God, she was a child.'

He covers his face with his hands.

'Please do not cry. It is not your fault.

We are all suffering, all of us. We just need to talk about it.'

I know he needs comfort right now, but he does not talk enough about pain.

Catalina tells me later, 'I wish I could change my DNA. I hate that he is my father.'

'Your black hair makes you look very dramatic and more like our mother,' I tell her.

'You look lovely, especially with golden skin, Catalina but a little thin….'

'You are the one who is so like her, Fiorenza.' She smiles.

She does not want to talk about her eating problems, always changes the subject.

'It is strange, seeing you after two years; you are the image of our mother.

You are fiery, argumentative, and wild.

It reminds me so much of her, as if she lives on in you. I feel better seeing you. Less sad.'

If only Catalina knew that I really did feel possessed by this spirit of our mother.

'And I am so sorry for what I said years ago…….about François, about little Marina.

It was our bitchy relatives; they said this poison.'

'You were hurting, Catalina. We both were,' I tell her.

'I would hate to lose you, Fiorenza,' she says.

After Catalina's visit, in between François working abroad, we scream and shout non-stop.

I do not want to carry on with our 'living arrangement' and he sees it as his goddamn right.

I know Marina witnesses some arguments, but most of the time we argue at night, full of rage and resentment.

At Easter, François persuades me that as I am tense, we need a break in Mallorca.

I do not want to go, and I will not go.

Natalija is in Dresden. She told me of it very early on, back in December.

She even spread out her entire three-year schedule, encouraged me to write European dates in my diary.

She spoke of her apartment in Milano and said she would love me to visit when she performs in La Scala. I do not think Italia is a good idea, but I like the thought of Dresden.

'I am doing five performances of Carmen, so I have over a month in Dresden.

I would really like you to visit, Fiorenza,' she had said.

'Write this in your diary.'

I had told Natalija my fears about visiting her in Milano. She performed in La Scala two or three times a year.

'I want you to stay there, feel like it is your place too.'

It was a big step for this diva to want me to feel at home in her own apartment.

She told me she understood I had this fear of my evil stepfather, but this is my life too.

He is in prison.

You cannot live your life governed by this hateful killer.

I understand Roma has memories, but you fly to Malpensa, come to my apartment by La Scala and stay.

Your sister lives in Milano.

Fiorenza, you cannot let Andrea ruin your life more than he has. He already stole so much.

Except now François is going to book Mallorca.

He says it will be good for us, not too hot this time of year.

'Fiorenza, you have worked so hard, got an internship for summer.'

'Which is exactly why I want to go to Berlin alone for five days. Please can you take Marina to Mallorca?'

'But surely Mallorca is warmer than Germany?' he says to me. 'Why not come too?'

'Please, François. I really need a break alone.'

He is puzzled and I do not dare say I am really in Dresden.

Dresden is a little off the map and if he studies the opera schedules, he could easily work it out. Carmen is on and that means the famous Hungarian mezzo he despises will be there.

Marina nods happily when we tell her François will take her to Mallorca to the beach and I go to Berlin. She wants to know why I am not coming, but I say I need shops.

'Berlin has many shops and I hear the Opera is beautiful.'

François reluctantly agrees to take my daughter to Spain for ten days; he does not mind being alone with her, but he wishes I were with him.

I really think it is such a bad idea, sharing hotel rooms as well but I do not want an argument now.

I fly to Berlin then get on a train to Dresden.

Natalija has the best room in the Kempinski in the Old Town.

When I knock on her door late afternoon, she is looking very beautiful; sparkling black dress and her raven spirals of hair pinned into a glamorous creation.

She takes my hand and pulls me into her suite, ever the seductress.

'Come along, my lovely Italian treasure.

And you still wear my necklace. How sweet.' She traces my collarbones with her fingertips.

'It means a lot to me,' I tell her. I look out of the window at the view over the spires of the Old Town. Dresden is so pretty; the old town is compact, the Opera House beautiful. I love it.

Tomorrow I will see her in Carmen.

Natalija gets out the reviews and spreads them over the table, showing me her opening night success.

'Everyone falls in love with me as Carmen.'

Then she left me alone as she took a call on the balcony. I knew from her expression it was her husband, but she kept it short and I did not hear a word.

'Sorry,' she says, placing the phone on the dresser.

'It is okay, really,' I tell her.

'He is so boring. I said I had to go to Opera for an extra rehearsal.'

The truth is I have a beautiful Italian I want to take for dinner.

I do not love my husband, Fiorenza.

I chose Diego because I wanted a designer kid.'

She sighs, looks pensive, despite her careless remarks. Did she coldly calculate it all from the moment she met this young tenor?

I notice she has a photo on the bedside table of her and Lucia.

The child looks even prettier now she is a year old.

'I really love my daughter. I know everyone thinks I am a lousy mother.

I hated kids.

I did trap poor Diego when he was only 25. He is young and naïve, flattered to be with this world-famous diva he met on Carmen as my co-star.

Then a few months later I announced I am having Lucia. I did not care what he thought.

But he was happy, asked me to marry him. Lucia was really what I wanted, not him.'

She looks at the ceiling. I cannot read her thoughts.

'I know you love your daughter, Natalija.

 Maybe you wanted her for all the wrong reasons, but she changed you.'

Natalija turns to face me.

I wonder if she is angry, but then she laughs so much and then her laughter turns to tears.

The great Natalija lies on the bed and cries into her hands.

She is weeping like the end of the world.

'Oh, Natalija, carissima; I am sorry if I upset you.

Please do not cry. Tell me what is hurting.'

I hold her close, and her Coco Chanel perfume is an intoxicating scent.

'This life is fucking lonely, Fiorenza.

I must seem such a bitch to you, marrying some young tenor…. the marriage will not last…..'

She cried some more, and I tried to comfort her.

'Dear Natalija, you are not a bitch.

You are scared to feel, just like me.

 You really miss your little girl, don't you, carissima?' I ask.

'Yes,' she says, and wipes the tears from her face.

'It hurts, as if I left a part of myself behind every time I travel. I am not a good mother; she has au pairs, but I miss her.'

Then as soon as she has betrayed some vulnerability, she snaps back into Carmencita; flirty, singing lines from the Seguidilla as she twirls round the room, urging me to get ready for dinner.

She turns her emotions on and off so fast. I guess she finds this easy as an actress, but it is how she lives in her real life too.

It is hard to separate the stage from reality, my mother always said.

Especially when we play other characters all the time.

'Fiorenza! Make it fast; I am hungry!' Natalija shouts through the bathroom door.

I manage to see Carmen twice and both times are just as amazing. First time I see her perform her signature role and she is Natalija, just a more exaggerated version of the flirty diva.

She is a hypnotic and hungry seductress with an outstandingly beautiful voice. No wonder she is rated as the world's best Carmen.

I notice the extras which elevate an opera singer into star status; it is not purely her voice, beauty, acting and dancing. Natalija has added coquettish movements: spitting oranges at the soldiers, licking her lips, tossing her hair and at one point removing her underwear with a wicked laugh.

The critics always call her 'the most physical, seductive Carmen in the industry'.

She is always virtually seducing her co-star on stage, sitting astride him as she sings or rolling around on the stage.

No wonder that young Diego fell in love with her as her co-star.

The curtain calls last forever and afterwards she takes me backstage, proudly showing me off to everyone as her 'wonderful friend, the daughter of Marina Valentino'.

The great Marina Valentino? Everyone asks me.

You look so much like your mother. We remember her. Such a

tragedy.

Then I am crying in the hotel, crying over Natalija. I am full of emotions I do not understand.

I loved Carmen, was uplifted and dazzled by her performance, and now I am crying champagne tears because I miss my mother.

And I have more feelings than I wanted to have for this mercurial Hungarian girl.

'I just saw Carmen and I am crying. I miss my mother,' I tell Natalija.

'Carmen is an uplifting Opera. Why am I fucking crying?'
'Baby, it is okay.

Sometimes we cry after wonderful music and a night out.

Opera, it is strange; it unlocks a secret door within our hearts even after a good night with no sadness.

I cry too at the craziest times. Especially after having Lucia.'
'I do not want to be weak,' I say.

'You do not want to feel. You do not want to feel anything, do you?' Natalija says.

I look at her heavily made-up eyes, the glittery cheekbones, the inconsistent exotic diva.

This beautiful temptress. I want to feel nothing for her, but that is changing way too fast.

'You do not want to feel for me?' she asks, pulling me closer.
'No,' I say. 'I am afraid to feel for anyone.'
'Let it go. Trust me and just let it go. Please, Fiorenza; if you do, I will too.'

Catalina is 17 this May and will graduate from La Scala ballet academy. She could join the company in Milano, but she has to become a soloist, being too tall for the corps de ballet.

One tutor suggests a year in another country.

François wants her to audition for Paris ballet theatre.

If she stays alone in Milano and pushes herself even harder, she could die from anorexia.

I want to help her, but I will be going into my fourth year at university, and I am stressed.

A visit is nice, but not a whole goddamn year.

When I arrive back in Paris, I have some days alone. I enjoy the space and now my sister will be coming to stay. It is too much for me.

Just after François and Marina return from Mallorca, Catalina arrives in Paris to audition.

She is very considerate, lovely towards me and plays with Marina, helping to prepare the cake for Marina's fifth birthday.

Catalina loves food, just not eating it.

At just 17 years old, she is still a little young, but she is an exceptional dancer, so she has the chance to study in Paris with the company. She will only make it as a soloist in Paris, just like Milano.

She will train over the summer for September season, and she has a year to prove herself by dancing minor solo roles.

There might be an opening with the company full-time by the time she is 18 years old, which is the minimum age requirement.

I do not think this is healthy to put herself under even more stress in a prestigious place. She would be better off in a small company, although she tells me she wants the big time.

The ballet academy in Milano wants an exceptional ballerina, at the expense of Catalina's health.

My mother always visited Catalina in the apartment for the first year she was in Milano, even when she did not perform in La Scala. She always took a night or a weekend to see her.

Catalina was happy then. She always looked forward to seeing our mother.

After her death, Catalina was alone, unless François was performing in La Scala and she had been frosty and uncommunicative until a few years ago.

She had hated me, until we went to that prison together.
Paris is highly renowned for helping dancers who struggle with eating disorders.

'If she stays in Milano, she could die,' François says.

'She can have my room,' I tell François.
'You can stay in the master bedroom,' he says.
'Are you out of your fucking mind?' I ask him.
'The room is the biggest and you need space to study, Fiorenza.
Besides, I am away so often next season.
You cannot share a bedroom with Marina or sleep on the sofa. What else can you do?
The master bedroom has a balcony, so you can have space from the girls for studying.
There is a sofa I can sleep on if you want.'
I glare at him.
'The living room is very comfortable, and I will use that sofa. I can use your room but not when you are in it! No way when Catalina is here.'
I hate him for giving me no choice about my sister's visit. One whole fucking year.
'Fiorenza, I need you to help Catalina.'
'I am not playing nurse for my sister!
Everything depends on getting into law school or my career as an advocate is over.
I am no fucking psychiatrist!' I shout.
'Fiorenza, we have the au pair to help. You just study and try to get Catalina to eat a little more.'
He tries to hold me, but I push him away.
'Fine, I tell him.
'But I do not trust Loredana. She is asking Marina too many questions.
I want to find another au pair.'

'Oh, Fiorenza, I am sure Loredana does not think anything malicious. We have a normal life as far as she is concerned.

It would be difficult to find someone as good as her.'

'Whatever,' I say, and flounce off to prepare my room for Catalina.

I plan to sleep on the sofa.

I am not going to be in his room for a whole damn year unless he is away.

Normal life. Like hell.

I look at the master bedroom. I love the stuccoed ceilings, the ornate mirrors, and chandeliers and the large balcony. It is my favourite room.

The au pair says how lovely my sister will stay with us in Paris.

'She is so thin; she needs help. But where will you go, Fiorenza?' Loredana asks.

'If you stay in Marina's room, you will be woken up early.'

'Catalina is staying in my room, so I can sleep on the sofa in the living room.

When François is away, I have his room then.'

Something about Loredana's expression shows she doubts my story.

'At 22 years old, you sleep on a sofa?' She stares at me unblinking.

I am dismissive, as if this happens all the time.

'He is out a lot even when he is working in Paris. Next season, he has so many commitments abroad.

Besides, I am happy to sleep in the living room. The sofa is so comfortable. And when he is out, I can study in his room, sit on the balcony to have space.

Listen, Loredana, I need help with Catalina; she is anorexic.'

I really do need help with my sister.

'Now the weather is warm, it is nice for you to study in the evening on this lovely balcony to have space from the girls.

I guess if François is away, it can be your room.
And I really will try to help your sister.'

'If you bake those delicious melanzane dishes, Catalina will be tempted.'

I smile. Loredana loves food, being Sicilian.

'Fiorenza, listen; I have known you since you were a depressed 17-year-old.

I watched you grow into this beautiful confident young woman, but I still feel I do not know the real Fiorenza.

You have a mask for the world. If anything is troubling you.......'

She places her hand on my arm.

'I have this mask because of everything horrible in my life; all that darkness.

And now, I am also extremely stressed about my career.

There is so much pressure.'

'I know it is hard for you, but please confide in someone. You hold too much in.'

I promise I will.

THE WICKED FAIRY

When Catalina arrives in June, I have an internship for a month with a criminal advocate, a woman I admire called Arianna. It is hard to find internships before law school, but this woman was very taken by me when we met backstage at the Opera.

Just like me she is half-French, half-Italian.

She also loves Opera, and she was a corporate guest at Christmas, when François was performing Rodolfo in La bohème.

Paris Opera is a fantastic place for networking and being the social butterfly I am, this is how I managed to get my Italian perfume advertisement.

Looking as good as I do in my evening dress is halfway there; I look a million dollars, so I have a stack of business cards from politicians, lawyers, media people, and just interested suitors.

Most of the law students at university are just students, but I told the advocate a few months ago, when she asked me to attend a formal interview, why I had chosen this profession.

I told her about my mother's murder, how determined I was to make it as an advocate after confronting Andrea in his Italian jail.

I was not just Fiorenza the glamorous Italian girl in the Opera and beautiful daughter of Marina Valentino, I was the determined Fiorenza who spoke three languages and was top of her university class.

'No one should live in fear,' I told Arianna in the interview.

'I am totally committed to law.

Maybe you know of my mother's reputation in the Opera World and her high-profile murder six years ago. She was never free because of her fame.

The Italian legal system failed her because my stepfather was free before trial

My mother's death did at least result in sweeping changes to Italian domestic violence law.

I am sure you know of 'Marina's law'.'

Arianna rarely took on trainees for an internship until they completed the exams for law school in the autumn after the fourth year, but then I am unique and have self-belief to the point of arrogance.

My mother taught me this. She said talent was only half of success; absolute self-belief and determination and beauty formed the rest.

Arianna told me rarely did she meet a young person with such drive and ambition.

'Suffering so much, Fiorenza; it made you the strong woman you are.

I know of 'Marina's law' and the tragic circumstances surrounding your mother's death.

I once saw her perform Madama Butterfly in Paris and I will never forget that night.

She felt tragedy like no other singer I have ever seen on stage.

You are so like her; very intelligent and very beautiful. Beauty should not be underestimated in our profession. See it as an extra weapon.'

I never saw being beautiful as anything but good.

Arianna was very attractive in a Parisienne way. She clearly valued appearance as much as me and we could also speak Italian with each other, talk about our home country.

She had grown up in Genova before moving to Paris.

'You are looking so good, carissima,' my father says, after my first day at work.

I pull away from his embrace and kiss Marina and Catalina.

'How are my lovely girls?' I ask them.

I give Catalina a plate the size of Marina's, encourage her to help herself.

As promised, Loredana made some wonderful Sicilian food which she thoughtfully placed on little plates and Catalina allows herself a few tiny bites.

François is very stupid when it comes to women.

He tips dinner on big plates and covers it with butter or olive oil. My mother always snapped at him, scooping half her dinner off her plate. She would eat from side plates or saucers.

'These fucking plates are too big!' she would complain constantly. 'I do not want to get fat!'

Even when she was pregnant with Catalina, I remember her shouting at François when he tried to encourage her to eat more.

She loved her rich Italian breakfasts but for dinners, she only ever ate off small portions.

'Fuck, François! You know nothing about women! I do not want this child anyway!' she had shouted at him.

He had also gently suggested she moderate her high caffeine intake and her curses were unrepeatable. Nothing came between my mother and her beloved coffee.

Poor Catalina was hated before she even arrived in the world.

François would look sadly at his beautiful Marina with her smouldering vitality, as she cursed and carved up her plate in a bad mood.

I knew it wounded him when she was cruel, but he loved her too much to criticise.

He knew just how badly she had been beaten and terrorised by Andrea.

Catalina speaks to me one evening when François is performing in his outdoor concert. I know she has noticed the way I am towards him and is puzzled by it.

'Fiorenza, you seem cold and yet he adores you. I just wondered why; what upsets you?'

I put down the law book I am studying.

'I am stressed, and I have to make sure I never neglect Marina,' I tell her.

'I do not want the au pair to take my place, although it will be hard when I qualify as an advocate.'

'Our mother was no good when we were young,' Catalina admits.

'She hated me.'

'Catalina, she thought she was a useless mother when we were very young, due to her terrible depression.

Life was hard for her as an opera star.

She also lived a double life, constantly having to hide the domestic violence from the world.

She always said, you are only as good as your last performance.'

Catalina still has this feeling our mother loved me more than her.

'Anyway,' I continue.

'Me and François only had each other after mamma died. He wanted to give up his beloved Opera, but I made him carry on.

I am mean to him, but I am still angry about life.'

Catalina clearly does not think this is the only answer.

'Does François want you to stay because you look like her? He is not seeing the real Fiorenza.'

She looked at me with her innocent expression, all dark eyes and seriousness.

I know she is emotionally repressed; many ballerinas are. She just thinks François worships my looks.

I sigh.

'Yes. I am not Fiorenza when he takes me to premières.

I am not me to the other singers either, Catalina. They all see Marina Valentino too.'

Catalina looks at all the framed photos on the living room wall, traces a photo of her as Tosca, her signature role.

'I still have all that pain inside from mamma's death, from those horrible prison visits….'

Catalina nodded.

'I do too, Fiorenza.'

'How about you eat something healthy with me?' I asked her gently.

She shook her head.

'Just come and have a look, Catalina.' I hold out my hand.

A huge problem was getting my sister to eat. She counted calories on everything.

François told her to stop counting calories and I said to leave her alone. She will only do it in secret.

François moans that Marina will end up anorexic.

'Marina will pick up on her food disorder, Fiorenza. Catalina is her auntie after all,' François said to me.

'Let me worry about Marina. She is not going to get anorexic! And leave poor Catalina alone; always you stress about food, and it makes her worse. The company doctor is helping her.'

'I want her to see a shrink, but she refuses,' François said.

I would not have seen a shrink either at 17 years old about anything.

I would not see a shrink now.

When François returned from his concert, I was asleep in the living room. He was in his black suit, and he slammed the front door, complaining about the heat.

'You woke me up!' I snap at him. 'Fucking close the door and do not slam it!'

I threw a book at his head.

'God, Fiorenza! You are so moody!' he says, picking up the book.

'All we do is argue these days.' His voice is sad.

I flop away and face the window.
'Sleep if you hate me that much, Fiorenza.'
There are tears in his voice.
'What did we ever do this for?' He traces his warm hand down my back, rests it on my spine for a few moments.
'I never wanted this. I was afraid of you hating me so much I could lose you forever.'
He gently caresses my hair as it spills over my shoulders.
'If you do hate me, I want you to know I never ever imagined our lives would turn into this.
Are you listening?'
I bury my head in a pillow, but he still crashes around.
Damn selfish man.

Catalina is watching me sleep in the living room.
'Catalina,' I say, stretching my arms. 'You are up early.'
My sister says she feels so bad for taking my room.
'You are on the sofa. Fiorenza. I thought you would sleep in the big bedroom on the sofa bed.
I should sleep here not you. I feel awful……'
'It is fine,' I tell her.
'The sofa is soft, and I can watch TV when everyone is in bed.
I am asleep when François comes home. Besides, he is away half the time, but last night he woke me up. I prefer to be in the living room.
I want you to feel at home,' I tell her.
'You always look so lovely, Fiorenza. You wear such beautiful things even in bed,' she tells me, admiring my silk nightwear as I get up.
'It is very important even if you live alone. Mamma taught me this,' I tell her.
'You are so slender, but you have curves; I wish I had a body like you,' she says.

'I was too thin until I had Marina. Then I got this figure. God, I was happy!

Catalina, you are a ballerina.

I had food issues too when I was 16 years old. You will be okay.'

She looks doubtful.

I take François a coffee.

He looks so peaceful, not the sinner he really is. I hate him as I place the coffee on the bedside table.

'You leave so soon?' he asks sleepily.

'See you later.' I manage a smile.

Loredana is hovering around outside the door when I leave the room. I am sick of her interrogations. She should stop trying to listen at doors too.

'Everything okay, Fiorenza?' she asks me.

Stop fucking asking, I think. Stop listening and spying all the time.

'My advocate lady is amazing. I am lucky to get this month with her.'

I am about to take my taxi which will drop off Catalina for her ballet, on my way to the law office. Loredana is here to take Marina to school. She has already whined about why I waste money on taxis. What is wrong with the Metro?

'Everything is wrong with the Metro. Dirty, sleazy and I have agoraphobia.'

I am irritated when she questions my use of money. If I ran a car, that would cost too.

She does not know what happened to me in Roma, and I do not want to tell her.

Let her think I am just a spoiled rich girl.

I have my mother's black Gucci suit on and high heels, my hair up and I look as sharp and as beautiful as I feel.

'All of you managing without any arguments?' Loredana probes again.

'Yes,' me and Catalina both say, as we exit the apartment.

'Mamma and François still shout,' Marina says.

'Marina!' I say to her, annoyed.

'It is nothing,' I say.

'Me and Catalina hate his big portions and he does not understand women at all.'

I see in the elevator mirror Loredana is looking at me as if she can see my guilt. I am paranoid.

She is probably just admiring my outfit.

I have become so good at lying, I even say Arianna wants me to travel to London for a meeting in September.

As she practises international law, she wants me to attend with her. It seems a credible reason; I speak fluent English. François does not doubt me and says how good that I have these languages at my disposal.

I am seeing Natalija, just before my 23rd birthday.

My agoraphobia seems under control as I forget we are in a busy street, outside Covent Garden.

I am laughing with Natalija, after we leave stage door. I forget all the people around us as we walk to the front of the building into the warm cocoon of night.

Then I remember the crowds and cannot breathe.

I begin to panic a little and then even more, until Natalija sees I am in absolute meltdown.

She quickly gets us a taxi, holds me close and tells me we are safe now.

'Something really bad happened to you, didn't it?' she said.

'Something you cannot talk about? This is why you have this panic?'

'Yes,' I say. 'I never told anyone.'

And finally, when we are in the half-light of the hotel room, I manage to tell someone about that terrible day in Roma when I was 19 years old.

'Oh, my precious Fiorenza,' Natalija said, as I cried.

'I knew something was wrong; your mask for the world, your fear of trusting people, your strange set up in Paris. And believe me, I do not judge you for that.

I knew all this was more than just suffering after your mother's death.'

Finally, I feel some of the vile poison leaving my wounds.

I beg Natalija to see me as the beautiful, confident Fiorenza and not a victim.

She holds me close, whispers into my hair that I am still her lovely Fiorenza. She only wishes she could hunt down the bastards who hurt me.

'Baby, you are so like me in many ways, hurting inside and confident for the whole world.

You know that I do not think any less of you?

God, that evil fucking stepfather ruined your life.'

When I arrive back in Paris, Catalina prepares a wonderfully rich chocolate cake for my birthday treat. She takes a wafer of a slice and I know she will push it around her plate, take a bite and then leave it.

That night, I am getting a drink and I see most of the cake has gone. Marina never eats without asking me first and she went to bed hours ago.

I find my sister throwing up and crying in the bathroom.

I kneel next to her.

'Dear heart, you need more help,' I tell her, stroking her hair as she leans over the toilet bowl.

'I should have hidden the cake. I have a friend; she is a famous opera star, and she nearly ended her career with bulimia.

It is so dangerous, carissima.'

She rests her head against the wall.

'I could not stop. Starving is easy, Fiorenza but one bite of the cake…..'

'It's okay, let us get you to bed,' I tell her.

'You are such a lovely mother, Fiorenza,' Catalina says.

'Maybe you should have more children.'

'God forbid,' I tell her. 'Marina is everything.

You sleep now, Catalina.'

'Thank you, Fiorenza,' she says.

I leave her some soda water, and then I set about hiding all the trigger foods in the kitchen.

Natalija talked about her terrible bulimia when she was a young opera singer. She damaged her vocal cords by constantly bathing them in acid.

She could have even had heart failure.

Sweet stuff was the absolute worst trigger food, she told me.

The biscuits, chocolate and the jar of Marina's Nutella get hidden in my closet for Catalina to be safe.

Natalija said she got so mad at her lover, Krisztyna, who always had Nutella in the fridge.

'I could empty a jar in a few minutes,' she said.

'I hurled the jar at the wall once, or maybe she did. I cannot really remember.'

I wish Natalija was in Paris, just to speak with my sister. She had always been honest about her bulimia and the treatment she received.

I had asked her, 'what happened to Krisztyna?'

Natalija immediately shut down on me. She did not speak until I went to get my taxi to the train station.

As I was zipping my suitcase together, Natalija finally spoke. 'Krisztyna; I loved her, Fiorenza.

I have not talked of her for years.' Her eyes were clear and sad.

'It's okay. I understand,' I told her.

'I hope to meet your Marina,' she told me.

'Each time we meet, I want to know you even more; everything about you. You are such a lovely girl. I feel you understand me more than anyone in my life.'

It was such a compliment from an opera star who could choose anyone in the world.

'Marina would be delighted to see you, but I am never bringing her to Milano.

Never Italia,' I said.

'But you should visit Milano alone,' Natalija insisted.

'Think about what I told you, Fiorenza.

Do not let your stepfather steal more of your life. God knows he took enough.

This is your home country. Milano will be safe, I promise.

I will make sure.'

François is away until the next day. When he returns from Barcelona, he has spent a lot on all of us, but especially me. He has bought expensive earrings, even though I have plenty of my mother's jewellery.

He feels he has to buy my affection, especially as I am bitchy and mean these days.

'Who bought you that necklace?' he says, touching Natalija's gift to me from last year in Madrid. 'Why don't you wear your mother's diamond?'

'Oh, this.

I bought it some time ago on one of my shopping trips. I am afraid of losing that beautiful diamond, so I keep it for the Opera.'

'And that bracelet? I never saw this.'

That was a birthday gift from Natalija. I tell him my mother had it right at the bottom of the jewellery box.

There is so much there, so how would he remember?

Catalina has a small solo role as Carabosse, the wicked fairy, in The Sleeping Beauty.

Ballet does not interest me at all.

I took Marina to Romeo et Juliette once and enjoyed it as it was a tragic story, and more like the Opera, but I still would not go to the ballet.

During the performance, I am astounded by my younger sister's ability. Our mother had been a gymnastics champion when she was 12 years old and was tall and graceful like me and Catalina.

She did splits and somersaults in her twenties to warm up in Opera rehearsals, maintaining it opened her chest muscles.

As I am thinking of her, I feel a chill on my neck as we are in a box alone.

I keep turning around and looking at the blackness in the back of the box.

At one point I swear someone rests their hands on the back of my chair and the scent of Hypnotic Poison is overpowering. I am wearing the same perfume, but this is a very different scent; the warm sweetness of my mother's body mixing with the fragrance. I remember it so clearly.

Just like in Anasztázia's apartment.

I turn round in fright, dropping my programme on the floor. I expect to see her, full of hatred for me. But no one is there.

'The stage is there!' Marina pointed. 'What is it, mamma?'

'I think this box is haunted,' I whisper.

'Theatres are full of ghosts,' Marina said so seriously, sending chills down my back.

François is leaning over the edge of the box, not noticing my edgy behaviour.

I try to focus on Catalina who is transformed with her ragged tutu and make-up. On stage she is confident and although the ballet is tedious overall, I think her role is best. Every other dancer is sugary sweet.

Catalina looks older, with her elaborate make-up and dramatic costume, and she owns the stage with the kind of magic a prima ballerina does.

Even compared to the brilliant dancers in the company, Catalina has something truly unique.

On stage those long limbs create such perfect lines, so she does not appear as thin as she is in real life. I see why ballerinas starve themselves; thin, graceful arms and legs look more aesthetically pleasing.

It must be a terrible trap for those who are ill.

Marina loves watching her 'famous' auntie perform, says the wicked fairy is best of all.

That night as put Marina into bed, she asks me did I see the pretty lady who lives with Ana?

'Marina, like me. She was on the stairs at the Opera, mamma. In her black dress and tiara.'

I believe my daughter because I felt my mother's presence too.

'No, Marina; she likes you.'

I close the door feeling sad and empty.

Catalina has been better after a 30-year-old principal dancer told her she could make it as a prima ballerina. But if she kept starving, she could irreparably damage her body.

I was happy to see her eating chicken salad.

'Marie told me I need energy.

I do not want the life I worked for gone. If I have five to ten good years, but not for it to end next year.'

Her casual acceptance of ruining her joints by the age of 40, combined with a short shelf life for a top ballerina seemed depressing. Compared to an opera singer, five to ten years of a career was nothing.

I am happy that my daughter shows no interest in ballet when

I see Catalina wrapping her toes with an ice pack each evening and placing hot water bottles on her aching left hip.

She is 17 years old, for God's sake.

Marina still wants to be an opera singer after watching Anasztázia perform. She says the beautiful Marina in the photos is an opera singer. She wants to be just like her.

Catalina is promised bigger roles if she returns to Milano in March. Paris Ballet loves her, but she has only had a couple of very small solo roles after The Sleeping Beauty.

She has been promised work in Milano and she misses her own apartment

I give her a gift of black silk nightwear from my favourite boutique.

'You wear these and you are instantly beautiful. I want you to put the nightdress and robe on tonight and love yourself.

And remember what Marie told you.'

'Thank you,' she hugs me. 'I promise.'

I then surprise her and say I am flying with her to Milano. François looks worried but I tell him I will go to Milano for the weekend.

'And it will be nice to see Catalina's place, as it was my mother's apartment. It has been years since I last stayed there.'

I have an invite from Natalija. I will go without Marina, and I can do this.

As Natalija says, I cannot let Andrea ruin my life more than he has.

Of course, this is all about a visit to Natalija's apartment and La Scala.

Catalina was surprised when after looking round her apartment, I announce I am staying with a friend. I am also feeling terrible nostalgia when I remember running around the apartment as a child when my mother drank coffee on the balcony.

'I am only a few streets away, Catalina. Natalija just texted to say she is in the street now.'

Catalina had rushed to have a look at this 'friend' I was visiting. 'She is so beautiful,' Catalina exclaimed.

Natalija had insisted that we walk the few streets without taking a taxi. For me and my fears.

I wanted to try, I told her.

I love this district of the city; five minutes from La Scala and the Duomo. I do feel safe.

I spent the weekend in Natalija's apartment, visited La Scala for Aida.

Her place was beautiful; top floor with a rooftop garden and I felt safe in the apartment, safe in the Opera.

'You could return, baby,' Natalija told me, as we sat on her balcony on my final evening.

'Not to Roma but Milano. I mean return to live. I know you still feel Paris is not your true home.'

'I will be an advocate in France, in French law. It is not so easy. But yes, I could find work in Milano.'

I had the feeling I achieved so much, so that when I said goodbye to Natalija I was in tears because I missed my home country, would miss her too.

'It is okay to feel, Fiorenza,' she reminded me.

'You hold too much in.'

As I passed through security in Malpensa airport, I felt overcome by emotion.

I had broken the fear Andrea had cast over my life for so long.

I would never risk taking my daughter, but I could be here alone.

A whole glittering world had now opened to me; visits to Milano to see Catalina, Natalija and La Scala.

To drink coffee and eat cornetti and then take the easy flight back to Paris.

Catalina had forgotten an important document in Paris and called François to mail it on to her.

When he asked after me, my poor sister said I was staying at a friend's, a few streets away.

Oh, a girl called Natalija. An opera singer. Very beautiful. She waited in the street for Fiorenza, and I saw her from the balcony.

I did not think to warn my sister, was feeling too elated about breaking my stepfather's evil spell.

François is furious with me.

He shouts I am a disgrace, lying about it all.

'If only you told the truth! But I find out when Catalina calls me!

Then it all made sense, those weekends away. You went to see her every time!

All this jewellery, that trip to Geneva in December when you said Arianna was taking you for a conference!

You lied every single time!'

'Fine, and I am still going to see her!' I shout at him.

'She is one of the only good things in my life right now!'

'No, she is a messed up obnoxious diva who married some poor guy to have a kid she does not even want! She is married, Fiorenza!'

'She loves her daughter! You do not know her! I have been with her enough times to know the sweet woman she can be! I have been in her bed enough times too!'

He slapped me across the face. He never hit me in my life.

'Bastard!' I screamed at him and locked myself in my own room all evening.

It is not about the fact I date a woman, but because I am slowly shutting down on him.

Marina acts up on account of our continuous arguments; she demands, and François gives in and buys her everything.

'She is my daughter! I will suffer because you buy her so much,'

I tell him.

'She is a happy well-adjusted child, Fiorenza,' he tells me.

'It never did you any harm, having designer frocks and diamond earrings.

And you have been thinking about yourself too much.'

I am sarcastic, full of venom for him, shouting that I was ruined with expensive gifts at Marina's age.

And just look at how I turned out.

FIORENZA

I need to change my appearance.

Nothing so drastic, just enough to feel as if I am defining myself as Fiorenza and not Marina Valentino. It is making me feel strange every time I see her reflection in the mirror.

Even worse, I have become my mother in a permanent bad mood when I am in Paris.

The only time I am in a good mood is when I see Natalija.

My mother was so volcanic, interviewers and critics referred to her as 'Vesuvius'. Her temper was legendary in the Opera World.

She could also be very cruel towards her lovers.

Her Art came before happiness, which is why she became so successful.

But I am not a diva, yet I am acting like an entitled prima donna.

I am not liking my behaviour right now and apart from seeing Natalija, who fills me full of light and hope, I am afraid of the person I am becoming.

When I went to my hairdresser the morning of April 1st, I asked, 'can you put some lighter shades at the front? I have an Opera première tonight.'

'You are so dark, I don't know,' she said, looking worried.

'You have such beautiful hair, Fiorenza.'

She runs the length of the silky black waves through her hands as they fall down my back and looks in the mirror.

'Well maybe just a few streaks could work.

If I just put some lighter brown shades in round your face.

Most women would kill for your hair. Your mother's hair was beautiful; I always loved styling it.

You want to wear it up tonight for your première?'

'Yes, thank you.'

I looked in the mirror and I felt different already. Lighter streaks were framing my face and it was good. I felt as if I were emerging from my chrysalis, showing I was not just someone's image.

All my life I had raven hair. My mother hardly changed her hair in a lifetime. Even at 50 she still had no strands of grey even though she looked for them obsessively.

She was known for refusing to wear wigs in every opera house she worked in, because she had such wonderful hair.

'I do not wear wigs with this hair,' she told me, shaking her luxurious raven mane.

After the hairdresser, I bought clothes in colours my mother hated; the rule was blacks and reds, maybe silver or gold for an evening dress or shoes.

A rule I followed religiously until now. I still would stick to black, like the stylish Parisienne women in my district.

I bought a canary yellow dress with black trim for the première, some blue and purple dresses and an emerald green coat. Then I found a fur coat in bright blue.

The sales assistant advised me that bright blue is very good for fur. It just looks like velvet to the untrained eye and keeps away anti-fur protestors.

My mother stuck to black or red for coats. I still love her clothes: the beautiful red mid-season coat, her black fur winter coat, all the dresses and shoes.

I can imagine her reaction to my recent purchases.

Ice cream shades are forbidden and who wants to look like a fucking banana?

And bright blue for a fur coat? Fiorenza! You must be crazy!

I also got a palette of coloured eyeshadow and a few brightly coloured bags and evening gloves.

I was dressed for the Opera by the time François arrived home.

Marina was already asleep, and I was waiting quietly in the living room waiting for Loredana to arrive.

He was not performing tonight but wanted me as his 'bride' for the Nabucco première. Marina would not enjoy it. It is too epic. She did not really object when I told her she would not enjoy it; she is a good girl.

Tomorrow François travels to Monte Carlo for Aida. Why he wants to go to that overstuffed bit of the world, I do not know. It looks truly hideous with all those high-rise buildings and if you have an apartment with a view, within a week guaranteed they build right in front of your window.

François walked into the living room and erupted with such volcanic rage as if I had dyed my hair pink.

'What the fuck have you done?' he said, his dark eyes full of angry ownership. Ownership of me.

I am his property.

He touched the loose strands of freshly cut lighter hair and looked disgusted.

'Why do you do this?'

'For God's sake! I am 23 years old,' I said.

'It is still the same length and colour. Only the front has lighter streaks in.'

'Dye it back!' he demanded. 'You dye it back tomorrow before I leave!'

'No!' I yelled at him.

'You want me to be just like her!'

He stares at me in my yellow and black dress.

'We need to be at the Opera, so take that awful dress off and change. You look like a canary.

Where the hell did you find such a monstrosity?

And evening gloves in yellow? Fiorenza! Go and find a nicer outfit!'

'I am ready.' I stare back at him.

'You have got to be kidding,' he said.

THE GODS MUST BE SAVAGE

I twirled a loose strand of my hair in my fingers.

It was a pretty outfit as it was edged with black lace and had an elegant black lace train.

It was expensive and I had applied make up to match. His anger has suddenly surfaced after so long, probably after my sulky attitude recently.

Now he has had it with me, and it is not just about the dress.

'Fiorenza! You have all your mother's dresses.

If you insist on changing your hair, then wear a black dress and a tiara. And put your dark eyeshadow on, get your black evening gloves and ditch those yellow things.'

'No!' I shouted at him.

'I am not your fucking slave!

You always told me not to wear her clothes and now you do not let me wear my own! You have made me her, François!

Don't you get it?'

'Get up!' he told me, angry with my continued moody defiance.

'No,' I said, looking away from him. 'Leave me alone.'

He was silent for a moment.

'Get up, you spoilt little bitch! I pay for everything, Fiorenza! Everything in your goddamn life: your daughter, your university, so many gifts.

You do not even spend a fucking euro!

All you do is disrespect me! You have this affair for the last God knows how many years with the worst prima donna in the Opera World and I find out from your poor sister!

You are well matched because you and Natalija are so alike!

Both spoiled, insolent and careless!'

He hauled me up roughly and dragged me to his bedroom by my wrists as I screamed at him.

'You are hurting me! Get your fucking hands off me!'

'I am not tolerating this any longer!' he shouted back.

'You are rude and obnoxious! You have every luxury on Earth! You seem to forget that I pay for all this, Fiorenza!'

I never saw him so angry in my life.

'I hate you! You try to buy me!' I shriek.

'And I have my mother's inheritance! It is not true you pay for it all! You never let me pay!

I want to pay!'

'I do not mind spoiling Marina, but I do mind an immature 23-year-old who is forever moody!

You were so sweet, now you are ruined! Natalija ruined you!'

'Natalija never ruined anyone!' I shout at him.

'Her heart is good! Yours is dark and twisted! You like showing me off, parading me round like…..'

He shook me hard.

'You shut up right now, you spoilt little bitch!'

We fought each other by the closet.

I beat his chest with my fists, screaming that I hated him. He tried to tear my new dress.

As I tried to get away, he twisted my arm behind my back cruelly. I cursed him, called him all the names.

'Take this black dress and change!' he said, holding one my mother's dresses.

'No!' I screamed at him.

'I wore her clothes and you hated me! I will not be my mother for you!

I am not your fucking wife, François!' I screech at him, holding my hands to my chest.

'And I love Natalija! Not you!'

He dropped the dress and slapped me for the second time in only a few weeks.

Me and my mother screamed at each other, but she never raised a hand to me.

She would empty the contents of the fruit bowl and throw

things across the room, but never did she even threaten to hit me.

For a few seconds there was silence. I held my face.
It did not hurt, but I was shocked.
'God, Fiorenza, I am so sorry……' He reaches for my arm as I fly out of the room.
'Get your fucking hands off me! Hitting a woman! My mother would be so ashamed of you!
You are just like fucking Andrea!'
I break free of his grip as my comments wound him.
'Mamma! François! Please stop!' Marina wails from the doorway.
'I am so sorry, Marina! I have to go!'
I run out of the room, grabbing my evening bag and shawl, and scooping up my shoes from the hallway.
'Fiorenza!' François shouts. 'I am sorry!'
'Mamma!' Marina wails.
Loredana is standing in stunned silence by the front door.
The au pair had let herself in and we did not hear the keys. She has heard it all too.
Loredana is calling, please wait, Fiorenza.
I do not wait. I run out of the apartment.
I am spoiled. He is right about that. Once I was so grateful for the life and riches he gave me, how he paid for everything and paid for Marina without question or resentment.
Although I had money from my mother and rent from the Napoli apartment, he told me to keep it in the bank.
I sit by a fountain near the Opera even though I am cold as I forgot my coat and my shawl is thin. The chill is in my bones; it is a miserable night for 1st April.
My phone is on silent.
I never felt so alone in my life, but I cannot sit here much longer. He will find me front of house, especially in this bright outfit. I

wish I had worn black now so I could hide.

I wipe the tears from my face and glide into the Opera House. I grab a coffee from the bar and take it to hide down some back stairs. I know everywhere to hide in this theatre, and I cannot face happy people tonight. I sit on my hidden steps hearing the buzz of people filling the Opera bars.

I make it to the company box three minutes before curtain up.

I considered not going at all, but I am dressed for the Opera and no way did I want to return to Loredana tonight.

As I take my place next to François, he tries to take my hand and I pull it away.

He cannot say much, as there are two other singers with us.

'Fiorenza,' he whispers during the overture.

'Fiorenza. Please forgive me.'

I do not look at him and run out before the interval to take another coffee.

One of the stage crew passes me sitting on the stairs; exotic plumed bird in all my finery, hiding from the world. He gives me a strange look.

I do not care.

As soon as the show comes down, I run out of the box in the dark.

François will not follow me as it is bad luck to run out before the applause, disrespectful towards the performers. Like my mother, he believes the superstition that if he leaves before the curtain call, there will be no applause on his next performance.

I have bruises on my wrists and the imprints of his hand on my arm when I took my evening gloves off to wash my hands.

I wander the streets feeling cold; no friends and nowhere but hotels to go to.

Finally, I call Alain, ask if I can stay in his spare room. It is starting to rain.

Alain was good, let me sleep in his spare room without questions, and said if Marina needed to stay anytime, she could.

'Your father? You had an argument?' he asked, as he brought me some towels.

I nodded.

'Try to sleep. I am sure when you go home tomorrow, it will all be resolved.'

The more I think about my life, the worse it seems.

Everything is awful at 03.00 in the morning.

When Alain brings me a bowl of coffee and a croissant in the morning, I feel like hell.

'You could stay here?' he suggested kindly.

'That is not a good idea.' I tell him.

'Listen, I would drop you home, but I have to get to work so I will call a taxi for you.'

I have never taken public transport in Paris. After the Madrid Metro, I am not repeating that experience.

I have done well, travelling to see Natalija, managing trains and airports but I draw the line at an underground train unless it is the Eurostar.

'Are you okay going home?' Alain wants to know.

'My father leaves for his flight to Monte Carlo at midday. I will be fine now.'

'I am sure you can work it out, Fiorenza,' he says.

'The argument will be forgotten especially as he is in Monte Carlo for a month.'

I doubt it.

Worse still, I have to see Loredana when I just want to sleep.

I check my phone; endless missed calls and pleading texts from François last night. I had my phone on silent.

Loredana calls me as I finish another coffee.

'Fiorenza, are you okay?

Your father has taken Marina to school. I will collect her as he leaves at midday for his flight to Monte Carlo.

He is worried sick about you.

Can you come back to the apartment?'

When I arrive home, Loredana looks sorry when she sees I am still in last night's outfit, my make-up smudged, face tear-stained

'Sit down Fiorenza,' she said.

'Marina is in her room, I need to speak to you alone, cara.

I told your father you were safe. He is away now which is best for both of you.'

'Thank you,' I tell her.

She poured a coffee.

'Here, take some biscuits. You are upset and shaken.

You look so much like your mother, just like that beautiful woman.

But this is the whole problem; you have taken her place in his life.'

She looks at me as if she has it all figured out. Half sympathetic, half triumphant. She has been spying and listening and looking through the whole damn apartment for years.

'I am sorry for yesterday, Loredana.

Please forget everything, it was nothing. Just an argument and it is over now.'

She looks at me so seriously.

'Your daughter should not have to witness arguments and violence in the home.

He is a bad man, Fiorenza. He loves you, but not the kind of love you need.

What I heard yesterday; well, I was shocked.

Marina heard it all, saw him hit you. And look at your wrists, my love.'

She touches my bruises where François dragged me out of the

living room.

'He did not mean to hurt me. It got out of control,' I tell her.

She rests her hand on my arm.

'Fiorenza, listen to me….'

Loredana told me that if I did not remove myself from the apartment, she would report the case to Social Services. She said I could lose Marina.

'I am sorry, Fiorenza, but I have to think of Marina. She can be here, but not you.

I always hoped you were close because of your mother's death.

But after last night, it is impossible to ignore this strange set up at home, also Marina says things.'

She took my fingers gently in her hand.

'My dear girl; when you stayed in his room that time your sister was here…….'

I helped my sister, for God's sake.

'I gave my sister my room for a reason! Catalina was sick!

I slept on the sofa after studying! I stayed in the master bedroom when he was away.'

She does not believe me, even though this is partly true. Maybe there was a night here and there when I did stay in his room, but I am trying not to.

'Not every time,' Loredana says.

What has she been doing? Taking notes? Marking the days in a fucking diary?

'I know you were kind to Catalina, but I did wonder.…..

And that glow you have, that sensuality; this only comes from a lover.

I know Alain is Marina's father now, but I admit I worried if this was true when I first worked for you.'

She thought this? She actually thought that about Marina?

'I told you about Alain!

I told you my lover had left me! He was married and now he is divorced! I stayed in his apartment last night!

And I do have a lover, only she lives in New York!'

'Fiorenza………' she says and cannot hide her disgust.

We trusted this wretched woman, paid her extremely well and treated her like family.

'And I cannot believe what you are saying about Marina!

All that time you even thought…….no, I cannot even repeat what you thought!

Don't you ever think my daughter is not pure!' I am spitting fire at her.

'Please sit down, cara,' she tells me.

'All this talk is really troubling me….'

I flop back in the chair, only because I am so fucking tired.

She carries on, her eyes sad.

'You said you loved this Natalija. This New York lover, I guess. Now this is not right……

First François, then the opera star…. Fiorenza, this is unnatural.

All those little shopping trips and work trips abroad; Marina talks.

You are jetting off to do 'unnatural' things with this girl. You are a good liar, Fiorenza and you should pray more and sin less.'

Wait a fucking minute, lady.

Unnatural!

'Lady, you have one hell of a nerve!

I love Natalija; she is an opera singer and François hates her! This does not make me 'unnatural', as you say. She is a friend, and my daughter has not even met her!

You judged me because I was a young unmarried mother.

You have different values. I do not judge you for living like a vestal virgin!'

'Fiorenza, please,' she says.

'I am concerned about you, about your life.'

I put down my cup. I can get rid of this woman right now.

I get up and grab my cheque book from the bureau.

'Loredana; how much money do you want?' I want her to vanish this second.

'I will write you a cheque.'

I look at her, my pen ready to write whatever amount she needs to buy her silence.

She needs money, for God's sake.

She stares at me, shocked that I am doing this.

'Fiorenza, please do not give me money.'

'You think you can buy my silence?' she asks me.

'Money buys everything you want, including happiness!'

I thought money was the answer.

'No, my love, and you are unhappy even with all your wealth.

I have a duty to report this unless you take yourself out of here and give Marina a normal life.

That poor child needs stability.'

This life is normal for Marina: luxury apartments and hotels, designer dresses, Opera premières.

'You were just a girl who lost her mother.

He has made you his wife and you hate him for it. I see your anger.'

'There is nothing like that between us, Loredana,' I tell her.

'And Marina has everything in her life!

She is spoiled by me, by François and her father! She could not have a better home.'

Loredana seems not to care about this.

'This is not an environment for a young child; one with unnatural relationships.

No, my love. You cannot behave like this. You should be married at your age for your daughter's sake, not running around as you do.

It is not fair on her.

Marina is a spoiled child, and it is not healthy for a little girl to have designer dresses and diamond earrings.'

'My mother gave me everything! You judge us because we are rich! We pay you well for years, treat you well, so what is the fucking problem?'

I remember her asking when I was 18 or so, was I taking the contraceptive pill.

I immediately got defensive. I had the IUD after Marina as a long-term solution. Why do you even ask me?

Maybe Loredana found it strange that a beautiful girl is not dating.

Hell, I would not have admitted anything to a devoutly Sicilian Catholic who insisted I marry at the age of 23.

And now because she overheard me say that I loved Natalija to my father, I see it is a problem to this wretched Sicilian.

I date one opera star and that has been all since Alain.

Even if I had affairs all over the globe, if Marina was well cared for, Loredana has no right.

I stare out of the window. 'Fiorenza! Are you still listening to me?'

'What?' I say, irritably.

'I have to sleep now. You should leave, Loredana.'

I get up and spill the coffee over the table.

'Fiorenza, you cannot live like this,' Loredana tells me, wiping up the spilt coffee.

'I know; I am untidy, careless and spoilt!'

'Please agree to my conditions.'

God will she ever give up??

'Marina said she has heard you and François fighting many times.

She has not met this Natalija because I asked her.'

I hate Loredana for asking Marina about my life.

'When I go to the Opera, I take Marina as long as it is not a violent performance.

I did not take her the other night as it was a 14-age rating.

I will be attending Natalija's performances in La Scala or London or wherever.

And I will still go to Paris Opera. You have no right to tell me how to live!'

Loredana looks at me sadly.

'Fiorenza; I cannot stop you living in such a fashion, but you have to leave this apartment before he returns from Monte Carlo. I cannot sit by and watch Marina be here whilst you commit such sin.

You really should be alone and have your daughter live with him or her own father.

You are not fit to care for a child.

Maybe go and live with students…..'

I turn on her.

'Loredana! You think I can crash on a student sofa?!

And how dare you say I am not fit! I give Marina everything!'

She softens a little.

'Look, the Opera has a list of places for visiting performers. Why not see if there is an apartment?

Promise me, Fiorenza?'

'I will ask at the Opera House this afternoon.'

'You should have friends your own age, not constantly mixing with these stars.

You are vain, Fiorenza. I see your mother brought you up in a similar fashion….'

'You dare say a word about my beautiful mother! She was everything to me! Just get out!'

Hateful jealous bitch.

I go to my room and slam the door.

'Mamma,' Marina knocks on my door. 'Please let me in.'

I open the lock and take her inside.

'Come here my love. I was upset with Loredana. I am so sorry about yesterday.'

Marina's dark eyes are sad and serious. She understands that something awful is going on but blames the au pair for everything.

'She is a bitch,' Marina says. 'She asks questions about you.

Mamma, I do not want to see her again.'

How dare that woman threaten me with Social Services. I adore Marina.

When I hear Loredana slam the front door, I am raging to myself.

I am a rich girl, and she suggests I can crash on some student sofa; the kind of place when everyone drinks all the time, the kitchen is filthy, and people have loud sex. Probably in the kitchen over the dirty plates.

And that is before all the hairs in the bathroom and the disgusting men who spit in the shower.

Damn her.

LIBERTY

I do want to have my own space away from François, but I want a decent apartment.

And in this district too. When I ask at Opera, Vincent, one of the resident opera singers sees me; he is wanting to give up his studio, but still has two months to pay. It is less than ten minutes' walk from the apartment.

He is happy if I can take it from him so soon and I can stay long term as his friend owns it.

François will be in Paris until July so Marina could stay with him in the apartment.

Vincent's studio seems a good solution, so I agree to go and see it later.

But I am still mad at Loredana.

Marina is hardly at risk. She is a spoilt little diva who has everything. François treats her like a princess.

I was dragged around by my mother to wherever she performed when I was four years old.

I know I had Roma as a home city, and Paris as well but my schooling did suffer.

My little girl has so much, and she has stability, something I never had. My mother was so impulsive, leaving me with my auntie and then next day, flying us to wherever, as the mood took her.

Marina likes adult company. She is generally a good child, just a little precocious and confident but that is all.

Damn Loredana for threatening me with Social Services as if I am a bad mother, neglecting my daughter. One of the reasons I do not have friends is because Marina takes my time.

She comes first after my studies, and aside from Natalija and my visits to see her, I see no one else. Anasztázia has stayed with us, but Marina is very much a part of that too.

What business is it of the au pair?

The only time I even go out in Paris is my visits to the Opera.

I sacrificed friends for my daughter, and I am studying hard to be independent, to have a well-paid career for her just as much as for me.

It would be easy to live off my inheritance, but no way would I want that.

Vincent meets me at the studio that evening, after his rehearsals for Otello.

It is free in a few days, if I would like to pay his rent.

'I am either working or at my girlfriend's place, so it seems a waste, Fiorenza.

And this district is expensive. My friend owns it, and he is happy for you to pay instead.

He knows of François and most of the top performers in the Opera.'

The studio is small but very bright and as it is top floor, it has plenty of natural light. There is a high ceiling with a chandelier and a twisted iron bed and a big TV. It has everything I need.

Vincent shows me the little balcony which has space for a table and chairs.

'See, this place gets the evening sun. I like to sit out, and the neighbours are very quiet people. It is a good place for you, Fiorenza. Very safe and secure and right by Opera.'

The bathroom is neat with a washing machine, but only an alcove of a kitchen which folds away.

'I only make coffee, Fiorenza,' Vincent says apologetically.

'Working evenings; your body has a different routine, but there are plenty of nice places to pick up decent food.'

'I do not cook either,' I tell him. Kitchens are low on my priority list.

There is a tiny cupboard like room with some shelves which Vincent uses as a walk-in closet, but you could squeeze a small fold-up bed in.

Vincent has a fold up bed, and he says he can leave it for Marina.

It fills the whole cupboard, but it is kind of him. She will hate it and she will hate me too.

I have to make sure she does not have to stay overnight, find a new au pair and get rid of that interfering Sicilian.

The studio costs less than the money I get from renting out the apartment in Napoli so I will use that to cover it. I have a place of my own to escape to, away from all these toxic arguments.

'A different district would have been better,' Loredana tells me, when I say I have a new place just five minutes from here.

I nearly shout I do not need her fucking permission to live my life.

And you knew you should have got rid of the au pair before now, Fiorenza.

But as she starts to set more rules for me such as no staying here when my father is home, I feel the volcanic lava rising

'That is it! Give me my keys back! Marina does not want you around and I want you to leave.

Here is a cheque, and it is very generous.

Me and Marina are going to the studio but consider your employment terminated.

I heard you saying on the phone only the other day that you are wanting to leave for Sicilia.

You are not the only person to listen at doors, Loredana!

This money should cover your father's medical treatment in Catania.

Consider this cheque an appreciation of your services all these years.

Go back to your village by Etnea and never ever contact me or anyone else in Paris again!'

She turns on me for the first time, cold and threatening.

'Fiorenza, you will be very sorry when Social Services take your daughter away.'

'Do not threaten me, you vengeful bitch!' I shout at her.

'Leave, lady! Get the hell out of my apartment right now, you nasty Sicilian money-grabber!'

She turns into a shrieking vile woman, betraying her real feelings and all this resentment clearly goes back years.

'You are a promiscuous teenage slut, Fiorenza!' she is spitting at me, hands on hips.

She still takes the damn cheque, gathers up her bag.

'I do not care what you think,' I say coldly. 'And I never did.'

'You dare hurt my, mamma!' Marina screams, running into the room.

I did not want her to hear, but she is upset by Loredana's shrieking.

'You heard mamma! Get the fuck out!'

Marina points at the door.

Loredana is pale with anger, hearing this language from a little girl.

'Your daughter has picked up your cursing, you foul-mouthed little whore!' she says, putting the cheque in her bag and throwing my house keys on the table.

'She will be a slut, like you, Fiorenza!'

'Get the hell out!' I scream.

'Expect a visit very soon from the Social Services!' she threatens. Her expression is full of contempt but also almost mocking. She is finally speaking her mind, throwing out the poison she held in for years.

'Get out of our house. Just get the fuck out this minute before I throw you out of here!'

Marina clings to me, scared by Loredana's anger.

Neither of us have seen her lose it before.

Once she has slammed the front door, I sit down and cry angry tears.

How dare she say my lovely little girl will be a slut?

'Mamma, she has gone. She cannot hurt you. Please don't let them take me away!'

'She was nasty, my darling. No one is taking you away. Ever.'

I sit her on my knees, and we cry together.

'I love you more than anyone in the world,' I tell her. 'That woman, she is jealous and evil.'

François is supposed to be in Monte Carlo for three and a half weeks although he is constantly texting me and saying that he will leave early. I am irritated.

My mother went through hell, and she never quit, unless she was ill. She would have to be virtually dragged off a show.

She had refused to cancel Norma in Buenos Aires after spending the summer as a psychiatric outpatient in Roma. Poor Romeo was terrified she would end her own life in Argentina.

A couple of times, my stepfather had beaten her so badly she had to cancel performances, once an entire run because the costumes would not have hidden her injuries.

And here is François, a short plane ride away in Monte Carlo, wanting to quit his show because of a stupid argument. My mother would shake him. He is weak.

Marina happily skips alongside me as we walk the short distance to the new place. She likes the studio and balcony, but sulks when I show her the closet.

'You want me in this closet?' she says, turning bitchy and mean.
'You hardly need to sleep here but if you do……'

I hung a string of fairy lights and put some pictures on the walls. I had made the tiny space look pretty and put a floaty shimmering curtain in the doorframe.

I hoped she would like the novelty for a night or two, but she hates it.

'Why can't you sleep in the fucking closet?' she demands.

I get mad at her and say I am the adult, and we can stay in the old apartment when François is away. We have our first argument.

'I hate you, mamma! Next time wear the fucking dress when François wants!' she shrieks.

I tell her she is spoilt, like I was.

'Marina we will stay in the old apartment too. You can stay most of the time over there if you hate this place.
And stop cursing so much!'

'Loredana asks me is François my daddy and are you my sister as well as my mother!' she says.

Marina does not understand what that vengeful Sicilian hag meant by it, thank God.

I burn thinking of Loredana asking her.

'He is not your father, and I am your mother! I am not your sister! You know this, Marina.'

'I really hate you and that Loredana bitch!' Marina is shrieking at me.

'Loredana is gone, Marina, back to Sicilia. Please calm down, my love.'

'No!' she shouts at me. She flops on my bed and sulks.

I curse non-stop at I place ornaments on the shelves, strings of fairy lights round the twisted iron bed and a wind-chime by the balcony doors.

It is a lovely bright little place and if I were alone in Paris, I could be perfectly happy here, high above the world. But after the huge apartment, I am spoiled, just like my daughter.

I had taken two of the large Opera photos of my mother; one of her in Tosca and the other from Anasztázia's La Scala dressing room, where she is in her jet beaded dress and ruby tiara.

I should order some black roses just like she is holding in the picture.

Maybe that will help. Anasztázia says you can find them on the internet.

'I love you, mamma,' I say to her.

I set up a little altar beneath this photo and lit the candles. I told her image that I was sorry, that I missed her, to please stop haunting me.

On the opposite wall, I place the one with her as Tosca in a glorious red cape, hands clasped in prayer after singing Vissi d'arte. Tosca should always wear red.

I touch the diamond on my necklace.

The nightmares have stopped for the last few days.

I waited for François in his apartment. He texted to say he was cancelling his final two shows in Monte Carlo. He will be home five days early.

I cannot tell him to finish his run, but his weakness angers me. He even pretended he was ill.

I am staring at her photos in the living room as I wait for him.

Marina Valentino as Butterfly, Tosca, Adriana Lecouvreur, or dressed in her spectacular evening dresses. She is eternal here.

'I thought I lost you,' François says, as he stands in the living room doorway.

I did not hear him open the front door. He drops his suitcase and bag in the hallway.

He is handsome in his black suit, but looks tired, with dark circles under his eyes and his thick black hair is untamed.

I get up and embrace him quickly and then sit down.

'Carissima, why so cold?' He asks.

'You should have finished the run. My mother would. It is so bad to drop out like that.'

I think he is very stupid for this.

'I know but I am not as strong as she was.'

I hand him some camomile tea and his favourite cookies, but it will not soothe his nerves.

He confesses he could not concentrate, and it never happened in his life before.

He reaches for my hand.

'There is some dinner in the fridge. Want me to heat it up for you?' I ask.

'I am not hungry, Fiorenza. Where is Marina?' he says, looking around.

'Marina is in my new apartment,' I tell him.

'I have a new au pair, Fleure. She is sitting with her. Loredana is gone.

It was Vincent's studio and now I am renting it. It is very close, only two streets away.'

I do not add just before I left the studio this evening, Marina accused me of 'ruining our fucking lives' in a very adult tone of voice.

Then she cried in her closet. I felt awful. She likes Fleure but hates me.

I even promised she could stay in the apartment at nights when François is home, but it has not helped her mood tonight.

'You left me?' François says, pain showing in his dark eyes.

'And you are with Vincent? Why, carissima? You said you loved Natalija.'

'François, I am not with Vincent!

Loredana insisted I move now, or she will report me to Social

Services.

Vincent wanted to rent out his studio, so I took the place.

Blame Loredana. She knows everything thanks to that argument we had before the Opera and Marina hates me for having to move to the studio.

Loredana called me 'unnatural' for dating a woman so I told that hateful au pair to leave and take a big fat cheque to Sicilia.

You know she was planning to leave?

She called me a teenage slut and a foul-mouthed whore.

She insulted my mother and I screamed at the evil bitch.

She will report us to Social Services, but I could not have that woman around any longer.

Marina will have to stay with you, as there is no space in my studio.'

'Whatever you want,' he says.

He looks so broken. He really hoped everything would be fine between us once he left Monte Carlo.

'I lost too much in my life already. Please come home, Fiorenza,' he pleads with me.

He takes my hands.

'I am so sorry that I was angry about Natalija.

If she is good for you, then see her. She clearly cares very much for you.

But remember she is married. She has a family in New York. I do not want you hurt.'

'She is not happily married but she loves her daughter,' I tell him.

I am irritated that he still thinks I can live here, with him.

'Come home,' he tells me.

'As you said, Loredana has gone back to Sicilia. She would not dare call Social Services.

And even if she does, they will see this beautiful home and…….'

'Stop it!

Give me some space, François! Opera is your greatest love!'

Natalija had a point about people begging and pleading. I hate it too.

'No, your mother was my greatest love. And you are. Opera is behind that.'

'François, Opera was my mother's greatest love.

Everyone else came second, including me and Catalina, including you.

Why can't you be like that? I thought you were.

My mother always told me that Maria Callas made the fatal mistake of sacrificing her Art for love.

You never sacrifice Art for love.

Ever.'

I look away from him.

'And Marina saw you hit me that night, heard the argument.'

'Fiorenza, carissima….' he gently strokes my face.

'I am so sorry I hit your beautiful face, but please come back. I will give you space.'

'No! Stop pleading!

This is not the ambitious opera singer I thought I knew!'

He puts his head in his hands and cries. He never cried like that, even when my mother died.

'Please do not cry,' I tell him.

'It is not the end of the world.'

'I wish God would strike me down. You look so like your mother….'

He looks at me, tears on his face.

'François, I am not her.' I get up.

'Please stay………' he asks me again.

'God will not strike you down, François because he does not exist. You never believed in Him anyway.

I renounced God years ago.

You need to let me go.

You never walked out on an Opera before. You let all those colleagues down in Monte Carlo for nothing.'

He nods but he is so broken.

'Listen, my studio is small.

Marina is there tonight, but after this Fleure can come here to look after her.

She is very good.'

'Whatever you want,' he says sadly.

'I am tired, François; I am just so tired of arguing.'

I get up and feel exhausted.

'François, come and look. I am not far away....'

I point to the pink stuccoed apartment block opposite.

Its windows have coloured squares of yellow in the misty swirls and the streetlamps look eerie in this weather. Such strange weather for the end of April.

'See that street on the right, by the pink apartment block. Just further along is my new place.

You can almost see it from the balcony,' I tell him.

'I have to get back to Marina now. I need to find a new au pair for autumn as Fleure can only work until September.'

I put on my emerald green coat.

'You look lovely,' he tells me. 'I cannot believe I was so stupid about your dress.

The last month was hell for me, carissima.'

He should have focused on his work. My mother's turbulent personal life made her work harder, so she could lose herself in her Opera and become someone else for the night or the run.

'I am Fiorenza, François. That argument was not about the dress.

You need to let my mother go. You thought you found her spirit in me, but it was only an illusion, a trick of the light.

That night you hurt me; that is not love.

What we had was sick and twisted. I am sorry it ever happened.'

'I am truly sorry I hurt you…...' His voice trails away.

'I have to go now.'

He nods but he still clings to the hope I will return as his love reincarnated.

'Goodnight, François.'

'At least stay a little longer tonight,' he pleads.

He tries to take my hand again and it slips through his fingers.

'No, I have to go.'

I walk out of the door.

DARK SOUL

As I step out of the elevator and exit the building, I shiver in the damp Paris night and there is a chill in the air. It could be November between the mist and the temperature.

Or maybe it is the spirits of my ancestors rising up to protect me.

I am comforted by this thought, of my mother's spirit spreading over the city like a sweet shroud.

But I am lonely; I miss Natalija, and I want to see more of her.

And life is lonely. It is horribly lonely, and I want my mother.

I hear François shouting Fiorenza! from the balcony as I walk down the street. He calls my name again, but I do not turn round. He is not the answer to my loneliness.

As I see my new apartment building appearing in the mist, I know I need to pray for strength at the altar beneath my mother's photo.

I will ask for her forgiveness.

The next day, the mist has melted into a beautiful sunny morning when I wake up.

I call my wretched little princess from her closet bedroom, and she refuses to speak.

As I look at soon to be six years old Marina who carves up her toast, I blame that hateful Loredana.

Me and my daughter never fell out before.

This is all Loredana's fault.

Marina never sulked before, never shouted. At most she was a little lively but that was all.

Loredana has damaged my relationship with Marina and put her at risk; Marina has been shrieking about running away to Roma every single day.

I tell her there is no need to run away; she can stay in the big apartment or with Alain.

She is going to the apartment as soon as François returns from the dentist.

Fleure cannot be available at such short notice, so sometimes she will need to be in the studio in the afternoons and this makes Marina mad.

I guess at some point, she was going to start throwing shouting fits and this is just a temporary phase, I hope.

Fleure explained that in autumn, she will be busy with a new job.

This is good enough for spring and summer, but I need to find a long-term solution.

Over the next two weeks in the studio, I know I have given Marina way more freedom than is good for her. It becomes all too apparent when she is behaving like a spoiled diva.

Take away a tiny bit of luxury, even for a few hours and Marina is a different child.

I always tried to encourage her to have friends, but she is morbidly uninterested.

She likes adult company and hates school. The teachers say she is very intelligent but disruptive; she constantly answers back in class, does not take part in any activity with the other children.

François is rehearsing for Il Trovatore, although he finishes early, so I take my wretched little princess to the apartment.

She is arguing with me again, telling me I should do as François says. That I should be with him, not in this 'fucking studio'.

I am close to shaking her when she breaks an ornament I love out of sheer spite.

I pick up the pieces of the glass swan.

'Damn, Marina! This was my mother's swan!

Say sorry to that beautiful lady's picture right now

She is your friend after all.'

I thought she would at least apologise, given she has seen my mother.

She always asks about this beautiful lady called Marina.

But today her dark eyes are full of rage.

'No! I hate you,' she says to me.

'Fine, Marina. Go right ahead and hate me,' I tell her.

'I hate you too right now. Loredana was our enemy, and she is gone!'

Marina horrifies me when she announces again that she will run away to Italia.

'I will go there to Ana, who does want me!' she shrieks.

'I will run away! And beautiful Marina can be my mother!

I am sorry for the glass swan,' she says to one of the photos.

She taps the glass and turns to me defiantly. 'I want her to be my mamma! I hate you!'

I try to hold her, but she pushes me away.

'Marina, my love. You are upset but please listen; you never go to Italia.

Promise me?

Stay with François or Alain, but never run away. It is so dangerous out there.

And Anasztázia works all the time. You cannot live with her.'

She pouts and snaps, 'Marina lives in Ana's place, and she wants me!'

How can I begin to tell her that this lady adorning my walls is only a spirit?

I tried many times, but she saw her in Anasztázia's apartment, talked to her and says she sees her in Paris Opera.

Paris is dangerous too, which is as far as she would get. The thought of my Marina alone in Paris scares the hell out of me.

There are evil people in the world. Maybe there are men like Andrea in this district, or even worse than him. What if she runs and I never see her again?

I had been to the Opera with François that night, but it was Andrea Chénier., so I did not take Marina. The ending gives me nightmares.

Marina had screamed before I went out as she had to stay in the apartment with Fleure.

She likes Fleure very much, so I cannot understand the problem. She would not even enjoy the Opera.

She is in the apartment and not the studio so there is no need to behave badly.

One long Aida she fell asleep and said she was bored. She does attend most shows, but not every single one and until recently, she accepted this.

'I hate you and I hate Loredana! I want to go to the Opera!

You are a bitch, mamma! Teenage slut!'

I had slapped her legs and she howled and threatened to jump from the balcony.

She did not know what a 'teenage slut' was; she heard Loredana shout at me that day I threw her out.

Marina screeched about running away to Roma.

'You dare run and I will drag your ass back here, Marina Valentino!

Then I will not take you to any Opera for a long time!

You cannot attend tonight because it is a 16-age rating and you are six years old, and do not call me a bitch!

You are spoiled because I gave you everything!

Fine, hate me, but look at your life; stuffed full of designer dresses, five-star hotels and glittering premières!'

'I hate you!' she screamed again.

'Good! I am your mother and sometimes you will hate me! You are just like me and my mother when we shouted at each other!

I was spoilt, rich and ungrateful, just like you!

So go and sulk, Marina! Go to your room!'

Marina had slammed her door, crying hysterically for effect.

Little spoilt diva, I thought, as I put on my evening dress. I felt awful for slapping her.

I had a sudden flashback of my mother and me. She called me an 'ungrateful little bitch' when I was screaming as a child, and then we both cried together in our exclusive hotel suite in Paris. I hated travelling and wanted to go home to Roma.

She had hugged me all night and I remember her tears on my skin. She was lonely and stressed with her Opera and often short-tempered, but she loved me.

This memory stabs at my heart.

The next day Marina did run away. I had returned to my studio after the Opera and François had taken her to school in the morning.

Later that day, Alain arrived to collect her and called me distraught from the school gates.

Somehow, she had managed to run away just before he arrived.

For half an hour she wandered the streets, asking for the way to Roma, until a lady managed to persuade her to stay with her as she called the police.

Marina says she was trying to get to Roma. She had overnight stuff in her bag, had stolen some money from me. The clever child had also copied down Anasztázia's address.

If she hates me, I can fix it over time but never this. Anything could have happened on those streets.

I am so furious, and I go in and shout at the principal.

She was finishing at preschool anyway, but she is quitting today, I shriek.

The more the principal tries to apologise, the madder I get.

Alain has some holiday leave to take, Fleure can help as much as possible, and we will have private tutors to get her up to standard for a prestigious primary school for next term.

It is a school with small classes which caters for bright individualistic children.

She has calmed a little the next morning when I arrive at the apartment as François has rehearsals.

'She was fine last night but now she is refusing to get up,' he tells me.

He looks worried.

'Please can you talk to her? She is still acting out.'

Marina is lying in bed, so I try to be nice, but I am sick of her behaviour.

She is spoilt and the tutor is arriving to give her classes in half an hour.

'Marina, you do not have to return to that school or my studio. Could you just get out of bed and get ready for Francesca and her lessons? You like her and I am sure she wants to see you.'

She sits up and glares at me.

'I hate your fucking place, mamma!'

'Marina! You do not have to stay there again. Fleure can sit in the apartment with you when I am busy, or you stay with Alain. And stop saying fucking.'

'You say fucking all the time,' she pouts.

'God Marina! You are a little diva.

François is home until July so you can stay right here with him for now.'

'Good. I can have nice birthday! You do not care!'

She rolls herself tightly in the duvet.

'Listen, my love, I care about you more than anyone in the world.

I want you to promise never to run away. It is very dangerous on the Parisian streets.'

'I wanted to get to Roma.' She says this so carelessly, as if she would do it again if she felt the urge.

Then I am mad. I haul her out of bed as she whines.

'Get up, you spoilt little princess! Out of that bed!

Your milk is in the kitchen with cake. François left it for you.

Go and see to yourself since you want to be an adult, Marina!

You can start by getting your own breakfast and wash the damn plates!'

I take the duvet away.

I expect her to cry and scream but soon after, I hear the sound of rattling cups in the kitchen. She wants to show that she is an adult.

Then she silently watches me study on the balcony until her tutor arrives for Italian class.

I am done speaking to her.

Instead of refusing to be home-schooled, she does not protest. I am surprised, given her moodiness this morning. But this is what she wants, individual attention.

She settles down quietly with Francesca, opens her books and spends the rest of the morning on her Italian grammar.

'She is a very clever little girl,' Francesca told me afterwards. 'But she hates school.'

I will attend the Opera on Friday with Marina and François. It is Marina's birthday, so it is a nice occasion for her to celebrate.

I needed to study Thursday night and all of Friday, but I would be very happy to attend Tosca at the weekend.

I admit to François that I am still worried about Marina. She is not the same girl, especially with me.

'Marina is better now,' he reassures me.

'But we have to keep her safe. She is still angry and unsettled.

And she is attending primary school next term and having private lessons at home until then.

She will be much safer in her new school.'

I turn to go.

'I have to go back to the studio now, but tomorrow I come over for the Opera. It can be Marina's birthday night out and I bought her some presents, but God knows she is behaving badly.'

'Whatever you want,' he tells me.

'Please do not worry about her. Fleure will be here when I am in rehearsals.

I know Alain loves having her stay too, and she likes seeing him.'

I am the problem now Loredana has gone.

'We can manage just fine,' François tells me, as he admires me in my evening dress.

'You and me, carissima.'

His fingers are cool on my shoulders as he carefully pins up my hair into an elaborate diamond creation and he tells me I will be the most beautiful woman in the Opera House tonight.

I am wearing bright blue and François does not complain.

I have tattoos. I had them done when he was in Monte Carlo. It was supposed to be a kind of liberation.

'Your mother had tattoos and she was an opera singer. It is more acceptable now. They can easily be hidden with make-up.'

Vissi d'arte, Un bel dì and Casta diva decorate my upper arms and left shoulder. I also had a black rose on my right ankle.

'Vissi d'arte was your mother's favourite aria, Tosca her favourite role and favourite Opera.

She will always be Tosca.'

'It is my favourite too,' I say.

Especially now, with all that happened in my life. Except I no longer offer my prayers to God, only in my studio to the altar of my mother.

My mother had Casta diva and Sempre libera, but positioned lower on her back, so her opera costumes would cover them.

Marina loves Tosca and repeats how she will be an opera singer when she grows up. Going out for her birthday means she has forgotten to be mad at me.

Everyone in the company compliments me when we head backstage for the première.

They all tell me I look beautiful.

I wake up in the morning and feel a little hungover.

I stare at my dress on the floor which shimmers like a bright blue waterfall. It is as if I blacked out on champagne, but I never drink more than a glass after the show. Very rarely do I have two glasses. I had two last night, but I think I took a sleeping pill too when I got home.

I have some memory loss.

Then I see François.

He is asleep and I hate myself for being in his room. I get out of bed quietly.

I am disgusted with myself for being weak. I am going straight to Hell for sure.

For the first time, I feel sick with regret. I feel horrible, just like he once did. Only now he does not feel regret or disgust. Now it is normal.

I see the Fiorenza in the mirror as I slide my silk robe over my shoulders.

I am beautiful.

But reflected in my dark eyes there is sin. I shake my raven hair over my shoulders.

I thought I had escaped all this darkness; it is suffocating my soul. I want to stop more than anything in the world.

Despite renouncing God, I still half believe in Hell, and I fear it.

Beautiful sinner, I say to the mirror. Why do you do this?

Loredana was shocked that I taught my daughter, 'beauty is

everything' as I brushed her thick black hair, fitting diamond hair slides into her glossy tresses.

She had said that beauty was on the inside, surely that child is vain enough, Fiorenza.

No, I said. We live in Paris, for God's sake.

I was only passing down what my mother taught me.

Marina would repeat 'beauty is everything' when she was two or three years old.

Who cares for other people and their opinions?

You will burn in Hell, Fiorenza. Forevermore, with the screams of the sinners and the damned around you.

But life takes and takes from me.

It took so much already.

I scoop up my dress to take to my room and I place it carefully on the bed. Then I go to wake Marina with a glass of juice, take her to the kitchen and fix François his coffee.

Marina says that morning she hopes Loredana never ruins our lives.

She seems to be the old Marina after her night out to Tosca, but I still worry about Loredana and her threats.

She can attend most of the evening shows as I did from the age of three, unless they are age rated or violent. She made such a scene because she had to miss Andrea Chénier.

I remember in Bregenz when I was seven or eight and travelled with my mother to see François. She shouted and cursed at people for talking, saying I was only a little girl and I behaved better than the arrogant people in the audience.

She had hated the floating stage on the lake, hated the audience and hated Bregenz. I feel such nostalgia, longing for my mother to hug me, to curse in Italian in front of serious Austrians.

She was so beautiful, so fiery and full of life.

Women everywhere had jealous hatred in their eyes which now

follows me wherever I go.

I feel the urge to pray coming back.
I will pray in my studio beneath the altar to my mother. I will kneel on glass to beg her forgiveness for my sin.
I cannot enter a church now after I cursed God and threw my crucifix to the ground years ago.
And with my sinning I feel I will be struck by lightning if I enter a holy place.
But I can pray in my own home. I insist on keeping the studio.
'I understand you need your own space,' François said.
'It is good for your studies, or you can stay there if Catalina visits.
It will help you to know you have your own little studio.'
Really, I want to be free. I want to liberate myself from this darkness and live in my studio, however small it is.
I tell François I am going to the studio as I forgot a book I need. Really, I need to pray.

In my studio, I smashed a glass and knelt on some small shards after I lit a candle. I pray to my mother who looks so content with her bouquet of black roses.
The nightmares have not come back yet, but I am sure they will with a vengeance.
Some nights I take sleeping pills but not every night. I am fuzzy and uncoordinated in the morning, and they give me a metallic taste which seems to last all next day.
'Forgive me, forgive me for becoming you. I am so sorry.
I pray you do not break your heart.
Forgive me. I miss you so much, mamma. I will always love you, although I understand if you hate me for eternity.
I wish you could come back and just hold me. On my life, I swear I will live here, away from him. By the end of the summer,

I will.'

I cry and when I get up my knees are bleeding. I pick the shards of glass out of them, the blood running down my legs. I deserve to hurt. Luckily, the carpet is black.

Fuck it all. I find a black wraparound dress and clean myself up. I will tell François I fell on some broken glass in the street.

Later I inhale the spring air as I sit on the balcony of the apartment. It is warm and the heat is building up, promising a hot summer ahead.

François asks why I am so quiet.

'Just thinking……'

'My God, Fiorenza! What the hell happened to your knees?'

He notices my damaged knees, as my loose wraparound dress falls to one side as I cross my legs.

'I fell outside my apartment when I was getting the book,' I tell him.

'It's nothing, really.'

'Let me see….'

'No!' I snap at him.

I take two of the photos to mail to Roma taken on the night we went out to Tosca.

The Opera photographer always likes to take some of me, saying I remind him of my mother.

I select two of the best photos of me alone on the staircase where I smoulder in my evening dress.

I send one to my auntie and one to my grandparents.

I had written on the back

I am a success in Paris. You are all an insult to my mother's memory.

And God does not exist. You pray for nothing.

I imagine their anger when they open the mail and they see me; glamorous, beautiful and with tattoos. That should touch a raw nerve, as they are so conservative.

My grandmother hated my mother's tattoos.

The Opera was different; I could be a social butterfly with the performers and crew, and yet still retain my air of mystery. It was as if I could step into someone else's skin for night; usually Marina Valentino.

I realised how little I trusted people, how my world had closed everyone out.

Getting close to people was something I feared for many reasons, and it was not purely because of my strange life. I did fear anyone hurting me again, even a little; could not let someone into my heart.

When I get the results from my university exams, and they are better than I expected, I do not feel any elation or even a sense of achievement. Instead, I feel flat and full of shattered visions.

I have a month's internship after graduating.

Arianna, the advocate, is happy to have me back that summer.

I will do my practical element of law school with Arianna if I pass my autumn exams.

I tell François I still have the exam for law school in October, and I am holding my perfect results envelope.

Suddenly, there is black cloud in the sky and the perfect grades do not seem so good.

I drop the envelope to the floor. All this really means nothing.

I want my mamma. I want to show her my results.

I feel sad thinking about the fiery woman called Vesuvius by the Opera World, who ended up beaten by her husband, and eventually murdered after eleven years of living a double life.

She never truly escaped, even when she travelled, even when she was safe in Paris.

I go and take a shower and cry and cry and cry.

François breaks my dark thoughts as I sit with a coffee. I refused a drink of celebration champagne.

He cannot understand my reaction, wonders why I dropped the results envelope on the floor and do not want to celebrate my success.

'What is success anyway?' I shrug and stare moodily into the distance.

'I am sure you will feel good soon,' he says. 'You worked so hard for the exams, Fiorenza.'

I doubt it.

'I want to take you and Marina somewhere. She is still a little unsettled so I think a holiday will be good for her and for you.'

'Not a good idea,' I tell him.

'Well how about you both join me in Hungary in July? I am performing at the outdoor festival in Il Trovatore. It is only two performances over a weekend, but two weeks rehearsals.

I am sure you will like Budapest.

 It is hot, but you can relax in the hotel, enjoy the city with Marina when I am rehearsing.'

I hesitate.

'I have my internship next week. Marina is still having private tutors through June.

She is getting on well with her home tuition.'

'Your internship will have finished by the time I need to travel. And Marina is six years old. She needs a holiday after all the stress with Loredana.'

The real reason for not wanting to join him is because I know it is bad for us, for me.

And Natalija was promising to see me at some point very soon.

I would sooner François went alone.

Marina has been studying at home, behaving so well with tutors. She has not complained once about having to do her work.

As he will not let the subject rest, I finally agree. It is easier than arguing and part of me would like to visit Budapest, even though Anasztázia said she hates her home country.

Natalija said she never visits Hungary; it is full of dark memories and pain.

I feel I would like to see this country which is not so far away and why sit around waiting for Natalija to call? I have not waited for someone to call me since I was 16 years old with Alain and I hate the feeling of putting yourself at someone else's mercy and getting upset when they do not get in touch. It makes me feel powerless.

'Fine, we can go, but no visit to Lake Balaton.

Anasztázia told me never to go there in summer,' I tell François.

'The whole of Budapest heads to that overrated and overstuffed lake.'

HUNGARY

On the flight to Budapest, I reflect on Natalija and her life, just how this Hungarian girl had become the worldwide superstar she was now.

No wonder she put her career above every person in her world; she nearly lost everything at one critical moment, including her life.

Her rise to fame had involved sacrificing relationships, her family, happiness and even Europe.

She had confessed when she flew to New York, she did not even want to live in America.

She was a European, like me. My mother had disliked even travelling to America for work, although she did.

It made me assess my own life and I believe that we are shaped more by the bad than the good.

Pain, hurt, rejection, violence, and loss; they all turned me into the person I am.

It was the same for Natalija, from the child who lost her mother to the ruthless opera diva, she had been moulded into this woman who rejected everyone before they hurt her.

Damaged, vulnerable, and fragile, yet at the same time spoiled, arrogant, and vain.

I realised she reminded me of myself.

I was already in Budapest when I got her call.

Natalija said she now had a concert in Paris. She was a last-minute replacement for a mezzo who had fallen sick.

'Natalija, I am in Hungary. You should have called before I left Paris!'

'Sorry, but it really was last minute. Fiorenza, why Hungary? I never visit. My family are not approving of my cold heart!' She laughed, as if it was something to be proud of.

'But my parents and brother came to visit us in New York, see the baby.'

The word 'us' spears through my heart; Natalija and her perfect husband and perfect child.

I always hated people who say 'us'.

Why should I believe she does not love him? She is still in America, in their plush New York pad on Park Avenue.

'François is performing in the open-air Il Trovatore……….' I tell her.

'François! Well, Fiorenza!

Anyway, enjoy the open-air theatre on Margitsziget.

Oh, and enjoy François too!'

She laughed again in a wicked way, and it made me furious.

Was I just a bit of fun to this girl? Was she just playing before she cast me aside?

After all nothing lasted in her world.

The volcanic anger rises and bubbles over.

'Natalija, why the hell do you seem so oblivious to my weird life as if it is just entertainment?

Everyone else would be shocked if they knew the truth about me.

I hate what I did, and you just laugh………

And why are you going on about 'us'?

God, you have a husband and daughter, a perfect fucking life in New York!

Why do you cheat? Why?'

She is silent for a moment.

'Fiorenza, what can I say when I hear about your life?

I do not think it is my business to comment, and as for my marriage; I told you my husband is purely arm candy.

I mean 'us' as in me and Lucia; my family wanted to see her.

And I am divorcing as I speak because I am returning to Europe.

I have a residency at Vienna Opera for August. I wanted to surprise you.

It is horrible, these arguments. I get custody of Lucia because I am her mother and rich, but Diego is claiming I am unfit.

His lawyer insists I bring Lucia to New York when I work at The Met, which will be twice a year, or three times at most.

It is stressful……I NEVER EVEN LOVED HIM!'

She shrieks this last bit.

I speak first.

'Sorry, Natalija.

 It must be hard with the divorce and fighting for custody of Lucia.'

'Fiorenza, I have been in New York too long; I am still a European girl.

And I am a lousy mother. ….'

'That is not true,' I tell her. 'You know that, Natalija.'

'I even learned German the last few years. I planned Vienna before I met Diego.

Fiorenza; I am sorry for being brittle.'

She sighed.

'We are arguing non-stop.

He gets none of my money. I made sure of that before our wedding; only Lucia inherits my money. I did let him keep the apartment.

I paid for it, but I do not want the poor guy in a lousy district.

I cannot live a lie; stay in America with him.

I am a bitch. I did hurt him badly.

It is hard boxing up my possessions and shouting every day.

I have all these emotions flying around……'

'I am sorry, Natalija. I wish you said about your divorce.

I know how horrible it must be. I wish you were here.'

'Yes, I want to be there too. Vienna is close to Hungary. My

father is not so well…I need to be in Europe.'
She was crying and ended the call.
She is so volcanic; emotions spiking all over the place. The great diva's tough shell is splintering under all the stress.

Hungary is like no country I ever visited, with its strange language full of spiky accents, a place which feels European and yet is not the Europe I know.
Natalija and Anasztázia had both started their careers with The Royal Hungarian Opera, but not at the same time, Anasztázia being 16 years older.
Their backgrounds could not have been more different; Natalija was the spoiled daughter of a wealthy Budapest dentist, whereas Anasztázia's family were impoverished country people.
She had to fight for everything in life.
'Hungarian sounds like it comes from the moon,' my mother told me.
'A crazy tongue.
Every time Anasztázia speaks this weird language, I do not understand a fucking word.'
It is not a European language. I wonder about older people living here who only speak Hungarian, linguistically imprisoned in their own country.
I thought it was bad enough that my grandparents only spoke Italian, but at least you can always find someone who speaks Italian in most countries, and it shares similarities with other Romance languages.
But Hungarian is something else entirely.
The programmes and surtitles in the Opera are only in Hungarian. Not that I need them, but it is the first time I have seen just one language on the surtitle board.

'This language is so strange,' I said to François when we went to a traditional restaurant, and I studied the menu.

He agreed. 'Worse than Czech and I hate Czech for Opera. I only performed two operas in Czech language as I could never remember the words.'

The food was too heavy for summer. We only came here as we are tourists, but the hotel had suggested we go to Italian or French places.

We should have taken their advice.

The wine was an expensive red, but way too soporific for such a hot evening.

I remember Anasztázia laughed when I told her about Budapest; how in the baking heat of July, we had visited a Hungarian restaurant for gulyás and heavy red wine.

When Natalija's stepmother visited broken-hearted Anasztázia, after Natalija jetted off to New York, she had made my mother gulyás. It was a hot September night, and Lilla was so jealous of this beautiful Italian diva, she wanted to offend her.

Anasztázia told me Lilla was a terrible cook and the dinner was awful.

'You can imagine the curses your mother hurled at Lilla before she threw her bread across the table and walked out.'

Anasztázia hated Hungarian food; it reminded her of the country she felt rejected by, as well as her awful parents who cooked food laden with pig fat.

No wonder she moved to Italia.

She loved Roma, the Italian language, the warmth of the people and the delicious food.

Apart from her porcelain appearance and her sad spirit, she was an Italian woman and there are many Italian television presenters who are similar in appearance to Anasztázia.

I remember my mother complaining about 'bottle blonde' Italians who judged her for being 'dark' and 'southern', like my stepfather's parents, who were Venetian and aspired to be as pale as possible.

My mother was dark and beautiful.

I prefer being dark; it is an exotic, smouldering beauty.

Budapest is a beautiful city at night with the lights glowing gold on the castle, the Parliament and all the bridges. The island in the middle of the river, Margitsziget, is where François is performing. It is leafy, green, and cool in the heat.

And it is hot, that oppressive city heat which does not cool down at night. The temperature hovers around 40c at midnight.

In the day, we do not go sightseeing.

I watch the idiot tourists on sightseeing buses frying their brains in the midday sun from the shade of our balcony. Why would anyone do that?

In Paris and Roma, everyone stays in when the summer heat is unbearable.

Our hotel room has two balconies split over a mezzanine level with windows offering a panoramic view. Although at home, Marina knows never to go on the balcony alone, I still worry about the worst happening.

I am afraid of the savage Gods.

I am afraid of losing Marina or Natalija or anyone I love.

I lie in bed and watch the beautiful lights at night, but I cry silently as I sleep next to Marina.

For some reason I am feeling sad and empty.

I listen as François gets into his own bed.

I am so tired of our hideous parody of domestic life and know it is not what I want for my daughter or me.

After watching Il Trovatore, Marina is distressed as François's character, Manrico, is killed offstage in the dramatic finale. She has seen him die on stage many times, but Paris Opera is home.

Here, everything is strange for her.

As the flames flicker and the lighting state turns blood red representing the funeral pyre, Marina is weeping, although we never see his death. Azucena holds her arms to Heaven and sings her final dramatic lines and Marina is so upset.

I had not let her watch Il Trovatore before as it is so dark, but François reassured me that most of the darkness in the Hungarian version is in the lyrics.

It is not any more violent than watching Tosca.

I have seen violent versions, such as the Paris Il Trovatore, which I would never let her attend.

In Paris Opera, she always comes backstage with me and meets the cast reincarnated after their various stage deaths.

She can separate the stage from real life, but on this island with its cavernous stage space and large audience, Marina believes it is real.

I carry her in the hot midnight evening to the dressing rooms.

'Don't cry, my love,' I tell her.

'François is fine. Just like in Paris, he is ready to see you after the show.'

'François, your beautiful wife and daughter are here,' the stage manager calls.

They do not know us as he never performs in Hungary. They asked him to perform in the autumn season when the Il Trovatore returns to the Opera House stage, but his schedule is full.

Many know of his reputation, as he is famous across Europe, and I am sure they know of Marina Valentino. The whole Opera World was shocked by her murder, but no one here mentions it because they do not know my name. They only write 'Fiorenza' for my backstage pass.

The news and chat shows focussed on my mother's death and the topic of domestic violence, but

her personal life remained secretive.

Many of those working in Paris and Roma Opera did not know everything about her personal life either, even Anasztázia who was her closest friend.

My mother was always guarded but she was fearful of people finding out the great Vesuvius was stalked and beaten by her husband. She had such a mask for the world.

'François!' Marina leaps at him.

'You know it is just playing, Marina,' he says. 'Just like Paris.'

'Hello, beautiful,' he says to me.

'You are so fresh and lovely. I was melting out there on that stage. It is hot tonight.'

I smile. 'Marina is distressed tonight. We should have asked could she see the set first.'

'Marina, it is just acting,' he tells her, as she is still tearful.

I think, we are all acting one way or another. Hiding behind our masks.

Two days after returning from Hungary, I open the door to a young woman, called Solange.

It is at the beginning of August, and I have forgotten all about Loredana and her threats.

At first, I think Solange is some religious caller, preaching the word of God. I am about to close the door and tell her that God does not exist.

She is from Social Services.

Solange double checks the address with her office, convinced she has the wrong apartment, not this luxurious pad by Opera.

Solange stepped into the apartment and as I offer her a coffee, she gazes around her, taking in the opulence: the chandeliers, the paintings and sculptures and everything that speaks of an extravagant lifestyle.

She asked again who lived here.

Loredana has contacted my family in Roma. She wanted to

hear Auntie Luisa tell her the 'real story' and it was not a nice one.

I acted cool and composed for Solange, telling her this was all a misunderstanding.

'My father owns the apartment and I stay when he travels abroad, although I have my own studio nearby.

My daughter also lives here.'

'I am sorry,' she said. 'But I have to ask you some questions.'

'Oh, it is fine. Please, let me show you round.'

It was just a quick visit she reassured me, but she had to follow up a report filed back in June. She had called in July when we were in Budapest.

François put on his best act as he brought her a coffee.

My beautiful little Marina said, 'is this because of Loredana?' She takes my hand.

'She wants to ruin our lives,' she says to Solange seriously.

'Marina, go to your room, my love. I have to talk to this nice lady alone.'

'This is all very difficult,' I tell Solange in the privacy of my room. I sigh.

'I found our trusted au pair of six years helping herself to my mother's jewellery.

My mother was murdered by my stepfather in Roma when I was 16 years old.'

I wipe tears away.

'I am so sorry,' the lady says. She looks at all the photos adorning my walls and picks up one of my mother as Tosca in her flowing red cape and dress.

'She is very beautiful,' Solange says admiringly. 'Was she an actress?'

'She was an Italian opera star,' I tell her.

'Once or twice, money was missing from the apartment, but I thought I miscounted.

After all, I paid the cleaner and Loredana extremely well so never suspected them.

It was April when I caught Loredana.

It is more the sentimental value of my jewels. If she needed money, I would have helped.

I asked her to resign, said I would write her a cheque for a large amount.'

I place the jewellery box back on the table.

'She then got defensive and nasty and said she would report me to your department.

She told me I was a bad mother, a 'teenage slut' because I was only 17 years old when I had my daughter. That really hurt.

She even accused me of some terrible thing, horrible things I cannot repeat. God, I was so shocked.

I know she got this from my Auntie Luisa. I had fallen out with my very religious family.

My daughter was so upset, so I asked Loredana to leave the apartment.

Once I gave Loredana a large severance cheque, she said she was leaving for Sicilia.

It is such a betrayal.'

I cry a little more.

'It's okay,' the social worker said, placing her hand on my arm.

'Your aunt in Roma was worried for your welfare as well as your daughter's.'

'My family are strict Italian Catholic and were extremely disapproving when I had my daughter so young.

I moved to a studio in April after the au pair said I was spoilt and I wanted to prove her wrong, but it was no good for my Marina; she even ran away one day.

Now my daughter is very safe and happy again; she stays here or with her father.

I cannot believe such a trusted employee did this to us.'

I turn to face Solange.

'I am so sorry for any distress, Miss Valentino,' Solange tells me again.

'It seems to have been a mistake. I see you are giving your daughter the best home.'

I walk Solange to the front door. Marina appears and looks anxious.

'Loredana wants to ruin our lives. She hurt my mamma,' Marina says, gripping my hand.

'I can tell you, Marina, that you do not have to worry,' Solange says to her.

I waited by the living room window and watched Solange exit the building, heading in the direction of the Metro.

Only when I was sure she was safely on the Metro, did I scream so many curses.

'Loredana got a big fat cheque! How dare she call my bitchy aunt in Roma?!

Fuck them all!'

François tried to hold me.

'It's okay, carissima. It is over, Fiorenza.'

'Let go of me!' I push him away.

I could not have Marina growing up in this situation, not how I have been living in this horrible suffocating sin. François could still see as much of her as he wanted.

He could still see me. But not in his bed. Not one night more.

I sat on the sofa and wept.

'Mamma, please don't cry,' Marina said, crawling onto my knees. 'Loredana is a fucking bitch.'

I laugh despite my tears, wrap my arms round her, kiss her face.

'Marina you are a good girl,' I tell her.

'No one is ever taking you away!'

I hug her, tell her Loredana wanted to hurt us because she was jealous.

'This is what jealous people are like. Remember, my love; you will get jealousy in your life because you are beautiful.'

She nods, her dark eyes serious.

François is hands me a glass of wine when Marina runs back to her room.

'Please look at me, carissima,' he tells me quietly.

I do not want to talk. I drink my wine and start to feel a little better.

'Please do not worry now, Fiorenza.

Solange realised that it is malicious rumours, but I should call those women right now! That Luisa and Loredana.......'

The wine calms me, but I still want to be alone. I wave my hand to stop him reaching for his phone.

'No. Case closed, François. You call no one.'

I move away from him and go out on the balcony.

'François, I really need to be alone for a bit,' I say.

He leaves me alone with my dark thoughts.

IN BOCCA AL LUPO

My first ever visit to Vienna and I am feeling a sense of freedom.

It is August when me and Marina see Natalija in her new country. She arrived a week ago.

We are no longer divided by vast stretch of Atlantic Ocean. A short flight across Europe is nothing.

Natalija had laughed when she said she never thought she would be a resident in Vienna Opera.

It is not forever, but this is home for now.

After all, she still had Milano, would still return to The Met, but being close to Hungary was important to her. She did not want to discuss her father's ill health, but I knew she regretted jetting off to New York without a care for her family seven years ago.

The last time she was in Vienna, she had performed very badly as Mercédès in a rainy November production of Carmen. Still healing from her internal injuries after the stabbing incident, she was unable to sing her signature role. Instead, she accepted the role of Mercédès.

Everything had been disastrous, from a fire alarm on opening night, to one of the cast nearly dying from bacterial meningitis. Natalija's review was awful, as she struggled to sing to full capacity with her injury.

'I thought my voice was ruined, yet here I am, reincarnated,' she said.

'I think I cried every day last time I was here.'

When we arrived in the opulent theatre district and found the top floor apartment, I saw a very different Natalija.

She looked light and lovely in her black shift dress, her long jet hair loose over her golden shoulders. She seemed even more beautiful not playing the seductress role and she was also wearing very little make up, instead of her sultry smoky-eyed look.

Her usually over-powdered skin was fresh and clear. It was as if she had literally taken off her mask for me.

The woman who embraces me is nothing like the flirty prima-donna who had smouldered in a careless Carmen way.

Her eyes were gentle as she took my hands.

Maybe it was returning to Europe, or the influence of Lucia on her life.

I do know that she had been unhappy in New York for some years. I also knew that she trusted me; there was no need to play the bitchy careless diva now.

'What a lovely princess in her red dress,' she said, kneeling next to Marina.

'But you need this to be a beautiful Tosca.'

She placed a tiara on Marina's hair. It was too big, but Marina happily announced she was going to be an opera star too.

'Natalija, that tiara looks expensive,' I say.

'It is Marina's now,' she smiled.

'Besides, tiaras are not for me. Marina will be Tosca, just like your mother.'

After admiring my new tattoos, she tells me she is going to have her daughter's name inscribed on her skin.

'You have given me ideas, Fiorenza!'

She showed us round her swish new apartment, Marina taking her hand, loving the attention.

We always spoke Italian together and Natalija introduced me to one of the three Italian au pairs she had for Lucia. She took her pretty daughter from the au pair.

Lucia is very like Marina at that age, with black hair and dark eyes, but duskier skin.

'She is even prettier than her photo,' I say.

I explained to Natalija that Marina did not like children. 'Too many Opera stars in her life.'

'She likes my Lucia,' Natalija said approvingly when Marina begged to play with her.

'Lucia is only 16 months old,' I told Marina. 'She is not a doll.'

'Please, mamma,' Marina asked again.

'Just sit down and help her build something with these coloured blocks in the living room.'

I tip out the toy box on the floor.

'Marina is a loner,' I explain to Natalija, as she makes us drinks. 'She has no friends.'

'So was I, as an ice skater, kicking my classmates with my blades,' Natalija laughed.

'I wanted to be Olympic champion. I hated kids too.'

Natalija hoped I could manage to see one of her performances after my October exam.

She was performing in Nabuccco, the first opera of the season, followed by Adriana Lecouvreur. Then she had to return for a month to guest in The Met in November.

I really like Adriana Lecouvreur and promise that I will be here for that.

'Only problem with Vienna is that women see dark beauties like us, and think we want to steal their husbands,' she said.

I remember in Bregenz when the Austrians clung to their husbands and glared at my mother with jealous hatred. They behaved as if this impossibly glamorous Italian star would steal their men in the interval.

'I still have The Met in my schedules for the next few years, but I have so much in Europe and La Scala, where you can visit again too,' Natalija said cheerfully.

Then she looked sad and admitted how horrible her divorce had been.

'God, this last month has been hell, Fiorenza.

Diego called me a heartless bitch and cried every day.

I promised that Lucia will fly to New York when I perform at The Met, but I broke his heart.

Fiorenza, I think I am getting old; I seem to have a conscience. I am not that careless prima donna anymore.'

I comforted her as she looked tearful.

'Lucia changed you,' I tell her.

She watched Lucia and Marina playing together.

'She is going to be a heartbreaker,' I tell Natalija.

'One of those sultry Mexican beauties…I can see it now; Lucia the movie star.'

I thought this would make her happy, but Natalija wiped a tear away.

'Carissima, everything is good now; you are in Europe, close to your relatives.

You have your Lucia and this lovely apartment, Vienna Opera…….'

I put my arm round her.

'Fiorenza; Lucia is Mexican……..

I never even learned Spanish. No one uses Spanish in theatres, so I used Italian with Diego.

I gave Lucia his surname. He was fine with the Italian version of 'Lucia' when I chose her name.

Now he says it should be the Spanish pronunciation.

Literally, we shouted about everything.

I speak to my daughter in Italian and English and have Italian au pairs.

I am not teaching her Hungarian; she would never use it.'

'Lucia is European as well as Mexican,' I reassure her.

'And you named your daughter after the Opera.'

'Fiorenza, maybe it is unlucky to do this. I gave her Carmen as a middle name just in case.'

Natalija looked reflective and sad.

She had always sounded light and mischievous on the phone, but the stress has got to her.

'Here I am with my perfect life, and I know what people in the Opera say about me.

But I would have died if I left Lucia in New York, Fiorenza.

'You can still play that heartless diva and be the gentle Natalija at home.

Nothing wrong with having a mask for the world,' I tell her.

'And my mother had au pairs. What can you do as an opera star? You have to work and travel. It is part of the life. No one would judge you for this.'

I squeeze her hand and try to think of something to make her laugh

'Anyway, everyone will be bitching about someone else soon, like a singer who got too fat. What about the American soprano who just sang Rusalka?

I watched it online. I thought she might break the tree she was sitting in....'

Natalija does not laugh.

'Yes, I would sooner starve,' Natalija says.

I saw her immediate reaction, which was to assess herself critically in the full-length mirror on the kitchen wall.

She was terrified of gaining weight.

'You did not eat when you were going to have Lucia because you were afraid of getting fat.

It was not to keep performing and squeeze into dresses, was it?' I ask her.

She examined her nails and covers her face with her hands.

'No,' she answers quietly.

Her shocking and careless admission of starving to fit her opera gowns back in Madrid had been in line with her selfish personality. I had hated her then.

The real reason was much sadder; she was afraid of food.

'Fiorenza, I worry I damaged Lucia.

If I ate much, I knew I would start my bulimia again and never stop.

The shrinks could not help me………

I fitted my concert dresses at seven months and Diego called me selfish………..'

She left the room in tears.

I watched the girls until Natalija returned. I promised her that Lucia looked glossy and healthy.

I remember the photos of Lucia as a fat beautiful baby at five months.

'Dry those tears, carissima,' I tell her, wiping her face.

'The doctor says she is fine, but I still worry….'

'How are you about food now?' I ask. She served the girls cake and cut me a generous slice, but only had a coffee herself.

'You see me eat, but I remember how sick I was in Budapest. I nearly died, nearly ruined my voice.

No Nutella in the fridge, no sweet stuff.

I got cake for you and the girls, then you have to hide it.'

Despite her fame, Natalija was also anxious about returning to the Vienna stage. She associated it with her unlucky run of Carmen.

'In bocca al lupo,' I told her when I said goodbye a few days later.

She had pressed a large silver object into my hand as I got in the taxi.

It was Tosca's crucifix with an amethyst at the centre.

My mother had given this piece of costume jewellery to Natalija for good fortune when she first met her in London. Natalija was 23 years old and hungry for fame, playing a small part in Manon.

'It did bring luck; I wore it to an audition in Hungary and my career turned into an overnight success.

But now, it is your turn. And it was your mother's gift; she was Tosca so you should have it, Fiorenza,' Natalija said.

I examined the crucifix as we headed to the airport.

'Mamma, does this really bring luck?' Marina asked me.

'It was from Tosca. You know she wears a crucifix? Yes, this one is lucky.'

When Marina chattered on about Lucia and Natalija and Vienna the moment we arrived back in Paris, François did not criticise.

I had told him where we were going and who we were seeing, and he just said it was nice for Marina to see another child.

I find out from Catalina and Alain that they had been contacted by Loredana too.

Was there no end to this vengeful hag's antics?

When Catalina visits for a few days, I find out damn Loredana called her in Milano.

Catalina confesses that she did not like to tell me because she never liked the au pair, found her intrusive and bitchy.

Loredana said that she would call Auntie Luisa in Roma, since Catalina was so evasive.

I was furious Loredana was suggesting that there was some sort of 'unnatural' relationship

between François and Catalina, or Marina and François.

That makes me burn. François adores Marina. He is not my stepfather.

'To be honest, Fiorenza, she was jealous of you because you are very beautiful, rich and successful. I noticed when I stayed here for my ballet.

She was even jealous of our mamma!

I remember her complaining about photos……….

I am sorry for not telling you, but I wanted to speak when I visited,' Catalina said.

'And please return to Milano again. My evil father is never going to hurt you again.'

I say nothing as I do not want her to know what happened to me.

'We buried him after that prison visit. You are safe now, Fiorenza.'

I confess that I was afraid when I went to Milano.

'But you were fine. You saw Natalija. You were safe and you can be next time.

Do not let my evil father ruin your life any more than he did.'

Natalija's words had been the same. They both wanted me to break my fear of returning to my homeland.

Then I say with a smile, how about a coffee?

There is fat-free gelato too.

Catalina looks at me so sadly, knowing I hide under my armour, just as she hides her pain by dancing.

Loredana even called Alain.

He is taking Marina to the coast for a weekend that August.

'It is very kind of you. She will love it,' I tell him.

'You could come too?' he says, tentatively.

'Thank you, but no. Besides everyone in Paris is at the coast in August. I need a break from my little diva.'

He understands. I like him but I see him as a good-looking kind friend, whereas I know he wants more from me. Maybe I cannot love anyone or maybe I did love Natalija.

I never said those words to her, but I had shouted it at François. I did not need to tell her, not now.

When Alain arrives, Marina is still packing.

'Make it fast! Your father is waiting!'

François is in rehearsals, so as we wait, Alain tells me about the phone call.

'You know I had this weird call in June.

You had exams, then your internship and then you were abroad, so I did not trouble you.

Loredana called me from Sicilia. I did not want to speak to her as she was such poison.

To be honest, I never liked your au pair.'

'Loredana heard a bad argument one night between me and my father.

Marina heard it too. It was just an argument.

I was screaming at François because I was wearing this crazy dress to the Opera.

The next day, she insisted that I move apartments, to be away from François or she would go to Social Services. She called me a teenage slut, all kinds of horrible names.

I asked her to leave when she insulted me, even though I found that studio.

She was nasty and spiteful, and I gave her a big cheque.

Poor Marina screamed at Loredana to leave me alone, that sweet protective child.

And evil Loredana even called my Auntie Luisa in Roma.'

I see Alain is not judging me at all.

'Everyone argues, Fiorenza. At least this woman is in Sicilia now,' he says.

'She was jealous,' I say, sweeping my hand over the living room.

'We paid her a lot, treated her well. I dated an opera star, but I cannot see her so often as she is the world's top mezzo. She lived in New York and now is based in Vienna.

Marina met her in Vienna, but the au pair said I was 'unnatural' for seeing Natalija.'

Alain is not at all surprised or shocked.

'So?' he smiles.

'What has Natalija got to do with this interfering Sicilian? It is your life.

Marina loves beautiful opera stars. She talked about Natalija and her pretty daughter.

Many people must fall in love with you, Fiorenza.

Marina did say something unrepeatable about Loredana, she is cursing a lot.'

I am quiet as I try to contain my rage against this hateful woman.

'Anasztázia found me a new au pair for the autumn. Fleure was lovely but she has a new job in September.

Yves is perfect and Marina likes him.'

Alain looks concerned. 'I am not sure about a man, Fiorenza.'

I touch his hand lightly.

'Yves is an old friend of Anasztázia, and he is gay.

His hours have been cut at the Opera in the costume department. I trust Anasztázia and when I met Yves, I knew he was right for Marina.

He lives with his partner, and he helps with the children's chorus too. I would not normally trust a man either, but he is the best for Marina. Do you want to meet him?'

'No, I trust Anasztázia.

I never met her, but I know of her, Fiorenza,' Alain says.

'After the summer, I need a lot of help as I am so pressurised.

He does not speak Italian, but I always speak Italian with Marina and she has been having tuition for her written work.'

Marina runs in with her suitcase excitedly.

'We get to go to the sea!' she says to me. 'But Papa wishes you were coming too.'

Alain looks hopeful again.

'Sorry, my love. Another time.' I kiss her goodbye.

After I wave them off from the balcony, I do what my mother

did once or twice a year, which is to light a cigarette.

Loredana left a pack of cigarettes in the apartment and for some reason, I did not throw them away.

My hands shake as I light one with my mother's silver lighter. Just lighting up is a ritual to calm down. I do not inhale.

I need to get out of this darkness I am living in, or it will destroy me. Anasztázia will help me break free and she will be in Paris soon.

I start to feel a little better as I watch the smoke drift into the hot afternoon sky.

My mother crashed her car once in Piazza del Colosseo and found her costume lady's cigarettes in the glovebox from a few days before.

She lit a cigarette and immediately stopped thinking about all the chaos and shrieking around her.

She was not hurt, just shaken. The piazza was notorious for accidents.

I had asked her why she carried cigarettes as an opera singer.

She said it was like wishing fellow performers 'In bocca al lupo' or 'Toi, toi, toi' before the Opera.

By invoking bad luck, the idea is that you attract the reverse. If she carried the cigarettes, she would hopefully not meet a stressful situation where she needed them.

I find that the act of lighting up with a beautiful lighter and watching the cigarette burn down was enough to calm any bad thoughts.

I look at my mother's lighter, engraved with her name and I long for her.

It had been in her handbag the night she died. Anasztázia had given me the gold Gucci bag a few days after my mother's death.

It seemed unlucky to take it, but I kept the lighter.

'You keep the bag,' I told Anasztázia. 'She would want you to have it.'

I feel a wave of terrible nostalgia, as if it were just yesterday when a tearful Anasztázia hugged me so tightly and we cried together.

On the balcony that August afternoon I wished I could reverse time.

But I know in my heart, there would be another night when she was not safe.

Besides, she would have to have been in Roma for the trial, where Andrea would be charged with attempted murder, domestic violence, stalking; the list was endless.

She would never be safe.

'Drinking wine alone?' François asked me when he arrived home from rehearsals.

He places his hand on my shoulder.

'Are you still upset about the social visit? My love, they will never come back.'

'Can you leave me alone for a bit. I need to think.'

ANASTASIS

I stare at the panorama of Paris and feel exhausted.

All the events of this year have sucked out my soul; even happiness has been draining.

So much has changed within me. It could be the negative energy leaving my body, as I have stopped with the black magic.

Anasztázia appears in my dreams many nights, like an angel.

Her name means resurrection, from the Greek word 'anastasis', which is fortuitous. She has resurrected herself many times, freed her soul from so much darkness and now she will resurrect me too.

She had a concert in Paris, and I tell her that she can stay in the studio.

'Fiorenza, you are thinking of the future?' Anasztázia asked, once we were safely in the studio.

'You say you wanted my help?'

'Anasztázia, I need cleansing,' I said.

'I am living without so called 'sin', but I feel my soul is still black. I am so tired of walking around in the shadows.

The curse of the savage Gods is hanging over me.'

'Fiorenza. I care so much for you,' she told me.

'We can begin to cleanse you right now. Whatever malevolent powers you have evoked, we need to send them back and I can start the process.'

I kneel on the floor as if she is Santa Anasztázia; she can lift me out of my dark place with her holy power.

Anasztázia gazes at me with her ageless complexion. I remember when I first met her as a teenager, she seemed to me like an angel with her porcelain skin, honey-coloured hair, and those eyes like clear water.

She kneels next to me and takes my hands.

As I close my eyes, she recites softly in Hungarian, touching me very lightly from my face downwards and I feel warm pink light encase my body.

It is a sweet feeling, like gliding into a giant bubble bath. I give in to whatever magic she is creating.

It is all white magic, she reassures me.

'I saw pink light, lilac too,' I tell her when I open my eyes.

'A warm bubble seemed to travel over me, like strange magic. But I did not understand a word of your prayer.'

She smiles and gets up. 'You do not need to understand the language.'

Anasztázia loves how I decorated my little space: the pretty ornaments and photos, the strings of coloured lights.

'You see this shrine to my mother below the photo you gave me? I pray here. I placed her Tosca photo the other wall.

Black and red either side.' I tapped the walls.

Anasztázia stepped outside to admire the view from the little balcony.

'It is beautiful with such positive energy, Fiorenza. Being high up is very good too; I always feel safe on the top floor.'

I was surprised that I had begun to appreciate this bright studio more each day, as I showed my friend around.

'Can you promise me you will be staying here once I leave Paris?' Anasztázia asked.

'Yes, I want to be free.' And I do.

Anasztázia gave me a gift of a book of spells as an early birthday present.

Casting black magic spells left me feeling tainted, sucking out the good energy, which is why I am tired, she explains.

'Fiorenza, take it; this is more healing than magic. Try a cleansing spell.

It is to cleanse the hurt and pain from the past, banish any bad feelings.

Just like I performed, except you can also do them yourself. It will keep you cleansed so you do not attract more negative forces.'

Anasztázia explained some time ago that black magic comes back on you threefold.

She is concerned that I have been casting spells, that the magic I have delved into is dark and evil and I need to focus on cleansing this from my life.

'And how is Yves? Does Marina like him?'

'He is like gold dust,' I tell her.

'Marina liked him as soon as we met.

I also found a very good private tutor to give her Italian written classes. This lady was recommended by the Italian language coach at the Opera.

She had some home schooling after that horrible incident where she ran away but now, she seems content in her new school.'

'I am happy, Fiorenza. As I said, I would trust him with my own child.

And Yves will not ask questions about your life. I am just hopeful your sweet Marina never runs again. I blame that awful Sicilian au pair.'

I nod. I blame myself too, feel it was not just Loredana.

After dinner that evening, I took Anasztázia down to the apartment block entrance. We waited for the taxi to arrive to take her down the road to the studio.

'Hear the latest about Natalija?' she says.

'No,' I lie.

'She and her husband are divorced, but she has custody of their daughter.

That poor Mexican tenor, only 27 years old and he cannot claim any of her riches.

She made sure of that.

She returned to Europe last month, to be resident in Vienna Opera. She always hated Vienna.

Somehow, she learned perfect German; in bed with some co-star, I guess.'

Anasztázia is full of contempt for her ex-lover.

'Anasztázia, New York is so far from Europe. I am sure she was homesick for this continent.

And maybe she truly loves her daughter,' I say.

'I do not believe she is so heartless.'

I wanted to defend Natalija but did not want Anasztázia to know the truth.

'European stars do find it hard to remain in America long term.

There is a kind of pull back towards the old world, but Fiorenza; Natalija is not fit to care for a houseplant!

She is the worst mother imaginable! He really should have custody of that child.

Natalija had a hot Mexican and now she is a Viennese tart!'

She laughs at this.

I am silent, hating myself for not being able to defend Natalija.

Then Anasztázia is suddenly serious, seeing my reaction.

She reaches for my hand.

'Sorry, that was mean. I do not like to wish bad luck on anyone, not even her.

Fiorenza, have you seen her?

Your Marina, she said something about Natalija, but maybe she saw her perform.'

I do not answer.

'You know something, don't you? You do not see a heartless woman.

She is not a prima donna for you.'

She reaches for my hand.

'Anasztázia, I am so sorry. There was never a good time to tell you.

I thought she was cold and heartless when I met her, but I have seen her for a few years in different countries. I saw a change in her every time, especially after she had Lucia.

I just visited Vienna with Marina.

She truly adores her daughter. The cold diva is a mask for the world.

It would break her heart to lose Lucia. And she left her husband the apartment. She felt awful for the divorce, but she was unhappy in New York.'

Anasztázia's voice is gentle. She is not angry with me.

'Sweet Fiorenza; she is history.

I found her photo in your studio, but there are a lot of photos.

I did not like to ask as maybe you just admired her as an opera singer.

And you say she loves her daughter?

Carissima, if she is right for you, then I am happy.

This situation in Paris is toxic, and I want you to be free of this.'

She hugs me.

As we kissed goodnight, she asked if I could manage alone?

'Yes, I promise,' I told her.

And I would keep my promise.

My grandparents' funeral is on September 12th. I find out because Catalina called me the night before at 22.00. Bitchy Auntie Luisa only just told her.

Luisa knew Catalina would call me, but I could never get to Roma on time.

I am not welcome at the funeral.

How dare Luisa? Funerals are a free for all.

I remember my grandparents and how they rejected me and Marina.

No, I would not go, even if I lived in Roma.
'Fiorenza, Luisa tells me that tomorrow we have the funeral. I hate her so much.'
I hate my auntie too and it burns.
I ask the question I am afraid of; was this a revenge hit ordered by Andrea?
'How did they die, Catalina?'
'Piazza del Colosseo, a road accident. They were not good drivers……'
'No one is a good driver in Roma. Our mother crashed in Piazza del Colosseo too.'
I am relieved it is a genuine accident. I despise them, but I do not wish them dead.
'Fiorenza, I have to cancel my ballet rehearsals in Milano, but need to go to the funeral.
Luisa called you a wicked temptress.
Doesn't every woman want to be a wicked temptress? Our mother was.'
'Catalina, you can be a wicked temptress one day.'

I feel sad about not living in Italia, especially now I have broken my fear.
I will return to Milano, maybe even Napoli too. I am not letting Andrea ruin my life.
I could return to Milano to live in the future. After all, I study international law as well as training to be a French advocate. It is possible.
Despite being a virtual Parisienne, I still feel Italian.
Deep in my heart, just like my mother, I am an Italian woman. Even down to preferring olive oil over butter, Italian designers over French.
My only French preference is perfume, Dior's Hypnotic Poison.
I sit in the studio alone. I feel a sense of calm, after all the

violent nightmares and the corrosive guilt.

In the September mornings and evenings, I sit on the balcony and think over everything.

Marina hates me, but I let her have her wish; to stay with François in the apartment or at Alain's house. Yves, the au pair is her friend and is good for her. He tries to speak with her about me, trying to rationalise but she still is full of rage for me leaving the apartment.

No pleading or tears from François would change my mind.

This dark life we have been living stops now.

Forever.

'We cannot live like this. Not for us, not for Marina.'

'Maybe you need space?' he said, hopefully. 'Please, carissima.'

He called my name from the balcony as I walked down the street, as if he were in one of his goddamn operas.

Marina had screamed that I was a lousy mother, that I hurt François.

He promised he will speak Italian with her, make sure she has her Italian tutor visit twice a week.

I worry she will suddenly refuse to speak the language if she associates it with me.

Yves told me he knew of children who did just this, after their parents' divorce or stress in their lives. It would be a tragedy for her to lose the language.

Yves reassures me Marina will soon forget her anger, but I cannot shake the feeling I lost her, if only for a short time. It breaks my heart.

She said she does not care if I stay in the apartment when François is away. I am happy in the studio; I will be doing it so I can see her every day.

'Go to Hell!' she shouted.

'You fuck up his life! Now he is sad!'

I do not shout at her for cursing. I just want her to love me like she did.

And she would have hated me forever if she discovered my terrible secret life.

I had cried on the phone to Natalija, told her about Loredana, about the whole horrible mess.

'My daughter hates me; she hates me for hurting François.'

'She will be fine; I promise you. She is young. And I will see you very soon.

Take your law exam, then we can arrange something. You can stay with me and Lucia and watch Adriana Lecouvreur. Can you look forward to this?'

'Yes, I would love that.'

When I return from the Opera that night after watching Madama Butterfly where I cry so much, I am alone in my studio. It is a very strange feeling to be alone after a visit to Opera.

Butterfly was a role close to my mother's heart, and I thought of her throughout the performance; that delicate, beautiful creature pinned to the wall, unable to fly away.

Everyone cried watching my mother perform Puccini or Verdi because she felt tragedy with every fibre of her soul.

I hoped to see her gliding along amongst the chandeliers and mirrors in the interval, but I did not.

I only saw myself reflected in the glass amongst the ocean of evening dresses and suits.

The beautiful woman everyone admires in the Opera House is me. For the first time, I am seeing Fiorenza and not the ghost of someone else.

I also realise when I arrive at my studio, that I just walked home at night without fear, even though it is only five minutes from Opera.

Somehow, I am conquering my agoraphobia, just like Natalija conquered her fear of returning to the Vienna Opera stage. Her first night of Nabucco was a success and she emailed me the photos.

I sit in my evening dress on the balcony with a coffee, reading Natalija's sparkling review as I play with Tosca's crucifix.

It seemed to be a symbol of good fortune, this jewellery from the Opera House in London.

I wonder how many opera stars wore this crucifix before Marina Valentino.

I had placed it on my altar. My mother pretended she had lost it in her dressing room after giving it to Natalija.

It still feels very lonely as I gaze at the lights of Paris. It is one of those warm and heavy September nights when I wish the weather could stay like this forever.

I go back inside and gaze for a long time at my mother's photos.

'I love you, mamma. I would do anything to be with you. Anything.'

I kneel below her beautiful image and recite the words for Vissi d'arte, Tosca's prayer-like aria.

My mother's favourite aria from her favourite Opera. She was made to be a Floria Tosca.

The candle-light flickers.

'Are you there?' I ask.

It has become a ritual every evening; to pray here as I atone for my sins.

I dream I die many nights, but there is a softness, a melting into spirit without pain. My mother is there to comfort me.

Only when I wake up do I feel disturbed, as if these dreams are premonitions of my death.

I can finally enter a cathedral without fear of being struck by a bolt of lightning. I pray, but alone at the altar.

As I lift my face towards Heaven, there is within me a strange dichotomy, one where there is great sadness yet immense hope.

I am her. I am myself once again and it feels good to be me.

I have resurrected Fiorenza Valentino.

ANGEL

I never saw such a beautiful white dress with dazzling beads and jewels encrusted over the fitted bodice and a sweeping diaphanous train. My black hair is half piled up into a crown of dazzling diamonds and loose spirals fall across my bare golden shoulders. I have glitter dusted across my cheekbones and diamond earrings. Did I go to watch *Lucia di Lammermoor* because I never wear white? The label says Christian Lacroix, so no wonder it looks amazing on me.

My mother never wore white even for her weddings, so this is not her dress.

Maybe *Natalija bought it for me? Yes, that must be it. She knows I love that Opera.*

I am full of life and vitality and hope.

'Fiorenza, you look beautiful,' I tell my reflection, as I touch my lips to the glass.

My mother gazes at me as I admire myself. She still wears her favourite jet evening dress and ruby tiara, her hair cascading in thick raven waves down her back, the colour shining almost blue-black in the light.

She seems even more stunning than when I last saw her, but there is a sadness in her darkest eyes.

'Mamma! You came to see me!' I say, turning round to face her.

'You look wonderful, my darling Fiorenza,' she says.

'You are so beautiful too!' I tell her, taking her hands in mine.

'My Fiorenza, I missed you so much,' she sighs, as she wraps her love around me in an enchanting bubble and I inhale her *Hypnotic Poison* perfume. Something about the scent is so nostalgic, almost melancholy, as if………no, the thought slides away before I can grasp it.

I rub a hand over my perfectly toned stomach, enjoying my beauty. I have always been so slender, so why am I admiring my body as if I have been fat?

It does not make sense but then my mother being here is strange too.

Today seems like a day full of mystery and a new beginning.

Yet my lovely mother remains haunted, her eyes full of pain.

'Mamma, why are you sad? I am sorry if I did anything....' I squeeze her hand and it is cool in my fingers.

'You have nothing to be sorry for, sweet Fiorenza. I have missed you so much.

But you do not remember this white dress? Or why you admire your body in the glass?

You are relieved to have your figure back.'

I look more closely at this sensational outfit; it is a wedding dress and I have a gold band and a large diamond engagement ring on my left hand.

'My wedding!' I say and laugh.

Maybe my mother is upset because she missed my wedding.

'But I married Alain.......' I hesitate.

It is strange............

He is Marina's father, handsome and kind, but I never wanted to marry him.

I never wanted to marry anyone. Besides, I thought I was with Natalija?

Now I am confused.

'Mamma, why do you say I got my figure back?

I never lost my figure, only when I had Marina.

Maybe it is just this lovely outfit,' I say, and twirl in the mirror, as shafts of sunlight fall on me through the window. There is a timeless feel in the air, like an endless spring.

My mother wipes a tear from her face.

'Mamma?' I turn back to face her. 'Please do not cry, mamma…
…..please tell me what troubles you.'

I step closer and she gently strokes a jet spiral of hair away from my face. Her hypnotic eyes, so dark they are nearly black, glisten with tears as she waits for me to remember.

Only my memory seems to be wiped clean.

Another tear falls and I catch it in my fingers, wishing it could turn to diamonds in my hand.

I open my hand; there are no diamonds.

'Mamma, I hate to see you cry.' I embrace her, feeling her soft skin next to mine.

She lets me hold her close and I inhale the warmth of her perfumed hair.

'Fiorenza your wedding dress was red,' she says quietly.

I could not remember.

'Why did I marry Alain anyway? I do not love him….' I look at her for answers.

'Fiorenza, you did not want the child. You admire your slim body because you hated losing your figure, just like me.'

I pull away, angrily. 'No!' I snap.

'I only have my sweet Marina!'

Why is she telling me these lies? No way do I have another child. That is crazy.

'Listen, my love; remember your wedding?' she asks, taking my hands again.

'That sunny April day? You did not love Alain, but he let you be free; the most important quality of all. You are a free spirit, like me. You loved Natalija.

Alain knew this and accepted it.

Remember?'

A snapshot of the wedding slides across my vision; my red dress shimmering the colour of fire, a garland of red flowers on my hair,

Marina throwing rose petals in the warm air.

I remember fragments of feelings; I was a respectable married lady at 26 years old and I felt content. I remember I had retained my Italian surname for me and my daughter, insisted the new child would take my surname too.

Maybe I could not love him, but I could be stable with Alain for Marina, and I would be atoning for my sins of the past. And he did let me be free.

Alain begged me to have the child, not to go to the clinic. Why the hell had I been with him in the first place? I have no idea.

I know I was with Natalija, and she accepted my fluid married existence.

Okay it will not last, Fiorenza, but for now it is good for Marina. That is so important.

Anyway, I believe we all need to get married once in life.

She was happy attending the wedding. How strange that is. I remember her in a beautiful gold dress, laughing with me in the sunshine and drinking champagne.

Then I have memory loss.

Last time my memory was clear, I was in my studio alone. I feel almost like time played tricks on me. It fast-forwarded and then it stretched like a Salvador Dali clock.

I stare in the glass. Did I divorce Alain? Did I have the abortion, as I wanted to?

'Fiorenza, do you remember the hospital?' my mother says.

A few jigsaw pieces of memory; the morning of 2nd November when I went to have the baby.

I hated this child, whereas I adored Marina right from the start.

I really did not want this second daughter, felt so miserable by autumn.

Alain waited at home with Marina when I went to hospital. I

was irritable, snapping at him all the time.

Visit me later, for God's sake. I will be home soon.

I remember the fruit I had waiting in the fridge to get my body back into shape and return to work.

I had worked from home in the last month, using holiday allowance to avoid taking time off.

I was young, had to prove myself as an advocate.

But in the hospital, I remember that I had cried for my mother, begged someone to call her.

Then it was night; I had lost a lot of hours.

I just thought *damn, I am still fat*. I was not sick so why was I still there?

I felt fragile and exhausted. I could see that I was full of tubes. Some were draining my insides, others were feeding me saline, blood, morphine, and antibiotics.

I wondered why.

I woke up as a nurse came to see me, her kind face full of anxiety as she adjusted my pillows.

I am fine.

My family had gone home, but did I want to see my little girl?

No, I did not want to see my daughter, Anasztázia.

'I want my mother,' I said. 'Please call my mother.' I reached for the nurse's arm.

I woke up at some dead hour between night and morning, and my mother was holding my hand, glorious and glamorous in her jet evening dress. She looked so beautiful.

The nurse had called her.

'Mamma,' I said, relieved she made it to see me.

'I am here, my dear Fiorenza,' she told me, and her perfume surrounded me in a sweet cloud of happiness, as she leaned over to kiss my face.

I drifted in and out of a twilight world; sometimes it was day and sometimes it was night, just like a Fellini film.

Marina, my father, and Alain visited, but I was always so tired. They told me Natalija was coming too, she was performing but she had three days free after Friday.

Whenever Friday was; time made no sense at all. I was too tired to read my watch.

My mother visited me, always very late at night. She would sit with me, stroking my hair.

'You are very, very sick, my love. Please try to fight,' she said.

I felt fine, just exhausted.

Then I remember the night of November 7th.

My mother kissed my forehead as she spent the night sitting with me.

It was so quiet and peaceful as she pressed my hand to her face, tears damp on her cheeks.

'I love you,' she said. 'I love you more than anyone in the world, Fiorenza.'

Now as we stand in this sunlit room with the ornate mirror and the timeless feel in the air, I am with my mother. I am feeling better than I ever did in my life.

'You visited me every night, mamma......' I say, twirling to admire my dress and how it glitters in the light.

'The nurse called you....' I smiled.

Her eyes were full of tears.

'The nurse did not call me, my darling.'

'What?' I stop and stare in the mirror.

A splinter of memory returns, sharp and jagged. This dress is not for my wedding, but for something far sadder. Did something terrible happen when I wore white?

A long time ago I think.......no, the splinter of thought is gone. It just explodes.

But I am fine.

'Fiorenza, you were so unlucky, carissima.' My mother tries to take my hands.

Then another snapshot; my mother died when I was 16 years old. She was at my bedside every night because I was dying.

'No! No, it is not true!' I step away from her in fear and shock.

'I am young and healthy! Look at me, mamma!'

I stare in the looking glass, and I begin to realise what all these fragments of strange memories are.

They are shifting together, forming a crazy jigsaw puzzle.

'Fiorenza, carissima; I am so sorry.'

Another bolt of memory hits me and I hold my hands to my face. The Fiorenza in the mirror does the same.

Where are we now? I struggle to place this sun-streaked room, which has huge windows and very little in it except this ornate mirror.

High stuccoed ceilings. Paris? Roma?

My elegant white dress is not for an opera or a wedding; it was chosen for my funeral. The diamonds in my hair and ears arranged by my Marina.

We dress mamma in white and diamonds as she is a beautiful angel.

'This dress is my funeral dress...... I do not understand....

I am only 27 years old!'

How could I die?

'Mamma?' I look to her for answers.

'My love......your insides were ruptured badly during the c-section.

Your poor body developed an infection; you just got weaker.'

I left the real world the night of 7th November with my mother beside me.

The vision of us in the glass looks so real, so how can this be the afterlife?

'I felt no pain; how could I die? No! It is not true!'

'Fiorenza, the morphine blocked the pain. And you were

beautiful, like a fragile opera heroine. You are always beautiful.

Natalija came to see you from Vienna, but she arrived a few hours too late. She was devastated. That once heartless diva broke her heart; she really did love you.

Maybe you would have gone to her one day. You knew it would not last with Alain.

You married for Marina.'

I sink to my knees. *I cannot be dead. I am not Violetta in La Traviata; to die so young and lovely.......*

'No!' I cry in her arms. 'I had so much to live for!

I will not see my Marina! Or Natalija!'

'Carissima,' my mother says.

'Your little Anasztázia is healthy.'

'Damn her!' I shout.

'Please do not blame your daughter, my darling. It was a terrible tragedy to happen to a young girl like you.........'

I cling to my mother. 'Why did I have to die, mamma? Why?'

I rest my head against her as she caresses my hair.

'Mamma.....why me?'

'I was too young to die as well, carissima. I had so much life left to live......'

'Mamma......'

'Shhhh, carissima,' she tells me.

'I am here. I am always here now andI loved you the most, more than anyone on Earth.'

As we sit on the floor in the dying light of the day which has no season, the room is split with a strange violet light. It reflects on us in the looking glass, sending a brilliant rainbow of colours from the diamonds in my hair and the beads and sequins in our dresses.

We are both so beautiful, I think.

'Yes, too beautiful,' she tells me softly. 'You and me. Too beautiful for this harsh world.'

'You read my thoughts,' I smile, as I wrap my cool fingers around hers.

'I missed you so much,' I sigh. I realise that I had always wanted to be with my mother, that this is the one wish I had since she died over eleven years ago.

I get one wish anyway. The savage Gods can no longer hurt me.

In Opera someone always has to die.

I surrender and let my mother hold me. Her eyes are even blacker than I remember, those eyelashes so long, her skin perfect and golden. I forgot just how hauntingly beautiful she is.

She has an otherworldly beauty.

After so many years of only photos or DVDs, or her appearing in my dreams, I missed the magic spell she cast when you were in her presence. She was a goddess.

And she loved me more than anyone. Maybe I did know it all along.

'You are Fiorenza, forever my Fiorenza, so young and lovely.'

I am Fiorenza. Forever Fiorenza. Young and lovely. I let the word 'forever' encase me like a sweet shroud.

The light fades and we remain entwined together, forever shadows in the twilight world.